SINGLE
MAMA'S
GOT MORE
DRAMA

USA TODAY BESTSELLING AUTHOR

KAYLA PERRIN

SINGLE
MAMA'S
GOT MORE
DRAMA

MIRA®

ISBN-13: 978-0-7783-2616-8
ISBN-10: 0-7783-2616-0

SINGLE MAMA'S GOT MORE DRAMA

www.MIRABooks.com

Printed in U.S.A.

For Leslie Gray, a longtime friend
and newly single mother.
You're beautiful, funny and talented,
and you deserve nothing but the best.

Here's to never settling and to hoping
that your true Mr. Right comes along.

I love you!

Prologue

"Ms. Cain?"

"Hello," I said, sitting up straight when I heard the voice on the other end of my line. It was Tassie Johnson's lawyer. My heart filled with hope after the message I'd left for him. I finally had a way to come up with the cash necessary to buy out Tassie's estranged husband's share of my condo, and hoped that her lawyer was calling to tell me that we had a deal.

I give Tassie Johnson a nice sum of cash. She leaves me the heck alone forever.

"I've spoken with my client," Bradley Harris said.

I crossed my fingers. This was it. The moment I'd been waiting for. My headache with Tassie was about to be over.

"However, Tassie asked me to tell you that she is rejecting your offer."

"What?" For a few seconds, I couldn't even think. Couldn't understand. Then I saw red. "How can she reject my offer?

Those were *her* terms. If I bought her out, I could keep the condo."

"Yes, but she's had a change of heart. She feels, having had time to fully consider the matter, that she would like to relocate to South Beach."

"And my apartment," I remarked sourly. *That evil, evil—*

"Your shared property."

Shared property, my ass. "So in other words," I began, anger brewing inside me like hot water in a kettle, "Tassie Johnson's only interest is in screwing me over. Do me a favor—tell her to stick it where the sun don't shine. Oh— and tell her I want my hat back."

And then I hung up.

If Tassie Johnson wanted a fight, it was *on.*

It was while I was gazing at the engagement ring Lewis had given me that I thought of something. Rather, made sense of something.

The day Alaina and I had gone to Atlanta, we'd seen Tassie near Eli's casket in the funeral home. I remembered that I'd seen a man beside her, offering comfort—an attractive man.

Tassie had tried to smear me in the media, making me out to be a manipulative slut while she'd been the doting wife, but it was unlikely that she had been sitting around waiting for Eli's return for seven years. She was an ex- tremely attractive woman, one who could have her pick of men.

She could have cheated on Eli for all I knew. What if she had some skeletons in her closet that she didn't want exposed?

There was one way to find out.

I searched for the *Miami Herald* reporter's card and dialed her number.

"Cynthia? This is Vanessa Cain," I said without preamble when she picked up.

"Hello, Vanessa."

"You said that you'd help me out if I ever needed anything. Well, I need something."

When I replaced the receiver five minutes later, I was smiling.

If anyone could help me bring Tassie Johnson down, it was Cynthia.

It was high time I played dirty.

1

Ten days later

I was locking the door to my condo when I sensed them. Sensed them and knew they meant trouble.

Securing my keys in the palm of my hand, I immediately reached down and scooped up my two-and-a-half-year-old daughter, Rayna, who was standing to my left. It was an instinctive, protective gesture—because I knew this was going to be bad.

Then, fearing the worst, I slowly turned.

My stomach lurched. Standing behind me were two very large men. One African-American, one Caucasian. Both looking like they abused steroids and had just escaped from prison.

"Vanessa Cain?" the white man asked, his voice raspy. Harsh.

I swallowed. Stalled for time.

"You *are* Vanessa Cain, right?" the man continued. Tattoos

covered both of his forearms, which didn't exactly give me a warm and fuzzy feeling about him.

Nerves had me shifting my weight from one foot to the other. "Who wants to know?"

"We're here to help you vacate Tassie Johnson's condo," the black man said, his words sounding like a threat.

I chuckled nervously as I met his stern gaze. "Excuse me?"

"It's time you leave," he told me. "And never come back."

"This is *my* home." I pressed my face to my daughter's. "*Our* home. You wouldn't take a mother and child from their home, would you?"

"I'm sorry, Ms. Cain," the white man said. "We're simply following orders."

"Whose orders? The court's—or Tassie's?"

"It's time," the black man began, "for you to leave. Tassie will send you your things."

"Oh, isn't that sweet of her?" I retorted sarcastically. "You want me out of here? You show me a court order. This is America. You can't just kick me out of my own home."

Neither man seemed swayed by what I said. In fact, they both took a menacing step toward me.

"Wait!" I cried. "Don't do this."

"It's time for you to leave," the black man said again.

Was that the extent of his vocabulary? Was he a robot programmed to say only six words?

The men took another step in unison, now invading my personal space. "But—but you can't," I sputtered, clutching Rayna to my chest while trying to block the men from getting to my condo door. They weren't just big—they could easily compete in sumo wrestling.

The big, bald, white guy wrapped his fingers around my upper arm. "Hey!" I protested. "You can't touch me! That's assault!"

"Then move out of the way," the man said.

Rayna began to cry. Tears filled my own eyes.

"But this is our home. Don't you have a heart? How—how can you be so cold?" I cradled Rayna's head to my shoulder to comfort her as she cried. Neither man batted an eye. I wondered if Tassie had hired them from Rent-A-Thug.

"I have a baby," I went on. "You can actually kick me out of my home with no concern at all for my child?"

"We have our orders," the men said in unison.

"Please," I begged, as Rayna cried louder. "Please, have a heart." One man took hold of my left arm, the other my right arm, which was secured around Rayna. "No," I said defiantly. *"Nooo!"*

I backed up until my body was against the door. I wriggled around, fighting to free myself. And then my eyes popped open. It took me a good couple of seconds to realize that I was in my bed, and that a pair of over-steroided thugs weren't in the room with me. I was sitting up, my body tangled in my sheets.

I'd been dreaming. *Thank God.*

I let out a relieved chuckle.

But my relief was short-lived. Because reality came crashing down on my shoulders, knocking me backward onto the pillow. Tassie Johnson, my late fiancé's estranged wife, wanted me out of the home I'd shared with her husband. Yes, it's a crazy and convoluted story, but I didn't know that Eli Johnson, my fiancé, was still legally married at the time I was involved with him. He'd romanced me, seduced me, then proposed. We'd moved in together and had been planning a life together. How was I to know that he had an estranged wife and a couple kids somewhere? But Tassie didn't believe me—or maybe she did, and she just didn't care. All I knew was that as his official widow, she was making my life hell regarding the property I'd shared with Eli.

Tassie had insisted that I buy out her husband's share of the condo, an all but impossible feat for a single mother like me. But despite the unlikelihood of me coming up with that kind of cash, I had. Only now that I'd come up with a way to buy her out and get her off my back, she up and changed her mind…and changed the game.

The sound of my door opening drew my gaze in that direction. The moment Rayna saw me, her face erupted in a smile.

Mine did, too.

"Mommy!" she cried, and sprinted toward me on the bed.

"Morning, sweetheart." I reached for my daughter and pulled her onto the bed with me. I hugged her against my chest tightly.

"It's morning," Rayna went on, her way of telling me that it was time for me to get out of bed.

"Yes, it's morning," I agreed, then glanced at the clock—7:12 a.m.

It was the perfect time to get up—if I was heading to work. But it was a Sunday morning, the perfect time to sleep in.

My nightmare had gotten me up, and now that Rayna was awake, I was up for the day.

I lay down with Rayna, tucking her against my side. Maybe we'd both drift off.

"Mommy?" Rayna said, her little voice sounding serious.

"Yes, sweetie?"

"Want Daddy."

"Oh, baby." I hugged her small frame. "I know you do."

Eli hadn't just been my fiancé, he'd been a father figure to my daughter, whose own father had abandoned her while I'd been pregnant. Since Eli's death a few months earlier, Rayna hadn't really asked for him much. I knew she missed his presence, and I'd tried to explain to her about heaven, but I also knew that she was too young to really understand that he'd never be coming back.

"Want Daddy come home," she said.

"I know, baby. We miss him a lot. And I'm sure he misses us, too. But we can't feel sad about that, remember? Because he's in heaven, a very beautiful place, and he's happy there."

"Want to go heaven," Rayna said, pouting.

"You will, one day. One day, we all will go to heaven. And you'll see daddy again."

Given the adulterous circumstances of Eli's passing and the numerous lies he'd told me, I doubted we'd be reunited beyond the pearly gates. But Rayna didn't need to know that. She never needed to know the ugly truth about what had happened. Some things, children deserved to be protected from.

I pressed my lips to Rayna's forehead, feeling a moment of sadness for her sake. Eli's public and scandalous death had thrown my life into upheaval and I guess, because of that, I'd had to quickly put the pain of his betrayal—being killed while in the arms of another woman—behind me. Certainly for my daughter's sake, because she'd needed me to be strong.

But I felt for her, worried for how she was dealing with Eli's sudden loss in her tiny heart.

"You want to go to the zoo today?" I suggested. "See all the animals? Maybe Amani can come with us." Amani was my babysitter Carla's daughter, and she and Rayna were only a year apart. They were playmates each day when I was at work.

Rayna clapped her hands together. "Party, party!"

The last time we'd been to the zoo, five months earlier, we'd gone for Amani's birthday party. Which is why Rayna was associating another visit to the zoo with another party.

"It won't be a birthday party," I told her. "But it will be fun. We can take that train around the zoo. And you can play at the park."

Rayna nodded enthusiastically. "Zebras!"

"Yes, you'll see lots of zebras." Rayna was a huge horse-and-pony fanatic, and hadn't wanted to leave the zebra exhibit the last time we'd been to the zoo. She literally could have stayed there for hours and been content. "And maybe after we can go to the lake and feed the ducks."

"Feed ducks, feed ducks," Rayna chanted.

There were countless small lakes in South Florida, most with ducks and herons and cranes. The ducks, of course, were the only animals that cared to get close to humans. Bring food, and you were their best friend. I enjoyed seeing

Rayna's face light up when she tossed bread to them, getting a thrill out of the ducks surrounding her feet for a feast.

Yes, Rayna and I would spend a fun day together.

Put all the men we'd loved and lost out of our minds.

I decided I'd wait until ten to call Carla about going to the zoo, it being a Sunday morning and all. On the weekends, I didn't like to phone people too early. It was sort of an unwritten rule with friends and family: I didn't call them before ten in the morning, and they didn't call me. In fact, I liked to laze around in my pajamas most of the morning, sometimes later.

When Eli had been alive, Sunday mornings had often become family bed time, with me, him and Rayna in our bed, watching the Disney Channel, snuggling and giggling—not having to worry about interruptions from the outside world.

So I was a little surprised, when, at 8:40 a.m., my phone rang.

I snatched the receiver off of the wall base in the kitchen, where I was mixing batter for pancakes. Seeing my sister's number on the caller ID and given the time, I couldn't help wondering if everything was okay.

"Hello?" I said.

"Morning, Vanessa."

My sister didn't sound stressed. "Morning, Nikki."

"I hope I didn't wake you."

"No, you didn't. What's up?"

"Well…" she began, then hesitated.

I frowned. Maybe everything wasn't okay. Was my sister having a problem with her husband, Morris? They'd gone through a brief rough patch, but as far as I knew, they were blissfully in love again.

"Nikki?" I prompted.

"I have something to ask you. Something important."

"Okay," I said cautiously.

"I know this is going to seem a bit weird, but given everything that's happened, I think it's right."

"Just tell me already."

"All right." Now, I heard a smile in my sister's voice. "I'm hoping that you'll agree…to be the maid of honor at my wedding!"

It took a good couple of seconds for my sister's words to register. And then I was confused.

Considering she was already married.

"Your what?" I asked.

"My wedding," Nikki repeated.

"You already had one of those. Eight years ago."

"I know, silly," Nikki said. "But Morris and I are renewing our vows."

"You are?" I asked, my voice a croak. Not because I wasn't happy for my sister, but because I vividly remembered her first wedding. It had been a very elaborate and expensive affair. Mostly, I remembered how my sister had turned into Bridezilla as she planned the most important day of her life. She complained about practically *everything*. The floral arrangements weren't big enough, not pretty enough, the bridesmaids dresses were too long, then too short. The menu changed at least once a week before it had to be firmed up. She wanted over-the-top elaborate on a scale that only celebrities typically indulge in. Anyone who tried to reason with her—namely, me, Morris and their wedding planner—got an earful and often a bout of tears thrown in on top of that.

Nikki is my only sibling, and eight years my senior. She can be trying on a good day, but when she's stressed out, she's pretty much unbearable.

"I know what you're thinking. That a second wedding now is at least fifteen years too soon. But after Morris's indiscretion, we felt it was best to have a brand-new start. You know."

"Hey, you have to do what you need to do," I said. If she felt a renewing of vows was in order, who was I to argue? "What are you thinking? A small ceremony somewhere?" Hopefully a city hall wedding, where she couldn't be too demanding. A justice of the peace could marry them, and then we all could be on our merry way without the headaches that would come from a bigger wedding.

"Nothing too big," Nikki said. "Maybe seventy-five or a hundred people."

"What?"

"And it's got to be on the beach. I said I want to go somewhere exotic, like Thailand. But Morris says the Keys will be fine, or maybe Jamaica or the Bahamas."

Was my sister serious? Or was she pulling an early morning prank? I didn't know what was worse—that she thought one hundred people constituted a small wedding, or that she expected a hundred people to travel across the world to Thailand for her second "once in a lifetime" day.

That had been her mantra the first time around. That she needed this extravagant thing, or that impossible to get thing because it was for her "once in a lifetime" day.

How nice she got to have two.

"Are you serious about Thailand?" I asked, half-chuckling. "I mean, you can't be—right?"

"What's wrong with Thailand?" she asked, sounding a little dismayed.

I felt the headache coming on already. Bridezilla Part Two. Oh, the joy.

"I hear Thailand is one of the most beautiful places in the world," my sister went on.

"I'm sure it is…but I don't think anyone has ever traveled there to have what they'd describe as a 'small' second wedding. Seventy-five to a hundred people? That's not a small wedding, sis."

"What's wrong with you?" Nikki asked. "Aren't you happy for me?"

"Of course I'm happy for you. I'm very happy that you and Morris are staying together and that you're working things out. It's just—"

"That it hurts you to see me having a second wedding when you haven't even had your first?"

I gritted my teeth at the comment. Counted to three. Made sure that when I spoke, I didn't say something I would end up regretting.

"No," I began. "I was going to say that what you're proposing sounds very expensive. A small, intimate wedding at city hall would accomplish the exact same thing. A renewal of your vows. And if you still want to go to Thailand, go for your second honeymoon."

Silence. Nikki must have been mulling over my suggestion.

"You think seventy-five of your closest friends will be

willing to hop on a plane to Thailand?" I asked, my tone saying the question was rhetorical.

"Probably fifty or sixty of them."

I highly doubted that. My sister's friends were all like her—married with children. Not to mention their careers. I didn't see that many of them being able—or willing—to head to Thailand for her second wedding.

"Will you do it?" she asked. "Be my maid of honor?"

"Yes," I answered. "Of course." I really didn't have a choice. I could only hope that as the weeks passed—and common sense set in—Nikki would decide on having her wedding a little closer to home.

"Good. I'm so excited!" she squealed. "A second wedding, a fresh start. This is going to be wonderful."

"I'm sure it is."

"I was thinking maybe December. Over Christmas, when everyone will have time off. That'll give everyone time to start making travel arrangements now for their trip to Thailand."

I suddenly realized that when it came to Nikki, "common sense" wasn't necessarily a factor. For some reason, she was stuck on Thailand. "I thought you said that Morris wanted to go to the Keys or the Bahamas," I said, hoping to steer her off the far east course.

"Yes. But I want to go to Thailand."

I shook my head. My sister. There was no getting through to her. When she got an idea about something, no one could change her mind.

I wondered if Morris even wanted a second wedding, or if he was strictly going along with the suggestion as penance for his sin of adultery.

"Oh, I have to run," Nikki suddenly said. "We're going to church."

"Okay. I'll talk to you later."

"If you want, you can meet us there for the later service. There are a few eligible bachelors in the congregation."

"I'll think about it," I lied. I wasn't against the idea of going to church. Eli and I used to go together sometimes. What I didn't want was my sister trying to hook me up between hymns.

"Don't just think about it," Nikki said. "Do it."

"Later, sis."

"'Bye."

Once I hung up with Nikki, I called Carla and asked if she wanted to go to the zoo with the kids.

"Oooh," she said. "That sounds like fun."

"Meet you at your place for noon?"

"You're on."

2

I was just about ready to head to Carla's place when my phone rang. Leaving Rayna in the doorway, I ran into the living room to answer the phone.

I snatched up the receiver. "Hello?"

Nothing.

"Hello?" I repeated.

A few more beats of nothing passed, and then I heard the dial tone in my ear.

I replaced the receiver, figuring someone had dialed the wrong number. No sooner was the receiver back on the hook than the phone rang again. I picked it up before it could ring a second time and said an exasperated, "Hello?"

Again, nothing.

"Stop calling me and get a life," I said to whomever was on the other end of my line. Really…prank phone calls? Twice in a row wasn't an accident—it was an asshole.

I was just about to pull the receiver from my ear when I

heard a faint voice. A whisper of something, but so low that I couldn't make out what the person had said.

"Who's there?" Was it actually not a prank call and simply a bad connection?

And then I heard the voice again. Definitely a whisper, but loud enough this time that I could make out what the person had said.

Bitch.

"Who the hell is this?" I demanded. But even as I asked the question, I realized I knew who it was.

Tassie Johnson.

"If that's you, Tassie—" I began, but the dial tone suddenly blared in my ear.

I slammed down the receiver, convinced that the person who'd called had been none other than Tassie "The Bitch" Johnson. The woman had to be close to forty, but it was clear that she got off on behaving like she was still in junior high.

Oh, I hated her. Hated her with a passion. Instead of Tassie trying to understand that Eli had lied to me about her existence, and accepting the fact that I hadn't "stolen" him from her, the woman was out for blood. She was living in the multimillion-dollar mansion that Eli had bought while he'd played for the Atlanta Braves. I'm sure she had cars, expensive jewelry and expensive art. Along with her Atlanta home, there were no doubt second and third homes in other cities.

Tassie Johnson didn't need my condo.

The only reason she was interested in it was because she wanted to make me miserable. Punish me for having been with the man who no longer loved her.

If her petty behavior with me was any indication, it was no wonder she had pushed Eli away. Of course, that didn't justify Eli's not telling me about her or the children they'd had together.

I checked the caller ID for the number of the person who had called, certain I'd see a 404 area code. But all it showed was Private Name, Private Number.

That wasn't surprising. And it didn't matter. I knew it was Tassie trying to get under my skin. And because I knew that, I didn't let the phone call bother me.

I headed back to Rayna, who was waiting patiently in the foyer. At two-and-a-half, she rarely waited patiently, which only proved how excited she was to get on with our outing.

"Okay, sweetie," I said. "Mommy's ready."

The phone rang again.

"For crying out loud," I muttered. I debated not answering it, but if it was Tassie again, I wanted to give her an earful before she had the chance to hang up.

I charged into the living room. Before picking up the receiver, I checked out the caller ID. Seeing my sister's cell phone number, my anger dissipated and was replaced by confusion. It was minutes to noon. Hadn't she gone to church?

I put the receiver to my ear and said, "Nikki?"

"What do you mean, I'm unbearable?" my sister asked, and now my eyebrows shot up.

"What?" I said, not at all understanding what was going on.

"Are you forgetting why we have to renew our vows in the first place?" she went on.

I got it then. She obviously wasn't talking to me. "Hello? Nikki?"

Nikki groaned in frustration. "Vanessa, will you talk some sense into Morris?"

"Nikki, what's going on?"

Nikki didn't answer. I heard some shuffling sounds and the faint sound of gospel music. But I also heard the sounds of traffic, making me wonder if they were in the car. If so, the music had to be coming from the radio.

"Hello?" I said.

"Hello?" Morris's voice.

"What's going on, Morris?"

"Your sister and I can't agree on this whole second wedding thing."

"It's not a *thing*," my sister said in the background. "It's about our *reaffirming* of our vows because *you* fucked up!"

"Nice post-church talk," I muttered. The minister must not have reminded the parishioners to abstain from cursing, I thought wryly. Morris didn't hear me, however, because he and Nikki were now bickering back and forth. I caught snippets of, "We've been through this," and "So in your mind everything's fine?"

I wondered if either of them would notice if I hung up the phone.

I didn't. Instead, I said, "Morris? Are you still there?"

"Yeah."

Rayna wandered into the living room and went straight for the box of crayons and pad of paper on the coffee table. One of her favorite things to do was draw pictures.

"I thought you were going to church," I said.

"We did. But we…had a disagreement."

"In *church?*"

"About the wedding," Morris clarified.

How had they had time to discuss the wedding during the ceremony, much less get into a disagreement? "What exactly is the issue, Morris?"

"I don't see why we can't take a trip to Key West with our closest friends. That way, Nikki gets to have her wedding on the beach. And we both get to save a ton of money. She watched some show where a couple got married in Thailand, and suddenly she's got it in her mind that that's the only place in the world good enough to renew our vows."

"You're lucky I even want to marry you again!" Nikki spat out. "After what you did."

"Where are the kids?" I asked.

"In the backseat," Morris replied. "Watching a DVD."

Good grief. "Put my sister back on the phone."

After a couple seconds, Nikki came on the line, saying, "You see what I have to deal with? Not only does he cheat, now he's got to make this difficult, too."

"Nikki, I understand you're upset," I said in a calm voice. "But you have the boys in the car. This kind of fighting in front of them is…well, it's crazy. You don't want them all involved in grown folks' business. Especially not this. Talk to Morris when you get home."

Nikki didn't say anything for a moment, which I took to be a good sign. Hopefully I was getting through to her.

"Be glad you're not in a relationship," she finally said. "Because men suck."

"Right, they totally suck," I said, feigning agreement. Rayna held up a picture with green and blue strokes, and I smiled encouragingly at her. "But please calm down until you get home. Don't let planning your second wedding send you to divorce court."

"Vanessa, I'm coming over."

"What?"

"I can't deal with Morris right now," my sister said, her voice cracking. "I just need to be away from him for a while."

"But I'm on my way out—"

"I'm gonna drop him off and head straight to your place."

No, not this. Please, God. "Why don't you call me back when you've gotten home?" I suggested. "Make sure the kids are fed or whatever, take a moment to calm down—"

Nikki started to cry.

"Nikki," I said after several seconds. "Nikki?"

"Morris thinks I'm overreacting," she sniffed. "Do you think I'm overreacting?"

I didn't want to answer the question. I didn't want to answer it truthfully, that is—not with my sister bawling on the other end of my phone line.

So I said, "You're emotional. That's understandable. But like I said, you have to calm down. If not for your sake, then for your kids. This can't be good for them."

"Okay," Nikki said, and I heard her inhaling some deep breaths. "You're right. Mommy's sorry," she said to the boys. "I'm just a little bit mad at your dad right now."

Understatement of the century. "Call me when you get home," I said. "We'll talk some more."

"We're almost home, so I'll drop Morris off, then head straight to your place."

"You'll what?"

"I really need you right now, Vanessa." Nikki's voice broke. "I really need my sister."

"Yes, but, I made plans. How about later?"

The dial tone sounded in my ear.

Oh, for God's sake. Had my sister heard me? Was she going to go home and stay there—or would she soon be on her way?

With any luck, Nikki's spat with Morris would be resolved by the time she got home, and she'd call to tell me that she was no longer coming over.

I reached forward and pulled Rayna into my arms, frowning as I did. Nikki being Nikki, if she *did* come here and I wasn't around, I wouldn't hear the end of it.

"Let's go zoo!" Rayna said.

Damn, this wasn't fair. I had a fun day planned for my daughter, and now it was ruined. "Maybe we can go see the monkeys and all the animals another time," I suggested. "Your cousins are coming over, so you can play with them."

"Monkeys," Rayna said, pouting. "Zebras."

"I know. But, your Auntie Nikki is coming over. And she's on her way right now, which means we can't leave." I kissed Rayna's temple. "Next weekend, I promise."

Rayna's pout grew larger.

Beside me on the sofa were two of her ponies, her favorite toys to play with. I lifted both and gave her one. "How about we play ponies? Is this one Rainbow Dash?" I asked as I held up the green one, knowing full well that this one's name was not Rainbow Dash.

"No," Rayna admonished with a smile, happy to be able to correct me. "That's Minty."

"That's right. Green tea."

"No! Minty."

"Ohh. Minty."

"Yes, Minty."

"Rayna, do you want to play with me?" I asked in a high-pitched voice, prancing Minty around.

Rayna giggled, then began playing with her own pony. We played together for several minutes before I remembered Carla.

"Just a minute, sweetie. Mommy has to make a call."

I lifted the receiver from beside me on the sofa and punched in the digits to Carla's number.

"I'm sorry, Carla," I said after I filled her in. "But you know my sister. And I can live without the headache of her freaking out when she comes over and finds I'm not here."

"I understand," Carla said.

"Next weekend?"

"It's a date."

I brewed a fresh pot of coffee, figuring I'd need the extra caffeine if I was going to have to spend the next several hours drowning in a sea of my sister's issues.

Not something I relished, considering I had enough problems of my own.

I waited.

And waited.

Nikki didn't show.

3

By the next morning, I still hadn't heard from my sister—but I also hadn't heard from the police with any bad news. I was pissed that she'd had so little regard for my time that she didn't have the decency to call and say she wasn't coming over.

I wondered if she'd even given me a second thought. If she'd considered, even for a moment, that she'd done anything wrong.

But I soon stopped thinking about Nikki when I got to work and saw the temp receptionist behind the desk in the entrance to the office. She had frizzy red hair and a face full of freckles, and looked nothing like the woman she was filling in for. Though the temp had been there for the past two weeks, it still caught me off guard to see her sitting behind the broad desk.

Still made me feel a moment of sadness and anger that she had to be there at all.

Alaina Rivera, my good friend and the agency's regular

receptionist, was home recovering after a vicious attack by her jealous and out-of-control ex-husband. She'd been banged up pretty good, had spent a week in hospital, and God only knew how much longer she would be off of work due to her injuries.

I pushed aside my feelings about Alaina and smiled at the temp as I strode past the reception desk. "Good morning, Nora."

"Good morning."

I was almost fully out of the foyer when I heard her ask tentatively, "Um, Ms. Cain?"

I halted, turned back. "Yes, Nora?"

"There was a call for you about ten minutes ago. From a Bradley Harris? He's from—"

"Harris, Lawton and Stein. Yes, I know."

"Oh. Well, he said that you two have been playing phone tag and it's crucial that you call him back today."

Bradley and I had *not* been playing phone tag. I'd been avoiding him after his phone call a week and a half earlier, when he'd told me that Tassie no longer wanted me to buy out Eli's share of my condo—she wanted me out, period.

The way I saw it, I didn't have much to say to Bradley Harris on the matter, because I wasn't planning on moving.

Nora extended a sheet of paper to me. "He, uh, left numbers where you can reach him."

"Thank you." I walked back to the reception desk, where I took the slip of paper from Nora, though I didn't have any intention of calling Bradley back.

I mean, what was the point? We didn't see eye to eye on this issue, and likely never would. I figured if I avoided him long enough, Tassie would give up on her demand and they'd disappear from my life forever.

A girl can hope, can't she?

I continued on to my office, where I crumpled the note with the lawyer's phone numbers and tossed it in the trash.

I didn't want to call him. I'd played nice, danced around like a puppet as Tassie pulled the strings and got a good laugh out of making my life hell. Trying to "come up with a solution," as the lawyer had suggested, had resulted in Tassie changing her mind. So really, could my plan to ignore her and her lawyer put me in a worse position than I already was in?

Though I'd had that nightmare about being forced out of my home, I didn't believe for a second that was going to happen.

I settled in behind my desk and booted my computer up. It was a Monday morning, and I needed to get schedules in order and start on the mid-month payroll. Agent expenses had to be calculated. There was a lot to do, and calling Bradley Harris simply wasn't on my list.

But first, I allowed myself to think about the one person I knew I was better off forgetting.

I opened my drawer and withdrew the framed photo of me and Chaz. We'd taken the photo when he'd come to Miami to visit me and explore the possibility of signing with the agency I worked for. Believe The Dream, Change Your Life was an agency that represented motivational speakers and life coaches. Chaz was one of the hottest names in the business, and he worked alone. Had I been able to sign him to my agency, I would have had my shot at becoming an agent, which was my ultimate goal.

It had almost happened. But a little white lie I'd told Chaz had come back to haunt me. Chaz had dumped me because of that lie, and as a result, had walked away from the opportunity to work with me.

Chaz had always said that the one thing he couldn't deal with was dishonesty. I'd learned how serious he was the hard way.

In the picture, Chaz was smiling widely, a spark in his eyes. I was smiling just as happily, a woman who'd finally found the man of her dreams.

How could Chaz and I have gone from this happy moment to utter despair? As long as I lived, I would never forget the look of utter disappointment on Chaz's face when Byron, my daughter's father, had shown up in the restaurant that day. Having told Chaz that Rayna's father was dead, Byron's appearance—and theatrics over possibly losing his daughter—had been a double shock.

Why hadn't I told Chaz that Rayna's father indeed was still alive, but a total deadbeat dad?

My phone rang, startling me out of my thoughts. I jumped in fright, then reached for my phone.

"Vanessa Cain."

"Hello, Vanessa." A woman's voice.

"Yes?"

"My name is Charlie Mann. I'm with Real Life Pictures in Hollywood."

I sat up straight, wary. "Yes."

"I heard all about your ordeal with Eli Johnson, and I'd love the opportunity to speak to you about the option of buying your story."

"Buying my story?"

"I'd like to make it into a movie of the week."

I frowned into the receiver, wondering if the person on the other end of my line was playing some sort of a joke on me. "Are you…is this a friend of Tassie's?"

"You mean Tassie Johnson, the wife Eli never told you about?"

The woman sounded almost gleefully excited as she relayed the facts I had wanted to put behind me. Like someone sharing a piece of gossip.

No, she wasn't a friend of Tassie's.

"This is for real?" I asked.

"Absolutely. And your story has the right amount of sex, deception, twists and turns that would make a fantastic movie. The secret wife and kids, being murdered in his lover's bed. The whole 'celebrity behaving badly' angle is a huge sell."

"Right," I said absently, the woman's retelling of what had happened in my life making my stomach twist.

"Of course, you'll be paid," Charlie went on.

"Oh?" I rolled my chair forward and rested my elbows on the desk. "How much?"

"The exact amount will have to be negotiated, but it would be…significant."

Possibly thousands of dollars, just for sharing my story with America. A story they already knew, quite frankly, so it wasn't as if I would be airing my dirty laundry.

Of course, a movie would get into much more detail, like how I'd met Eli, our courtship, his life with Tassie.

My life with Rayna.

"When can we meet, Vanessa? I'd be happy to fly you to L.A."

"You know what, I'm not interested."

"I think we should meet face-to-face, and you can hear my ideas."

"I really am not interested," I reaffirmed. "I think the story has been exploited enough, and I didn't exactly come out of it smelling like roses. Then there's my daughter…"

"I promise you, we'll handle the story sensitively."

"Short of when my parents died, what happened with Eli was the worst time of my life. I have no desire to revisit that tragic time." Not even if the money sounded appealing. "I'm sorry, but that's my final decision."

"If you change your mind—"

"I won't. Thank you for the call, though."

I replaced the receiver, then exhaled sharply. A producer wanted to make a movie out of my life?

Unbelievable.

When my phone rang again, I assumed it was the producer calling back, and I debated not answering it. But there was one thing I couldn't do as the agency's office manager—ignore my phone.

I picked up the receiver and put it to my ear. "Vanessa Cain."

"Hey, girl."

"Alaina," I said, feeling immediate relief. "How are you?"

"Better. I'm feeling a lot better than yesterday."

"Oh, I'm so glad to hear that."

"I figure I'll be back to work in no time."

"Of course you will. You're a fighter." I said the words

not only to support Alaina, but also because I believed them. In the face of a horrific assault, she was finding the courage not just to go on, but to not let what her ex-husband had done bring her down emotionally.

"So, any office gossip?" Alaina asked. "I'm going through serious gossip withdrawal."

"Not really," I said. "Well, that's not true. You'll never believe who just called me."

"Chaz?" Alaina asked excitedly.

"No. Not Chaz." Hearing and saying his name, I felt a pain grip my heart.

"Tassie?"

"No, not Tassie."

"Then who?"

"A Hollywood producer," I said, enunciating my words. "Would you believe she wants to make a TV movie about my story? My relationship with Eli, how he was killed, the fact that he had a secret wife and kids. All the drama that made my life total hell."

"Oh, my God! How much are they going to pay you?"

"I don't know," I said. "I didn't stay on the phone long enough to ask."

"*What?* Tell me you did not just say what I think you said."

"You heard me."

"Are you crazy?" Alaina asked. "You turned the producer down?"

"I just said that all that drama made my life total hell. I don't want to relive that."

"But you could probably get rich! And then you wouldn't

have to marry Lewis, because you'd have the money to buy Tassie off yourself. It'd be a nice way to profit from something so horrible."

"And all I have to do is let them exploit me," I said in a fake-cheery voice. "It's not like I haven't had enough stress because of the media covering the story to last me a lifetime."

"I guess I can see your point. But still…"

"No buts. If I do this, I'm not only letting myself be exploited, I'm letting my daughter be exploited. And I've got to protect Rayna at all costs."

There was a soft sigh on the other end of the line. "I didn't think about that. Still, it's pretty cool that a producer wants to make a movie about your life, even if it's not going to happen."

"I guess," I agreed noncommittally.

"So what's going on with Debbie?" Alaina asked, referring to the ownership of the agency. "Is she still screwing Jason?"

"Actually, I'm not sure about that. She hasn't mentioned him, so maybe that's a good sign. I hope it means she's decided to stop her affair and concentrate on her family."

"You never know with Debbie." Debbie and I had been friends since I'd started working for her, but we didn't see eye to eye about her affair.

"This is true. Other than that, nothing much new here. Other than we all miss you and can't wait for you to return."

"I'm hoping next week. The doc says my ribs should be healed by then." Alaina paused. "But enough about me. How's Lewis?"

At the mention of his name, my stomach tightened. Not exactly the appropriate reaction, considering he was my fiancé.

"He's all right. I guess."

"You guess?" Alaina asked. "Haven't you spoken to him?"

"We've talked."

"When was the last time?" Alaina asked, her tone saying she didn't believe me.

"A couple days ago."

"Mmm-hmm. Are you avoiding your *fiancé?*"

"No." And I didn't like the way Alaina had said *fiancé*— as though she were mocking me.

"When are you gonna tell him?" she asked.

"Tell him what?"

"That you don't want to marry him."

"I—" I stopped abruptly, unsure what to say. I had accepted Lewis's engagement ring, which had been part and parcel of his offer to help me come up with enough cash to get Tassie off of my back.

Lewis's proposal had trapped me between a rock and a hard place. I wanted—no, needed—his help. But I didn't quite know how to ask for his financial help and turn down his proposal. I'd loved Lewis once, but he had been a total player. I couldn't have been more surprised when he told me he'd help me with my Tassie problem—and then had proposed.

According to Lewis, he knew now that he loved me and that I was the only woman for him. He was done with his cheating ways and wanted to make a life with me.

"Vanessa?"

"Oh, sorry. What did you say?"

"I'll take that as a no," Alaina said.

"Ally, you know I love talking to you, but I've got a ton of work on my desk."

"You can't avoid this issue forever. Pretty soon, Lewis is going to start talking about setting a wedding date, and if you don't love him, don't want to be with him, you have to tell him. You can't marry him just because he's got the financial means for you to fight Tassie."

"I'll talk to you later, Ally."

"All right, girl. But think about what I said."

Think about it? I could do nothing but.

Like Alaina had said, Lewis was the only one who could help me fight Tassie. And I certainly didn't want to seem as though I would use him only for his cash. How could I turn down Lewis's proposal? Especially since he claimed to love me?

I stared at the photo of me and Chaz again, then put it back in the desk drawer. It was after Alaina had been attacked by her ex that I'd gotten a new perspective. That maybe passionate love was overrated. Passionate love led to seriously painful heartache.

The kind I was suffering now.

I'd come to the realization that it was probably far better to have a marriage based on friendship and respect. Sexual chemistry—like what Lewis and I had once shared—was a bonus.

Not that there was any sexual chemistry right now. Try as I might to convince myself of the non-passionate-marriage argument, I was still grieving over Chaz, and until I'd gotten over him, I knew I couldn't share my body with Lewis.

But perhaps some time soon…

Even as I tried to convince myself of that, my mind wandered to the photo of me and Chaz, and that happy time we had shared.

And I knew in my heart that I wanted that back.

Wanted him back.

4

I put Chaz out of my mind and concentrated on work. It was the only way. Actually, it was the best way. Focusing on work made me forget about the grief I was feeling in my heart.

At least temporarily.

There was still no call from my sister, but I took her lack of contact as good news. Trust me, if she had been planning to see a divorce lawyer, she would have called and made me join her.

Thank God she hadn't. I didn't need her drama on top of my own. Already, I'd missed out on taking Rayna to the zoo because of Nikki.

I glanced at the wall clock. It was almost three-thirty. I would try to leave a little early today, head home, get Rayna, then take her to the lake so we could feed the ducks. There was a spot in Coconut Grove we'd been a few times, and it was always a fun experience.

My daughter needed fun right now. We both did.

And she needed to know that even if the man she'd known as her father wasn't coming back, I would always be there for her.

I got up, stretched my body, then strolled to the window. As was typical every day during the summer months in South Florida, we'd have an afternoon downpour. I welcomed the short showers as they cooled things down. The sun always returned after the rain, and right now, it was shining brightly on downtown Miami.

My phone rang. I turned around and took three long strides back to my desk and snatched up the receiver before the phone could ring a third time.

"Vanessa Cain."

"Ms. Cain. Hello."

I swallowed.

"This is Bradley Harris."

The man didn't have to identify himself for me to know that it was the lawyer I'd come to dread hearing from. "Yes. I recognized your voice."

"I called this morning, but I haven't heard back from you."

"Really?" I asked, feigning surprise as I rolled my eyes. "You know, we have a temp receptionist right now. She must have forgotten to give me the message."

"That must be it," Bradley said, but I could tell by his tone that he didn't believe me.

"How can I help you?" I asked brightly.

"I'm calling to see if we can arrange a meeting to discuss the transfer of the condo to my client."

The condo. Not "your condo." As if I had no ownership of it whatsoever.

"You want a meeting," I repeated.

"Yes."

"You know, I've got a very busy schedule. Maybe we can arrange something in a few months."

"Ms. Cain, I know what you're doing." The lawyer sounded a little exasperated. "You think that if you put this meeting off, the problem will simply go away. I assure you, it will not."

I said nothing.

"There are two ways to do this. The easy way—and the hard way."

I rolled my eyes again. Now the lawyer sounded like a character out of a bad movie. "You don't have to threaten me."

"I'm not threatening you. But you do need to know that this is a serious legal matter, one that won't be resolved with stall tactics. And trust me, you don't want this going to court."

I frowned, thinking. I wasn't too sure that Bradley was right. In fact, I figured he was trying to scare me. However, I knew that going to court would cost money. Money I didn't have.

I didn't have even the slightest interest in meeting with attorney Bradley Harris and the woman who had been a thorn in my side. But despite the fact that I'd been avoiding Tassie's lawyer, I knew he was right. I couldn't avoid Bradley and Tassie forever. At some point, this situation would have to be resolved.

Fine—if Tassie wanted a meeting, we'd have a meeting. However, she would soon learn that I wasn't planning to hand over anything to her.

She was in for a fight.

"Ms. Cain?"

"When?" I asked. I knew I sounded testy, but I didn't care. "When were you and Tassie thinking of having this meeting?"

"Early next week would be good for my client. We can meet in Miami, as I know that will be more convenient for you."

"Very thoughtful," I muttered softly, not meaning my words. But the lawyer was right. I would have to meet with him and Tassie Johnson sooner or later.

It would just have to be sooner.

"Will that work for you?" Bradley asked.

"Yes. How about Tuesday? The afternoon will be better for me."

"Let me verify my schedule and speak with Tassie, then I'll get back to you."

"You do that."

I hung up the phone, emitting a groan as I did. Then I forced myself to draw in a few steady breaths.

I was looking forward to this meeting as much as a person looks forward to root canal. But on one hand, I was glad that the lawyer had forced this meeting. Because with a date set, I would have to take action myself.

The last time I'd spoken with Bradley Harris, I'd been determined to fight back. Determined to keep my home from the hands of a greedy, conniving bitch. I'd called a reporter from the *Miami Herald* who'd followed the story of Eli's death and asked for her help. But as the days passed and I hadn't heard from her, I'd put the whole matter out of my mind, wrongly hoping that Tassie would simply go away.

I needed to call Cynthia Martin back, see what the reporter had discovered. Perhaps she'd forgotten my request or had been too busy to do any digging. If that was the case, my call would prompt her into action.

And if she'd been unable to find any dirt on Tassie, then I'd have to hire a private investigator. Because I knew the dirt was there.

I felt certain that Tassie was involved with the man who'd been at her side at Eli's funeral. There was no law against that, especially since she and Eli had been separated for years. But it mattered in terms of the way Tassie had portrayed herself in the media—like the doting, grieving widow who'd never stepped out on her man, even though he'd had his own indiscretions. And she had painted me out to be a gold digger who had relentlessly pursued her pro-athlete husband for his cash.

Given her lies, I knew that for Tassie perception was everything. A woman like her would hate to have the truth about her own adulterous relationship exposed for the world to see.

And if she hoped to persuade a judge that she deserved my home because she and her husband had been very much together at the time of his death and that I was simply a woman on the side, she also needed to keep up her grieving widow charade.

With Cynthia's help, I was about to blow that plan up in Tassie's pathetic face.

Well, I hoped I was. Even if I believed that Tassie had

been living her own life and had been romantically involved with at least one man in the past seven years, I still needed proof. Proof was the only thing that would *persuade* her to leave me the heck alone.

My temples throbbed. Talking to Bradley Harris and thinking about my predicament had brought on a headache.

I withdrew a bottle of ibuprofen from my desk and downed two capsules with the dregs of my cold coffee. As I was swallowing, my phone rang again.

I hesitated—and then was angry that I even had to be wary of answering my office phone. Damn Tassie Johnson.

I picked up the receiver and placed it at my ear. "Vanessa Cain."

"Baby," came the smooth, sexy voice.

My stomach tensed slightly at the sound of Lewis's voice. It shouldn't have, of course, considering he was my fiancé.

Then again, he wasn't really my fiancé—well, not in the true sense of the word. He'd proposed marriage, and had assumed that I'd accepted. I'll admit, I didn't do much to let him think I hadn't accepted his proposal, but I hadn't really had a choice. He was the way out of a problem—the problem being the woman who wanted to take my home from me and my daughter. Lewis could easily give me the money to pay off Tassie Johnson.

The simple fact was that I couldn't afford to turn down Lewis's proposal. Not when I knew that it was part and parcel of his offer of financial help.

But I'd loved him once. I could love him again.

"Vanessa?" Lewis said, reminding me that I hadn't greeted him. "You there?"

"Hey, Lewis."

"What's wrong, baby?" he asked.

"Nothing."

"Then why do you sound stressed out?"

"I do?"

"Uh-huh."

"It's been a long day," I said. "I'm getting a bit of a headache, that's all."

"Maybe I need to come by and give you a nice back rub."

I smiled and said, "Nice try, Lewis. But I'll be fine."

"It would just be a back rub. Right in your office. With the door open if you want. So everyone will know there's no monkey business going on."

After realizing that I couldn't exactly turn Lewis's proposal down, I'd told him two things: that I wanted a long engagement, and that I wanted to wait until we were married to have sex.

Total stall tactic. I admit it.

"I'll pass on that, thank you."

"Damn," Lewis muttered. "You're being tough on a brother. But I get it, so I'm not complaining."

"Thank you for understanding."

"Any word from Tassie Johnson's lawyer?" he suddenly asked.

"As a matter of fact, yes," I said. "I got off the phone with him a few minutes ago."

"And?"

"And he's proposing a meeting. Next week."

"Good."

I drew in a shuddery breath. "Yeah, I guess it is."

"You've got to do this sooner or later, babe."

"I know."

"Did you tell the lawyer that you definitely have the cash and offer to buy out Tassie's share again?"

Lewis had advised me to do that, but I hadn't. "I didn't bother to call him back, because it's clear Tassie is playing games. I kinda hoped they'd just go away."

"Now you know he's not going away, so the meeting's a good thing. I'll go with you, we'll bring a check. Tassie's gonna be there?"

"Yes."

"I'll make it a cashier's check. When Tassie sees it, I bet she'll happily accept it and disappear."

I found myself smiling. Lewis was definitely being super-supportive, and I was extremely grateful for that. The idea of him being with me at the meeting set my mind at ease. Perhaps with Lewis by my side and a fat check in his hands, Tassie would give up on her latest plan. After all, I knew she was a greedy little witch, using her lawyer to push me around. The bitch was probably laughing her head off in her Atlanta mansion right now.

But she'd see who would have the last laugh.

"Not that you *should* buy her out," Lewis went on. "Now that we're engaged, we're gonna find our own place to live."

"You know why this is important to me."

"On principle, yes, I get it. It's just kind of a shame, since you're going to sell the place anyway."

"Not really, since we're going to have a long engagement," I pointed out. "As we discussed."

"I know. But that doesn't mean we can't live together."

"Yes, it does, because living together will compromise the no-sex rule," I said sweetly.

"Baby, I hear you. And I get it." Lewis paused. "When I was with you, I messed up. Big-time. That's why I'm willing to do anything I have to to prove to you that you're the only woman for me. I know you love me. But you can't trust me. And I'm going to change that."

Lewis was saying all the right things. I *had* loved him. Loved that he made me feel sexy and desirable with just one look. Loved that he made me laugh. I could have married Lewis and lived happily ever after if he hadn't been such a player.

But lately, my outlook on love had changed. I wanted the fantasy…but it had eluded me. Maybe I was far better off marrying someone I liked a lot and got along with as a friend—and that was definitely Lewis. Even after he'd cheated on me, we'd remained friends. Maybe that was a sign that we'd be able to have a successful marriage.

"Mostly, I'm thinking about Rayna," I said, which wasn't a lie. "Her little heart's been broken over Eli, and now Chaz is suddenly gone… She's the reason I want to make sure I keep our home, so there's some sense of stability for her."

"I think it'll help if she starts seeing me again. We should do some fun things together—"

"No," I said, cutting Lewis off. "I'm not ready for that."

I'd trusted Eli, and he'd hurt me. Now Rayna was without the father she'd known. She hadn't known Chaz long, but she'd taken to him immediately. Until I was certain that I'd be marrying Lewis, I didn't want my daughter forming an attachment to him, because the last thing I wanted to do was put her little heart at risk again.

"It'll happen," I quickly said, not wanting to offend Lewis. "Just…give it some time."

"What about dinner tonight?" Lewis suggested. "We can go over strategy regarding your meeting with Tassie and her lawyer."

I was about to say no, but stopped myself. Lewis was going to give me the cash I needed to take care of my Tassie problem. And I was engaged to him—officially, if not wholeheartedly. I couldn't avoid him.

"Actually, that's a good idea." I could take Rayna to feed the ducks after dinner with Lewis. "Why don't I call my babysitter, and if it's okay with her, you can meet me on Ocean Drive and we can have an early dinner? That way I won't be out too late, and I can spend some quality time with Rayna before she goes to bed."

"Sounds like a plan."

"I'll call you back to confirm."

"All right, sweetheart."

Sweetheart.

I swallowed at the term of endearment as I hung up the phone. If only when Lewis said that, I felt warm and fuzzy inside.

But I didn't, and I wasn't sure I ever would again.

5

Lewis and I made plans to meet at The Clevelander, a spot that had a lot of history for us. Sexual history. I could have protested when I called Lewis back and he suggested the spot, but I didn't. I knew that Lewis was hoping I'd cave to the emotional history the place represented for us. And for that reason, I knew I needed to go there as a test of my own feelings for him as well as a test of my own resolve to keep our relationship platonic.

As I waited for Lewis at a table on the patio, I gazed at the palm trees that lined the South Beach strip. The scent of the ocean filled the air, and I could hear the sounds of calypso, reggae and hip-hop coming from the surrounding clubs. At night, the strip lit up in an array of neon colors, highlighting the beauty of the art deco buildings. On South Beach you had the beach, the swanky clubs, architectural history and natural beauty. As far as I was concerned, South Beach was one of the most beautiful places in the world, and very likely the hippest.

I loved living here. It offered fun for the kids, excitement for the adults. Being on South Beach was like living in paradise. As I took in everything I loved about the place, I was more convinced than ever that I wouldn't lose my home.

At least not to a greedy, conniving, self-serving bitch.

"Hey, gorgeous."

At the sound of Lewis's voice, I looked over my shoulder. He looked sexy as hell in a tailored, pin-striped navy suit. Honestly, Lewis Carter looked like a top-paid model, or even a movie star. I had no doubt that his smile had gotten many a woman hot and bothered—me included.

Yes, Lewis's great looks had attracted me to him, but it was his ability to make me laugh that had made me fall in love with him.

As I stood to meet Lewis, I sensed eyes on us. A quick glance around and I saw that women in The Clevelander and those strolling the street were checking Lewis out. He had the kind of sex appeal that drew women's attention like white on rice.

Not seeming to notice the women, Lewis slipped an arm around my waist, drew me close and kissed me full on the mouth. It was the kind of kiss that at one time would have had me smoldering, but I didn't feel much more than a tingle now.

I was kind of hoping I would. Anything to show the feelings I'd had for Lewis once could return.

I broke the kiss and smiled up at Lewis. "As usual, all eyes are on you."

"But I only have eyes for *you,* baby."

Lewis gestured for me to sit, so I did, and he helped me ease my chair back under the table. Then he took a seat opposite me.

His eyes zoomed in on my left hand, then narrowed. I knew what he was thinking before he spoke the question.

"Where's your ring?"

"Oh." I drew my purse onto my lap, reached into it and opened the engagement ring box. Beneath the cover of the table, I slipped the engagement ring onto my finger. "I noticed someone following me when I left my office building," I lied. "I slipped it off my finger…in case the guy wanted to cut my finger off to get the ring."

Lewis's eyes widened. "You were followed?"

"I think so," I hedged. "I'm not sure. But, I wanted to be safe. Just in case." I placed my left hand flat on the table, showcasing the amazing engagement ring. "It's a big rock."

Lewis took my hand into his. "And no less than you deserve."

Smiling somewhat uncomfortably, I pulled my hand back and linked my fingers together, then rested my chin on my joined hands. "I want to thank you for offering to go with me to the meeting with Tassie and her lawyer next week."

"Of course I'm going with you. You're my girl."

"I think your being there is going to help a lot. But I have a couple other ideas I want to run by you."

"Shoot."

"First of all, I was thinking that it'd be really stupid for me to go to that meeting without a lawyer. I looked through the phone book for some, but I don't know who's good. I need someone who's tough. Someone who will push back when Tassie pushes. For the most part, she's been running the show with her demands, treating me as though I have to deal with *her* terms. That crap's got to stop."

"That's a great idea."

The waitress arrived, a pretty Latina whose eyes lit up when they landed on Lewis. Normally, Lewis might give a woman like her a sexy smile. But he looked her way only to order a half-carafe of white zinfandel for the table.

When the waitress was gone, I asked Lewis, "Do you know someone? Someone tough? In your business dealings, you must have a lawyer. If your lawyer isn't appropriate, hopefully they'll know someone who can help me out. I don't know what kind of attorney would be good in this situation—divorce, civil?—but I do know that I need a bull."

"I know a couple lawyers who'll be perfect for the job. Sharp, tough. Bruce Barnes. Neil Gorman. Neil's a shark."

"Perfect," I said, relieved. "You think you can put me in touch with him tomorrow? I need to get on this fast. I don't even know how I'll pay someone, but—"

"Don't worry about that," Lewis said. "You're my fiancée. I'll take care of you."

Nodding, I didn't meet Lewis's eyes. I was aware that with each step I was taking toward resolving my situation with Tassie, I was owing more and more to Lewis. Not that he would ever expect me to repay him—at least not monetarily. And yet I felt I owed him, so much so that I couldn't confess that I wasn't altogether sure about this marriage thing. I would far prefer to continue being friends with him and see how things went, but I just didn't know how to tell Lewis that.

"Vanessa?"

The sound of Lewis's voice jolted me from my thoughts. "Sorry. I was just thinking."

"It's gonna be all right," he said. "Trust me."

"I hope so." I gestured to the South Beach strip. "I can't lose my home, Lewis. Not to Tassie Johnson."

"You're not going to."

"What I don't get about her is that she's a mother. As a mother—one who's living in a multimillion-dollar mansion—how can she be so cold and callous as to take away my home? She doesn't have to like me, but where's her concern for my daughter?"

"You know this is about Eli," Lewis said. "This is Tassie's way of hurting you for hurting her."

"That's the thing. I didn't hurt her. She and Eli were married in name only by the time we got involved."

"She still wants to make you pay."

"Tell me about it," I agreed. Which was exactly the reason I would do whatever it took to get the bitch off my back.

When I saw the waitress coming, I lifted the menu and perused it. "How do you feel about an order of calamari?" I asked. "Maybe that and some bruschetta?"

"Add an order of beef fajitas to that and I'll be good to go."

The waitress placed the wine and two glasses on the table. "Are you ready to order?"

The question was directed toward Lewis, as though I weren't even at the table. I rolled my eyes. Some women.

"We'll have an order of calamari and bruschetta to start, and after that, we'll share a large order of beef fajitas."

"All right." The waitress collected the menus. I saw her gaze linger on Lewis even as he faced me once more.

I shook my head as she walked away. "Someone's got eyes just for you," I pointed out.

"Who?" Lewis asked.

I flashed him a mock-scowl. "Don't pretend you didn't notice how the waitress was drooling."

Lewis dismissed the comment with a nonchalant shrug. Then he poured us both wine.

He raised his glass in toast. "To life without Tassie," he said.

I clinked my glass against his. "Now I'll drink to that."

We both sipped our wine. As Lewis lowered his glass, he said, "You mentioned you had *ideas* about how to fight Tassie. What else were you thinking?"

"Right. Well, when Tassie's lawyer told me she no longer wants me to buy out her share of the condo—that she wants to move in instead—I got pissed. It's like you said, the bitch is just trying to mess with me. She refuses to accept that fact that I didn't destroy her marriage. Hell, I knew nothing about her. She can say what she wants to the press, but she knows the truth." For a moment, reliving the hell she had put me through, I seethed. Then I pulled myself out of my anger and continued. "I immediately called that reporter, the one from the *Miami Herald* I told you about?"

"Right."

"I saw Tassie at Eli's funeral. She seemed *very* cozy with a man by her side. I know she's got some skeletons in her closet. I was hoping the reporter could help me dig them up."

"And?"

I frowned. "And I haven't heard from her yet. I called her again today and got her voice mail. I'm starting to think there's nothing Cynthia can tell me. Well, at least nothing that she could find. I think it's time I hire my own investigator."

"Now you're talking," Lewis said. "I don't know why I didn't think of that."

"If I could get pictures of Tassie with someone else, establish some sort of proof that she was definitely involved with another man while Eli was in Miami, maybe I can use that evidence to get her to back down. She's made a name for herself as the 'victim' in the media. I don't think she'd want anyone to know that she was really crying in some other man's arms." I paused, remembering the hot stud beside Tassie at the funeral. I was certain he was her lover.

"And the way she didn't let Eli see his kids," I went on. "The way she threatened to cry child abuse if he didn't do what she demanded… A person should be put up on charges for that kind of behavior, not rewarded with more material possessions."

"Or get the shit beaten out of them," Lewis offered. Then smiled.

"Wouldn't that be nice," I commented. If the law allowed it, maybe I'd ask for five minutes alone in a room with Tassie—and one of Eli's favorite bats that he'd used when he played for the Braves. "I've thought about suing her for pain and suffering, but I don't know. Although this is America. Anyone with seventy-five bucks can fill out the forms to sue someone at the courthouse. Of course, you need the money to keep the suit going—something she has and I don't."

"You don't need to get into an ugly lawsuit situation. It's too time-consuming. What you need is for Tassie to back down. Immediately. I know an investigator. He can dig up some dirt."

"You do?"

"Baby, I'm a well-connected man."

That I believed. I didn't know the extent of Lewis's contacts, but I did know that with him being a real estate investor and developer, he knew a lot of people. Six degrees of separation and all that, he would certainly know someone who knew someone who could provide the help I needed.

"Now," Lewis said, his eyes brightening while his voice deepened, "let's talk about us."

I glanced away, suddenly uncomfortable. With Lewis, it would always come back to "us," I realized. We'd had some serious sexual chemistry that sizzled like eggs in a hot skillet.

"How late can you stay out?" Lewis asked me, the deep timbre of his voice making it clear exactly what was on his mind.

But still I asked, "Why?"

He reached for my hand. Ran his tongue along his bottom lip. "I was thinking…maybe we could go to my place for a few hours. Or, I can go up to yours."

I started to ease my hand out from under Lewis's, but he tightened his fingers, keeping my hand in place. "Lewis…"

"Would it be so wrong?" he asked me.

"I didn't say it was wrong—"

"Good, because I want to make love to you, baby."

I swallowed. "I know. But you remember what I said, don't you?"

"Yes, I remember. But come on, what's the point in waiting?" Lewis leveled one of his charming smiles on me. "It's not like we haven't been intimate many, *many* times before."

My face flushed, and I admit I felt something. How could I not? The times Lewis and I had been together had been electric.

"I was hoping I could change your mind," Lewis said, running the pad of his thumb over my inner wrist.

I pulled my hand away while returning Lewis's smile. "Oh, no you don't. You're not going to charm the pants off of me."

"No?"

"No."

Lewis reached for my hand again. Lifted it. Pressed his lips to the inside of my wrist. "Well, I'm going to have fun trying."

I felt another tingle then. Lust. I reached for my glass of water and took a sip.

"You want it, too," he said with his trademark confidence that had always turned me on. "You know you do."

I stared at him, checking out his handsome face. Could I fall into bed with Lewis? Sure. Could I fall into bed with Lewis as a way to try and forget about Chaz? Absolutely. It was the kind of thing I would have done in the past.

Lewis was guaranteed to perform in the bedroom, and he knew exactly how to please me.

But I couldn't—and wouldn't—sleep with him while

Chaz was still in my heart. Not until I'd made the definite decision to put Chaz behind me and move on.

"What I want," I began slowly and smiling sweetly, "is to wait until we're married."

"Are you sure about that?" Lewis challenged.

"Yes, I'm sure. It'll be easy for us to fall into bed together, but—"

"And fun," Lewis supplied. "A lot of fun."

I flashed a mock-scowl his way. "But," I continued, picking up my point where I'd left off, "if we wait until we're married, then I'll know for sure that your heart is in the right place."

"You still don't believe me?"

"It's not that I don't believe you," I quickly went on. "But come on, Lewis. You know me and you when it comes to sex."

Lewis wriggled his eyebrows. "How could I forget?"

"My whole point about waiting until we're married—instead of falling into bed together—is that we'll both know that we're getting married for the right reasons." I took a moment to let my words settle over Lewis. "Our sexual chemistry was never the problem. But a marriage has to be based on more than that."

Lewis nodded slowly, his lips pulling downward in a small frown. I knew he didn't like my position, but like the last time when we'd discussed this, he seemed to accept my terms without a fuss.

Two women in barely there bikinis strolled by the table. I watched Lewis, waiting to see his gaze follow the women as they passed.

Instead, he raised my hand to his mouth and kissed it. "You're worth the wait."

My lips spread in a genuine grin. Ever since proposing to me, Lewis continued to surprise me. I expected him to get frustrated with me over my no-sex requirement, but he continued to be patient. I expected the player I'd known to react to the beautiful women who flirted with him, or at least check out the eye candy. But he wasn't doing that, at least not in front of me.

Instead, Lewis gave me more and more reason to believe that he really did want to marry me for all the right reasons. And more so, that he really was in love with me.

Heck, he'd remembered my favorite wine, white zinfandel, something he hadn't done before.

Maybe this marriage thing to Lewis was going to work out just fine. Maybe, like I'd tried to convince myself, marriages built on a mutual friendship and respect were the ones that went the distance. It wasn't necessary for my heart to be overflowing with love for Lewis in order for us to have a good life together.

As long as he would be faithful to me, treat me with respect, be a good father to my daughter, that was all I could want.

Then why was it, I thought as I raised my wineglass to my lips once more, that I couldn't help wishing that it was Chaz sitting across from me?

6

"So?" Carla asked when I got to the door after my dinner with Lewis. "How did it go?"

"It was nice," I replied.

"Nice?"

"Nice dinner. Nice ambiance. Good company."

Carla raised an eyebrow. "Are you still engaged?"

I strolled into the apartment, sighing as I did. "I guess so."

"You *guess* so?"

"Yes," I said. Then with more conviction, "Yes, I am."

"Vanessa." Carla frowned. "I thought you were going to tell him that you don't want to marry him."

"I was?"

"That's what you told me last week, remember? Over a bottle of wine as you were crying about the fact that you weren't in love with Lewis."

"Vaguely."

"Vaguely?" Carla asked, her voice full of skepticism.

"I remember," I said as I plopped myself down on the sofa. "Of course I remember." I'd been extremely confused that night, pining over Chaz, but knowing that I needed Lewis to help me fight Tassie. "Well, I've changed my mind."

"Now you *do* want to marry him?"

"Where's Rayna?" I asked.

"She and Amani are snuggled under the covers on my bed. They're engrossed in that Barbie Island Princess movie. But don't change the subject. Have you really changed your mind about Lewis?"

"You should have seen him tonight, Carla. He ignored every woman who tried to flirt with him. Every single one. He even showed me this note our waitress had slipped him when she gave us the bill. The skank had the nerve to give him her phone number! Even though he was clearly with me."

"That's the way women are," Carla said sourly. "A man's more attractive when he belongs to someone else."

"Lewis ripped up the number right in front of my face. The old Lewis never would have done that."

"Score one for Lewis. But—"

"And he's going with me to that meeting with Tassie and her lawyer I told you about when I called you earlier. He's going to bring a cashier's check, which I think Tassie will happily accept."

"Again, that's nice—"

"And he's putting me in touch with a lawyer tomorrow. One who can represent me during the meeting. It'll be totally foolish for me to go without one."

"Definitely smart."

"*And* he's also going to help me find an investigator, because I need to dig up some dirt on Tassie before the meeting. Hopefully, if all goes well, Tassie will be out of my life forever after next week."

Carla crossed her fingers. "Let's hope."

"Yes. Let's hope."

"Any other wonderful things to tell me about Lewis?" Carla asked.

"No. That's about it."

"Then can I give you my opinion?"

"Of course." I pulled my legs up onto the sofa with me and stared at my friend.

"Everything you've said is great, and Lewis definitely sounds like he's changed."

"No one is more surprised than I am."

"But—" Carla said, holding up a hand to silence me. "Everything you've said also sounds like you're trying to convince yourself why you *should* go through with marrying him. And if you've got to convince yourself, then should you really be doing it?"

"It's not as simple as that," I said.

"Really?" Carla asked. "Because I thought it was as simple as if you love someone, you marry them. If you don't love someone—"

"I've learned that life isn't as easy as black and white, right and wrong. Being in love or liking someone. There are so many shades of gray, Carla, complicating everything."

"You're justifying," Carla said in a singsong voice.

"But how can I accept his help and *not* marry him?"

"With a 'thank you very much for your help, but I'm not

in love with you.' You and Lewis stayed friends after your relationship ended the first time. I'm sure you'll remain friends if you tell him the truth now."

"I don't know," I said, shaking my head. "Lately I've been thinking that love is overrated."

Carla laughed. "Love is overrated? This coming from the woman who has always been seeking the real thing? Hell, when you came back from the Bahamas, you had such a glow. And when Chaz came to visit you here, I've never seen you happier."

"And Chaz dumped me, remember? That's exactly why I say that love is overrated. No offense—I know some people find the real deal—but for others, maybe it's enough to find someone you like a lot, someone who makes you laugh. Someone who won't break your heart."

"Chaz is going to come around," Carla said. "I really believe that."

"I wish I could believe that, but he was very clear. He couldn't accept any form of dishonesty. I left him a couple messages, but he hasn't called me back." My throat grew thick with emotion, my heart heavy. "I'm not sure I'll ever get over him."

Carla patted my hand. "Oh, sweetie."

"Which is exactly why I need to marry someone I'm not head over heels in love with," I went on, trying to push my sad feelings aside. "Lewis and I can have the passion in the bedroom without love. I think it's a win-win situation."

"I saw the way Chaz looked at you," Carla said, her voice encouraging. "It was obvious how much he loved you."

I swallowed. Hard. I didn't want Carla talking about

Chaz—it was too painful to remember what I'd shared with him. "It's over," I said simply. "He made that very clear."

"But it doesn't have to be," Carla insisted. "Not forever."

"Carla—"

"A man wants to know a woman's crazy about him," she said. "Just as much as he's crazy about her. I say you fight for him."

"I tried that. It didn't work, remember?"

"You called a couple times. Maybe you need to call twenty times. One hundred. Whatever it takes to prove to him that he's the only man you'll ever love."

I lifted my left hand, showing the enormous engagement ring Lewis had given me.

"I've got nothing against Lewis," Carla said. "Except that you couldn't trust him to be faithful."

"But that's the thing. He's really changed."

"Fine. Let's say he has. If you could return from a date with him and be glowing the way you did after you'd met Chaz, I would wholeheartedly support any union between you and him. You're a terrific girl, Vanessa. You deserve nothing less than to spend the rest of your life with a man you're passionately in love with."

I held up a hand to stop Carla. "Stop, please. I'm confused enough already. Besides, I have the problem of Tassie Johnson. Lewis can make it go away." I wouldn't know for sure until after the meeting, but I was hoping that with a big check, Tassie would choose greed over her fight with me. And the only way for me to come up with that kind of cash was Lewis.

What else could I do? I had resolved to think of my

daughter's happiness instead of my own. Thinking of my own happiness had resulted in dating disaster after dating disaster. Personally, I was ready to close the door on my heart once and for all and deal with being a good mother. And being a good mother meant keeping my home for my daughter.

"I've given my opinion," Carla said. "I'm not going to browbeat you with it."

"Thank you."

"Because the truth is, whatever you decide, I'm going to support you. I just want to see you happy."

"Thank you." I leaned forward and hugged Carla. "That means a lot."

"You were there for me when I had my marriage crisis. The least I can do is support you."

Only a month earlier, Carla had contemplated an affair. I knew she didn't really want to do that, but she'd been missing her husband terribly, who was in Iraq on a tour of duty. Thankfully, she'd come to her senses and not jeopardized everything that mattered most to her.

"Have you heard from Paul?" I asked.

Carla's face erupted in a grin. "Just this evening, actually."

"And how is he?"

"He's doing well. He misses me like crazy, as I do him. And with every day that passes, I don't worry as much. The worrying was making me go insane."

Didn't I know it. The big issue that had had Carla very worried—and in my mind, thinking irrationally enough to even consider an affair—was her fear that Paul would die in Iraq and leave her a widow. It was a completely natural fear, and all any of us could do was pray for Paul's safe return.

"I'm counting down the days until he gets back," Carla said. "As soon as he's home, we're going to Disney World."

As I watched Carla's face light up as she spoke, her earlier words got me. The whole bit about being passionately in love with your partner and deserving nothing less than that.

Seeing the love in her face made me believe in the ideal. Wish for it in my own life.

Before I got lost in thoughts about Chaz again, I got up from the sofa. "Let me check on my little pumpkin."

I walked down the hall to Carla's room and peered inside. Amani and Rayna were lying on the bed, a comforter covering them as they watched the television.

Rayna smiled when she saw me, but didn't make a move to get off the bed. "I watching Barbie," she said.

I padded into the room. "Yes, I see that." I eased onto the bed beside my daughter and kissed the top of her head. "Is it a good movie?"

"Shh!"

"Oh, okay then." I giggled as I got up. "I'll let you watch the rest of your movie, then we'll go home."

I went back out to the living room, where Carla was still on the sofa. She had the television on to CNN and was absorbed in a story about a missing girl in Omaha.

"This is so scary," she said, turning to me. "The father was so pissed over losing custody that he took his little girl and took off. No one knows where they are. The mother is devastated."

"Of course," I said, only half-interested. Carla was

addicted to television. Soap operas and CNN. While she didn't say so, I figured she watched CNN all the time for any news about fallen soldiers.

"Do you mind if I head upstairs to shower, then come back down to get her?" I asked.

"Sure. Go on."

I left Carla's and headed upstairs to my place. In my bedroom, I stripped out of my suit.

That's when I noticed the red message light flashing on my phone.

I went around to the side of my bed where my phone was and punched in the code to check my voice mail.

"Vanessa, this is Cynthia Martin. I tried you at work, but you'd already gone. Call me back. It's important."

Cynthia then rattled off her number, but it wasn't necessary. I'd committed it to memory. I called her back immediately.

"Hello."

"Hi, Cynthia. I'm glad I—"

"This is Cynthia Martin. I'm unable to take your call right now, but leave me a message, and I'll be sure to get back to you."

I frowned, but left a message letting Cynthia know that I was home now, and that she could call me anytime.

Then I went to the bathroom and turned on the shower.

As I climbed into the tub, I was both excited and scared. Excited at the prospect that Cynthia might have gotten the dirt I needed, but scared that she hadn't.

I wished she'd said either way what she had learned. The suspense was killing me.

I showered quickly, hoping she returned my call soon.
She *had* to have good news for me.
I wouldn't allow myself to think anything else.

7

I called Cynthia Martin no less than five times the next day when I was at work, and was completely dismayed when I got her voice mail each time. How was it that the woman had called with news, but now wouldn't get back to me?

Every time my phone rang, I hoped it was her calling. All but one time I answered it, it was someone calling regarding my work. The one non-work-related call had come from Lewis, who'd let me know that he'd put in a call to both the lawyers he'd mentioned the previous night and was waiting to hear back from them.

I glanced at my wall clock. It was ten minutes to five. Disappointed that the whole day had passed without a word from Cynthia, I frowned.

And then my phone rang. I snatched up the receiver before it could ring a second time. "Vanessa Cain."

"Hey, Vanessa. It's Cynthia Martin."

"Cynthia," I said, my heart filling with hope when I heard the reporter's voice.

"I've got news for you," she practically sang.

"You do?"

"Yes. And you're going to like it."

I pumped my fist in the air and mouthed the word *yes!*

"Can we meet this evening?" she asked.

"Name the time and place."

"How about the Barnes and Noble on Kendall Drive? We can meet in the Starbucks café."

"Sounds good."

"I can be there around five-fifteen."

My office wasn't too far from that bookstore. And if I met Cynthia now, I wouldn't have to go home, only to head back into downtown Miami later. "I'll be there."

"See you then."

As soon as I replaced the receiver, I quickly finished with the file that was on my computer and logged off. I slipped into my slingbacks, which were beneath my desk, and collected my purse. Then I hurried out of my office, saying a quick goodbye to the co-workers I ran in to, before heading to the bank of elevators.

Hardly able to contain my excitement, I all but danced around in the elevator, ready to spring through the doors the moment they opened on the ground floor. I watched each floor light up during the descent, and inwardly groaned every time the elevator stopped on a floor other than the first.

About three minutes later, I was the first to get off the elevator when it landed on the lobby level. I caught Edgar's eye immediately. The building's long-time security guard raised his hand in greeting and offered me a meek smile.

I'm not sure what kind of look I leveled on him, but I know it wasn't pleasant.

"Come on," Edgar said as I neared the security desk. "Are you going to be mad at me forever?"

In reply, I scowled at him.

"Vanessa…"

Edgar and I weren't close friends or anything, but I hadn't expected him to betray me the way he had. Edgar was a friend of Rayna's father, Byron, and had told him about my involvement with Chaz Anderson. Because of that, Byron had shown up at the restaurant where I'd been having lunch with Chaz, confronted me about not wanting to "lose" his daughter—thereby exposing my lie about Rayna's father being dead—and that had been the end for me and Chaz.

"Come over here and talk to me," Edgar urged, motioning for me to go to him.

I paused, debating what to do. But after a moment, I sauntered toward him. Reaching the security desk, I blew out a heavy breath and stared down at Edgar.

"Yes, I'm going to be mad at you forever," I said. "Edgar, how could you have told Byron about me and Chaz?"

"I already told you. Byron said he'd changed—given up the gambling, you know? I know that was a big problem for you guys, and I figured, he seemed like he was telling the truth. And doesn't everyone deserve a second chance?"

Byron was a compulsive gambler. It was one of the reasons that our relationship was doomed to fail. I didn't know about his habit until we'd already been involved about a year, and when I found out he was in debt to bookies for thousands, he always had what seemed like a reasonable explanation for how the situation had gotten out of control.

Every time I asked him how the "situation" was going, he told me he was working off his debt. I believed him. And then I noticed that some of my jewelry was gone. Like a diamond-and-emerald necklace my father had given to my mother that I'd received after her passing. At first, Byron swore that he hadn't taken it. Then, he claimed he "borrowed" it.

I never saw it again, or any of the other jewelry he'd taken. I still remember thinking that the reason he was so upset that I was pregnant was because of the money it would cost to raise a child—money he was happier spending on placing bets.

"It was up to me to decide whether or not he deserved a second chance," I said to Edgar.

"I know. But he kept telling me how he'd changed, and was talking about how much he wanted a relationship with his daughter, that he was ready," Edgar went on. "But that you wouldn't give him the time of day. Then there was that article in the paper about you and Chaz, speculating that you'd get married." Edgar shrugged. "I felt I had to say something."

Edgar had explained himself already, but no matter how many times he told me the story, I would never understand. He had jumped the gun by talking to Byron about my relationship with Chaz, though he'd rightly assumed that it was serious. I guess it boiled down to the fact that Edgar and Byron had been friends from the time Byron had also worked security at the building, and despite Byron's shortcomings, Edgar must have felt some sort of obligation to tell him about me and Chaz.

What Edgar didn't understand was that Byron talked a good game. He said the right things about getting over the gambling and wanting to be a decent father to those who would listen, but in reality, he didn't try. He knew that if he admitted the truth—that he'd simply abandoned his daughter—his friends and family would see him as a schmuck.

"Well, you ruined everything," I said.

"I was only trying to help. Trying to be a good friend."

"You want to know something? Something that will show you Byron's true character?" I paused, made sure I had Edgar's full attention. "I haven't heard from Byron since that day he showed up at the restaurant. So. There you go."

"I'm sorry," Edgar said. "I really am."

"Yeah," I said softly. I still liked Edgar, even if I felt I had to keep up the pissed-off act with him a while longer. It was probably best I didn't get too chummy with him again, because I didn't want him running back to Byron with any more stories about my love life.

That was one of the reasons I made sure not to wear the ring Lewis had given me to work. And of course, I hadn't wanted any questions from anyone in the office. Only Carla and Alaina knew about my engagement. I hadn't even told Debbie.

"You have a good evening," I said to Edgar. I knew it wasn't his fault that Chaz had dumped me, but if only he hadn't told Byron. If I'd been able to broach the subject of Rayna's father actually being alive in some other way than the dramatic fashion with which it played out, Chaz might still be in my life.

"Yeah, you have a good night, too," Edgar said, but his voice sounded off, and he was looking beyond my shoulder, not at me. The wary expression on his face had me alarmed.

"What?" I asked, and quickly followed his gaze over my shoulder.

As I did, I gasped, feeling as though I'd been scalded by fire. *Byron*. Then I spun back around and glared at Edgar. "Did you set me up again?"

"No!" he protested. "He just showed up, I swear!"

I didn't know what to believe. All I knew was that my heart was suddenly pounding furiously. There was a chance that he wasn't here to see me, but rather Edgar. That's what I hoped as I secured my purse strap over my shoulder and started briskly away from the desk.

Byron promptly blocked my path.

I didn't say anything to him, just moved to the right to try to step past him. He matched my movement, which made it very clear that he was here to see me.

"Get out of my way," I said. I didn't care why he was in the lobby of my office building. I had nothing to say to him.

"We need to talk," he said.

"I don't want to talk to you." I was already frustrated and spoke louder than I'd intended. I glanced around surreptitiously to see if any people were staring. No one seemed to care about me and Byron as they headed toward the exit.

For now. If our "conversation" continued, I didn't doubt we'd end up with an audience. The last thing I wanted was an ugly conflict with a dozen witnesses. So I made a quick step to the left and moved around him, then hustled to the front door.

Byron was on my tail. I could feel him. But I didn't turn. I breezed through the door behind someone else who was exiting and hurried onto the street.

I took about ten steps before I felt a hand clamp down on my shoulder. Even though I knew it was Byron behind me, I flinched nonetheless.

"Damn it, Vanessa. You *will* talk to me."

"What?" I demanded as I whirled around. My chest was heaving, my breathing labored.

"I want to see my daughter."

"Excuse me?"

"You heard me."

"Yeah, I heard you. But considering you've been a deadbeat dad since before Rayna was born, what you're saying may as well be in Chinese, since it makes no sense to me."

"I want to see Rayna. Let's set up a time and meet somewhere you feel comfortable."

"Like in your bookie's office, perhaps?" I asked.

"I'm done with the gambling. I already told you."

"And I'm just supposed to take the word of a liar?" Byron had been around intermittently when I'd been pregnant. One of those times had been when my friends had thrown me a baby shower. He'd gathered the presents and driven me home from my sister's place—only he hadn't given me all the gifts I'd received for Rayna. Some ended up missing and—you guessed it—were never seen again.

"A guy can change, Vanessa. I'm ready to be a dad."

"Not gonna happen," I said.

"She's my daughter."

"No, she's not."

"Yes, she is."

"Maybe biologically, but not in all the ways that matter. And that was *your* choice, Byron. Not mine."

"Don't be a bitch," Byron snapped. "I'm trying to do the right thing here."

I laughed sardonically. "Better a bitch than a deadbeat. This conversation is over."

Turning away from Byron, I started to jog now. I pressed on even as my feet hurt in my shoes. When I was half a block away—and certain that my heels were destroyed—I finally looked over my shoulder.

Byron was nowhere to be seen.

Only then did I stop jogging. Stopped and gulped in air. Not just because I was winded, but because I was panicked. Panicked at the thought that Byron wanted to be part of Rayna's life.

I leaned my back against the exterior of a building, my stomach suddenly nauseous.

This isn't happening. This isn't happening. I repeated that line in my mind over and over, as though just by thinking it, I could make what had happened a bad dream rather than an ugly reality.

People gave me odd looks as they passed me, and I finally eased myself up off the wall. My heart was still pounding, and I felt sort of numb.

I made my way to the parking lot where my car was, and as I got behind the wheel, I noticed my hands were shaking.

Was Byron truly feeling paternal? Or was it once again a passing phase? I hadn't heard from him after that day at the restaurant. Not one peep. Not an apology. Not a request to see Rayna. I guess there were times when the reality that he'd fathered a child hit him in the head like a giant conch shell, and he probably felt a bit of guilt over not being in her life.

But the guilt would pass. It always did.

When I realized I'd been sitting behind the wheel of my car for nearly ten minutes, I started the engine and drove out of the parking lot. I was going to be late for my meeting with Cynthia.

I resolved not to let Byron get to me. It wasn't the first time in the past two-and-a-half years that he'd had an attack of conscience and had reached out to Rayna by sending a gift. Then months would pass without a word from him or even an e-mail.

I had a far more pressing matter to deal with. Getting to Cynthia Martin and hearing what she'd learned about Tassie Johnson.

8

I didn't make it to the Barnes & Noble bookstore until five-thirty. I rushed inside, hoping Cynthia wouldn't be upset at my tardiness. But when I saw her, she was casually standing near the perimeter of the café with a magazine in her hand.

Seeming to sense me, she looked in my direction. Then smiled.

I returned her smile. I never thought I'd be so happy to see Cynthia Martin, not after how some of her reports after Eli's murder had made me look in the press. But I couldn't help being giddy with excitement.

As I strode toward her, she replaced the magazine on the rack.

I'd prayed that she would come through for me, give me some kind of ammunition I could use against Tassie, and it looked like my prayers had been answered.

"Hello," I said as I reached her, and offered her my hand. "It is so good to see you again."

Cynthia took my hand and shook it firmly. "It's good to see you."

"Sorry I'm a bit late. Traffic."

"No worries," she said.

I glanced around the café. There were a number of available seats. "You want something to eat or drink before we sit down?" I asked. "A coffee, a sandwich? I'm buying."

"I'm fine," she said. "I don't need anything."

"No, I want to buy you something," I insisted. "It's the least I can do."

"All right, then. I'll take a latte and a scone."

I went to order while Cynthia sat at a table where no one was within earshot. A few minutes later, I joined her at the table, setting down two large lattes, her scone and a piece of carrot cake for myself.

After dealing with Byron, I deserved a treat.

I was anxious to ask Cynthia what she'd uncovered. But I decided to let her eat a bit of her scone first while I munched on my carrot cake.

That resolve lasted thirty seconds before I had to speak. "I'm dying here. You said the news is good?"

"Very." A devious spark lit Cynthia's eyes.

"How good? Or should I ask—how scandalous?"

Cynthia swallowed a mouthful of coffee before speaking. "Tassie Johnson has been a very bad girl."

"Meaning?"

"Meaning she was far from being a grieving widow."

My heart was so full of excitement, I thought it might burst. "The guy I saw her with at the funeral. He's her lover?"

"Ray Carlton," Cynthia said, nodding. She broke off a morsel of her scone and put it in her mouth.

"I *knew* it." I lifted my cup of coffee, but didn't take a sip. "She had the nerve to talk about *Eli* being unfaithful while flaunting her lover at her husband's funeral."

"It's worse than you think," Cynthia said. "Or perhaps I should say better."

I lowered my coffee cup. "Oh?"

"When I say Tassie Johnson has been a very bad girl, it's not just because she and Ray are lovers. It's because of how long they were an item. *Long* before she and Eli split."

"How long?"

"Try before she walked down the aisle."

My eyes narrowed in confusion. "What—like an old boyfriend?"

"Old boyfriends aren't scandalous. Everyone's had at least one lover before getting married. I'm guessing the average these days has got to be between ten and twenty other partners, but I don't have the hard data to support that claim."

I could care less about the average number of partners a person had before settling down. I moved a hand in a rolling motion to indicate that I wanted Cynthia to continue with the news about Tassie.

Her eyes danced with humor. "But it *is* scandalous when you marry someone, continue to see your old boyfriend and even have an *abortion* when you're still very much living with your husband."

"Tassie had an abortion!" I couldn't help exclaiming, then glanced around. A handful of people were suddenly intrigued by my conversation. "Wow, that's progressive for a soap opera, isn't it?" I continued loudly, hoping to kill any eavesdroppers' interest in what I was saying. "I thought people always end up having the baby or miscarrying on those shows. But a real abortion."

Cynthia edged across the table, and continued speaking in a lower tone. "I've got the records to prove it."

I wanted to jump up and down and scream hallelujah, but I remained seated. Remained calm.

"When?" I asked, keeping my voice down.

"A year and a half after she'd had her first child."

My excitement fizzled. "Then the baby could have been Eli's," I pointed out. "Maybe the timing wasn't right, and they decided they didn't want to have another baby."

"Eh, eh, eh." Cynthia waved a finger. She was clearly enjoying this, as though she'd always imagined herself being some sort of secret spy. I guess that's what journalism entailed…to a degree. "It was Ray's baby."

"It'll be my word against hers."

"But will she be able to explain why her ex-boyfriend took her to the abortion clinic? Why he paid for it with his credit card?"

I gasped, but quickly covered my mouth. "Oh, my God."

"Uh-huh."

"So she was having an affair right from the start," I said quietly. Another revelation hit me. "Do you think she was *never* in love with Eli? That she married him strictly for his money?"

"If I were a gambling woman, I'd guess exactly that. It doesn't look like her relationship with Ray has ever waned."

I sipped my latte, stewing over Cynthia's words. This was good. Very good. Once, I'd been dreading the meeting with Tassie and her lawyer, but now I couldn't wait to see her and let her know the skeletons I'd dug out of her closet.

"So, is that helpful enough?" Cynthia asked.

"Are you kidding? It couldn't be any better if you had photos of them in the act."

"Good. I'm glad."

"How did you find all of this out? Abortion clinic records?"

"A journalist never reveals her sources."

"Okay," I said. "I understand."

"But, I will say that it helps to track down a former housekeeper with an axe to grind."

"Oooh, you're kidding?" I asked, my eyes as wide as saucers.

"Not at all. Gotta love the hired help."

I laughed out loud.

"I won't tell you her name—since it's not important—but she pointed me in the right direction. It took me a while to find her, which is why I didn't get back to you sooner."

"Hey, you got back to me with gold. I'm not complaining."

Cynthia sipped her latte. "Keep that whole tidbit about the former housekeeper to yourself, though. I promised the woman I wouldn't say anything. In fact, don't tell Tassie where you got the information. She doesn't need to know."

I mimed pulling a zipper across my lips…then burst into laughter.

Cynthia sighed with contentment. "Ah, sometimes, my job is deliciously fun."

"I'll remember to stay on your good side."

Cynthia's expression grew serious at my comment. "You were never on my bad side. And for the record, I'm sorry about how the story of you and Eli played out in the press."

I waved away her apology. "I didn't mean that personally."

"Still, I'm sorry," she went on. "I was just doing my job, but I know that's little comfort."

"It's okay," I told her. "That's all behind me, and I'm moving forward. With your help," I added with a smile.

"Speaking of which, I have a copy of all the proof you need." She reached into her large purse and withdrew a manila envelope. She passed it across the table to me.

I accepted the envelope, fingering an edge as though I were touching the gilded frame of a priceless painting. "I'm meeting with Tassie and her lawyer next week. This is perfect."

"You'll keep me posted?"

I nodded. "Definitely."

"I hope what I've uncovered helps you keep your home. Tassie's hitting below the belt by trying to take it."

Cynthia's reference to "below the belt" had me thinking about the sin that Tassie wouldn't want anyone to know about. "An abortion. Her *lover's* baby." I shook my head. "What a conniving skank that Tassie turned out to be. She had the nerve to get on *my* case, accuse *me* of being a gold digger. At least I loved Eli. I never went after him because he had money, but because he knew how to treat a lady. He swept me off my feet."

As I said the words, my mind drifted to the charity function where I'd met Eli. I noticed him right away, but had been heartbroken over Lewis and not looking for love. Yet Eli had won me over with his charm and persistence.

In so many ways, our time together had seemed like years ago. If he were alive, we'd be moving full steam ahead with wedding plans.

How odd that that was all over, and yet, how odd that it had ever been. Eli was so firmly out of my heart now, it was hard to believe I'd ever been head over heels in love with him.

"So how are things going with you and that motivational speaker?" Cynthia asked, as though she'd sensed the direction of my thoughts.

I swallowed. Chaz. Just the mention of him had my stomach fluttering. Lord, I missed him.

"Aw, you should see the look on your face," Cynthia said, smiling. "I guess it's love."

"With all due respect, you're still a reporter."

"Ouch."

"No offense," I added.

"None taken."

"But," I went on, "if we get engaged, you'll be the first to know."

Somehow, I managed to smile through my words, knowing I was lying through my teeth. The chance of me and Chaz getting engaged was right up there with me discovering the cure for cancer.

Cynthia finished off her scone, then pushed her chair back and stood. "I'm sorry I can't stay longer," she began, "but I've got to head back to the office to write a story."

"Anything interesting?" I asked.

"An interview with Scott Meyer on his testing positive for steroid-enhancing drugs."

"Right. That story is huge." Scott Meyer, a running back for the Miami Dolphins, was currently dominating the headlines because of his steroid drug use. He denied knowingly taking anything, blaming his coach for secretly giving him the drugs. At issue were the countless records Scott had broken, now being contested based on the fact that the use of performance enhancing drugs had aided him in breaking those records.

"Read the paper tomorrow." Cynthia beamed. "I've got an exclusive!"

"I will."

Cynthia slipped the strap of her large purse over her arm and picked up her latte. "I've got to run. Stay in touch."

I watched Cynthia run off. Then I reached into my purse and withdrew my cell phone. I wanted to talk to Lewis about the lawyer, and also share with him the good news Cynthia had uncovered.

"Baby," he said when he picked up. "Miss me?"

I chuckled warmly, but didn't answer the question. "I've got some good news."

"Shoot."

I told him what Cynthia had discovered, and how this was going to make a world of difference at next week's meeting. Then I asked if he'd spoken to the lawyer yet.

"Neil Gorman got back to me. He's busy today, but said he'll reach out to you tomorrow."

"Excellent."

"And I spoke to an investigator friend of mine. He's

going to do some of his own digging. We'll see if he comes up with something else in addition to what the reporter found."

"Double whammy. I like it. Hell, maybe Tassie's got a whole closet full of dirty laundry."

"What are you doing tonight?" Lewis asked, his voice deepening. "Maybe we can meet for dinner?"

"Tonight won't be good. My sitter's got plans." A little white lie, but I wanted to spend some one-on-one time with Rayna, take her to feed the ducks as I'd planned before.

"We can go out with Rayna," Lewis said. "I know you want to take your time bringing me back into her life, but she knows who I am. She's not going to be traumatized by spending some time with me."

Lewis was right, I knew it, but I still wasn't ready. "Maybe another time."

"Babe, are you avoiding me?" he asked. There was humor in his voice, but I suspected that the question was quite serious.

"Avoiding you? Absolutely not, Lewis. We had dinner last night, remember?"

"I know. But we still have a wedding to plan, business to discuss. And I don't know if I'm being paranoid, but I'm sensing a bit of hesitation on your part."

"It's not you," I quickly explained. "I—I had a weird encounter with Byron today. He showed up at my work—"

"Byron?" Lewis interjected. "Rayna's father?"

"The one and only." I made a face at the idea of Bryon being a father. "Though I like to think of him as a sperm donor."

"What'd he say?"

"He was a bit of a jerk, quite frankly. Started demanding that I let him see Rayna."

"Really?" Lewis spoke slowly, his tone saying he was mulling over what I'd said. "Did he threaten you?"

"I wouldn't say he threatened me, no, but the whole exchange was a little frightening. He shows up when I'm leaving work, follows me out, says I need to let him see his daughter. You know his history, how he stole from me to feed his gambling habit. Not to mention some of his friends, who were downright scary. One of them even assaulted a guy downtown to steal his wallet because he needed cash to pay a bookie." I drew in a sharp breath at the memory. I'd put so much of what had happened with Byron behind me when I knew I would be a single mother, and I didn't like thinking about it. "I'll tell you this—it'll be a cold day in hell before I make any plans for him to see Rayna."

"I don't like that he came to see you," Lewis said.

"Tell me about it."

"The next time Byron shows up and starts making demands, you tell him to talk to me."

"That's not necessary. I can handle Byron."

"Maybe. But sometimes a man needs to know a lady has a protector in her life, someone who won't let her be pushed around."

"My protector, huh?"

"Of course. You're my girl. I'm always gonna protect my girl."

"That's nice to hear." And it was. It was nice to know that

Lewis had my back. If nothing else, I saw him as a friend, which was rare for me after a relationship had gone sour.

"And the sooner we get married," Lewis went on, "the sooner you get to have me as your bodyguard full-time. It's one of the perks of being Mrs. Carter."

"Is that so?"

"Oh, yeah." A beat passed. "I know you have some doubts about my feelings for you," Lewis said softly, his tone now serious. "But I really am looking forward to marrying you. And I can't wait to adopt Rayna, make her legally my daughter. I'd also like to get started expanding our family as soon as we're married. It'd be nice to have a couple more kids."

"Wow. You're turning into a regular family man."

"I've always wanted kids. I just had to wait for the right woman."

This was the first time Lewis had ever talked about being a father, and I was a little surprised. Sure, he'd gotten along well with Rayna when we'd been involved before, but I always saw him as the consummate player, and didn't see him as particularly paternal.

My call waiting beeped. A quick glance at the display told me it was Carla calling on the other line.

"Lewis, I'll talk to you later, okay?"

"Saved by the bell," he joked, then added, "All right, sweetheart. We'll talk later."

I clicked over to the other line. "Hey, Carla, I'm sorry," I began without preamble. "I should have called to tell you that I had to meet that reporter from the *Miami Herald*. But I'm on my—"

I stopped talking when I heard the sound of loud crying in the background.

Rayna's cries.

Goose bumps popped out on my skin.

"Rayna's hurt." Carla spoke in a rush before I could ask what was wrong. "And I'm not sure if I should take her to the hospital. She won't stop crying."

"I'm on my way," I said, already on my feet. I closed my phone, dropped it in my purse and ran to the car.

9

The moment Carla opened her apartment door, I rushed inside, my eyes frantically scanning the area for my daughter.

Rayna was on the love seat in the living room, her head resting on the armrest. She was crying incessantly, and the anguished sound broke my heart.

"What happened?" I asked Carla while I hurried to Rayna. I gingerly scooped my daughter into my arms. Normally, Rayna would quiet when I held her, taking comfort from my touch. But she continued to cry, a high-pitched wail that told me something was terribly wrong.

"She was playing with Amani and they fell," Carla explained. "I think they were both on the sofa, and rolled off onto the floor."

"You think?" I asked. I swayed Rayna from side to side. "You're not sure?"

"I was in the kitchen getting them a snack," Carla said. Guilt flashed across her face. "I only left them alone for a minute."

I understood as well as any mother how quickly disaster could strike, and that it always happened when your back was turned. "It's okay, Carla. But how long has she been crying?"

"She'd been crying for fifteen minutes straight when I called you, which had me concerned. That was half an hour ago and she's still crying. When kids get hurt, they cry for a minute and then it's back to business. But the fact that she hasn't stopped…"

"Oh, my poor baby," I cooed in Rayna's ear. "Mommy's here, sweetheart. It's okay."

Rayna continued to cry.

My throat filled with emotion, and I blinked back tears. There was nothing worse than seeing your child in pain and not being able to do a thing about it. "Did she hit her head?"

"I think she hurt her arm," Carla said. "After she fell, she kept touching her left arm."

I eased Rayna backward and noticed that even though I was holding her, she kept her hand on her left arm. "Heck, maybe it's broken," I said. An injury like that would explain why she hadn't stopped crying. "I'm going to take her to the hospital."

"Do you want me to go with you?" Carla asked.

I shook my head as I started for the door. "No, there's no point. You stay here with Amani."

Amani hadn't said a word since I'd arrived, and had looked pretty much shell-shocked as I'd gathered Rayna in my arms. But as soon as I got to the door with Rayna, she burst into tears.

"It was an accident," Amani said as she sobbed.

"Hey, sweetie." With Rayna in my arms, I walked back

into the living room and lowered myself to Amani's level. "It's okay. I'm not mad at you." I offered her a smile, even though I didn't feel like smiling. "Accidents happen all the time and it's no one's fault."

"Is Rayna going to die like her daddy did?"

The question surprised me, and also made me feel a jolt of pain. "No," I said after a moment. "Rayna's not going to die. I'm going to take her to the doctor, who's going to make sure that she's perfectly fine. She'll be back playing with you tomorrow."

Amani nodded bravely, even though the fear was still evident in her eyes.

I rose and faced Carla. "Can you help me get Rayna's shoes on?"

"Of course." Carla scooped up Rayna's shoes and slipped them onto her feet. Finished with that task, she first opened the door for me, then picked up Amani and kissed her daughter's cheek. Then she leaned forward and kissed Rayna on the forehead.

"I'll call you from the hospital, okay?" I told her.

"Please. I'll feel awful until I know what's going on."

Then I rushed out the door.

Rayna finally dozed as I drove to the Miami Children's Hospital, and that was the only time she stopped crying. When I arrived at the hospital and got her out of the car, she woke up and began to whimper again.

I nearly cried myself when I saw the emergency room full of people. I didn't want to be here for hours with my child, not when she was clearly in a lot of pain.

Thankfully, I'd taken Rayna's stroller from the car, because there was only one available seat in the waiting room. That and the fact that I would need my hands to fill out the necessary paperwork.

I went to the check-in counter, explained that my daughter had fallen and I didn't know what was wrong with her, and then I took the clipboard with paperwork to fill out. I stood to the side and filled out the form, not bothering to head to the only available seat in the crowded room.

Minutes later, I returned the clipboard to the woman behind the counter. She gave it a quick once-over, then instructed me to have a seat and wait.

Fifteen minutes later, I was called to bring Rayna in to see the doctor. I guess with her being so young and not able to describe her injuries, the hospital didn't want to take any chances that she had serious internal injuries.

"What do we have here?" the doctor, an older gentleman, asked in a kind manner.

"My daughter fell. It seems as though she really hurt her left arm."

Rayna stopped whimpering to eye the doctor warily. And she became especially uncomfortable when I laid her down on the hospital bed.

She started to squirm, trying to sit up. "It's okay, sweetheart," I said gently. "The doctor has to look at your arm so he can see what's wrong. Then he's going to make it better."

"That's right," the doctor concurred. "I'm not going to hurt you."

Rayna still eyed the man with caution and her back was stiff, but she didn't protest when he began his exam by touching her tummy. When she realized that he indeed wasn't hurting her, her body relaxed. I remained by her side, soothingly stroking her forehead.

I watched the doctor do his exam. It was really awful seeing my daughter's small body on a big hospital bed. She looked so frail and helpless, and I wished I could take her pain away.

The doctor very quickly surmised that she likely had a fractured elbow, given how Rayna began to cry when he tried to extend it. He sent her for X rays to be certain of his diagnosis, and I was by Rayna's side through what was obviously a weird and stressful experience for her.

"She's got a spider fracture on her elbow," the doctor announced after seeing the X ray. He pointed to four very thin lines that resembled a spider's legs on the X ray so I could see it for myself.

"What does that mean?" I asked.

"It means your daughter's going to have to have her arm in a cast until it heals."

"How long?"

"Four weeks."

Four weeks in a cast. I shook my head. "No wonder she wouldn't stop crying."

"It's a good thing you brought her in. This wouldn't heal on its own."

"My poor baby." I looked down at Rayna with sympathy and bent to kiss her forehead.

"You said she fell?" the doctor asked.

"Yes."

"That must have been a hard fall."

"I think her friend fell on top of her. They were playing in the living room."

"You *think?*"

"I wasn't there," I explained—and the doctor's eyebrows shot up. "She was with her babysitter. I was heading home from work when she called to say my daughter had been hurt."

The doctor didn't speak for a moment, and I'm not sure why, but I got a weird feeling. Almost like he was scrutinizing me.

"Have there been other incidents like this?" he finally asked.

"I don't understand the question."

"Other incidents where your daughter has gotten hurt while at the babysitter?"

"Of course. She gets hurt all the time. She's a kid. No," I amended, quickly backtracking. Did the doctor suspect I had abused my child? "I don't mean that she's always getting hurt. She's perfectly well cared for. I just mean that of course kids fall, get hurt. That's normal."

I was rambling, and I didn't know if the doctor believed me or if he thought I was a mother who abused her daughter.

Looking down at Rayna, he rubbed her belly. "Your mommy and daddy are going to have to give you lots of extra hugs and kisses."

"It'll just be me giving her the extra hugs and kisses," I felt compelled to say. "There is no father."

"There must be a father," the doctor said, meeting my eyes.

He was old enough to have been raised in an era when people didn't get divorced, but certainly he knew times had changed. I got the feeling that he was judging me as he stared at me, but maybe I was just extrasensitive. It wouldn't be the first time a person had assumed that because I was a single parent, I'd done something awful to deserve that status.

"I'm a single mother," I explained. *One who doesn't abuse her child,* I added silently, but didn't say. "One of ten million in America."

The doctor didn't respond. Instead, he turned back to Rayna and smiled warmly at her. "We're going to get your arm taken care of, sweetheart. You're going to be all better before you know it."

Rayna's arm was set in a cast, and I was advised to give her children's Tylenol for the pain. We were out of the hospital in under two hours.

The best part of the experience for Rayna was the red lollipop the doctor gave her after her arm was bound.

I called Carla the moment I got to my car. "'Rayna has a spider fracture on her left elbow," I explained.

"Oh, no."

"Yeah, her first broken bone." I'd lived my twenty-eight years without ever breaking a bone. "No wonder she was in so much pain, but other than that, she's fine."

"Thank God it's not a concussion."

"Yes, thank God."

"I feel so bad. If only I hadn't gone into the kitchen—"

"Don't beat yourself up over this. These things happen, and it's not your fault."

"I know. But I still feel bad."

"What matters is that Rayna's okay. And you should have seen it—her pain seemed to disappear the moment the doctor gave her a lollipop," I added with a smile. "It was like magic candy."

"At least she's not crying anymore."

"Now, she's as happy as a peach. After her crying for so long, it was nice to see her smile again."

"I'll bet. Give her a great big kiss for me, okay?"

"Will do. And let Amani know that Rayna is fine."

"I will. She's been asking about her ever since you guys left."

As I ended the call and started to drive home, I realized that with the drama of what had happened this evening, I hadn't gotten to tell Carla what Cynthia had discovered about Tassie.

It would just have to wait until tomorrow. Tonight, I didn't give a rat's ass about Tassie. I was going to head home and give Rayna some TLC. I would feed her ice cream and cuddle with her on the bed until she fell asleep.

10

The next morning, I fully intended to stay home from work to look after Rayna. But when she woke up in her regular cheery mood, despite the cast on her arm, I realized it wasn't necessary.

I also decided that it'd be good for her to head back to Carla's, in part to keep up her routine and in part to put Amani's mind at ease when she saw for herself that Rayna was perfectly fine.

Amani was as curious about the cast as Rayna had been the night before after it had been set. Amani stared at it, touched it, asked if it hurt…and then she was ready to play.

So was Rayna.

I smiled fondly as I watched my daughter and Amani settle on the living room floor and dig in to the tub of colorful ponies. Everything was back to normal.

"Call me if there's any problem," I told Carla as she walked with me to the apartment door. "Or if Rayna wants to talk to me."

"Of course," Carla said.

I threw one quick glance into the living room as I stepped into the hallway. Rayna was so involved with her ponies, she didn't even notice I was on my way out.

"Hey," Carla said suddenly. "You said that you met with the reporter yesterday? You never told me what she said."

"Right," I said. It was funny how I'd all but forgotten that. "Lots to tell, but let me call you from work, okay?"

"You're going to keep me in suspense?"

"Not for long. But it's a juicy story, and I want to savor every delicious moment of it as I tell it to you."

"Ooh, I can't wait."

No sooner had I settled behind my desk in the office, than Debbie appeared.

"Hey, Debbie," I greeted her warmly.

"Morning, Vanessa." She stepped into my office and closed the door behind her, and I knew instantly that she wanted to talk privately.

"What's up?"

"You know that I leave this weekend for Phoenix."

"Right." Debbie was heading to Phoenix to accompany Lori Hansen, the client she'd recently acquired, while she gave a series of weight-loss seminars. As the agency's office manager, I'd made the travel arrangements.

"Well," Debbie began slowly, "I need you to do something for me."

"Sure."

"Can you book Jason on the flight to Phoenix? Hopefully the same flight I'm on. Although, he'll have to travel coach."

I stared at Debbie, not saying a word.

"Don't look at me like that," she said.

A couple of months ago, she'd begun an affair with a much younger man. Though Debbie had promised to end the relationship when her husband discovered the affair, clearly she had no plans to do so. I couldn't tell her what to do…but taking Jason to Phoenix? That was going too far.

"Debbie, what are you doing?" I asked her.

"Taking Jason to Phoenix with me."

"Why?"

"I'm sure you can figure that out."

I rose from my seat and walked toward her, my arms folded over my chest. "Come on, Debbie. Ben already figured out you were having an affair. He gave you a chance to end it. And now you're taking Jason on business trips? What's next—are you going to have me sending your husband flowers to make up for you *working* late?"

"Cut the dramatics, Vanessa."

"No, you need to listen to me," I told her, feeling a little angry. "You keep up with this kind of behavior, and you're going to lose your husband. Your whole family."

Debbie waved off my concern. "The only reason I asked you is because I need to put this on the company account. It can't be on my personal credit card. In case…"

Her voice trailed off, but I knew what she'd been about to say. "In case Ben sees your credit card statement. For God's sake, Debbie."

"I'm not ready to end it," she said, smirking. "You know it's not serious. It won't last forever, but for now, it's fun."

"You think this is a joke?" I asked her. When she'd first

told me about Jason, I figured she was planning to leave her husband. She hadn't been happy with him for more than a year, so I'd assumed that her seeing Jason meant she was ready to file for divorce. However, Debbie had made it clear that she intended to stay married but mess around on the side—even in the wake of her husband discovering her infidelity.

"This is your family you're messing with," I continued. "You've got three children. When is this going to stop?"

Debbie's smirk disappeared in an instant. "Vanessa, remember who your boss is."

"What's that supposed to mean? That you'll fire me because I don't like the fact that you're cheating on your husband?"

"Of course not," Debbie said, her expression softening slightly.

"Then what are you saying?"

"I'm telling you that I'm not asking your permission. I own the agency, you're going to book the travel. Your lectures on morality aside, Jason is going with me to Phoenix."

I threw my hands in the air and let them fall onto my thighs in frustration. "Fine."

"Good."

Debbie turned, opened the door and left my office.

Great, she was pissed. Well, let her be pissed. I considered Debbie a friend, and true friends didn't have to pussyfoot around each other, trying to spare their feelings regarding serious issues. In the past, I had gently and not so gently tried to discourage Debbie from screwing around, but this was crossing the line. I hated being made to have even a small part in Debbie's affair, by facilitating her sex-fest with her lover in Phoenix.

But, like Debbie had said, she was the boss. The agency was hers. I could try all I liked, but I couldn't tell her what to do.

I called Renée, the travel agent I used to arrange all travel bookings for the agency, and gave the woman a cockamamie story about a junior agent needing to travel with Debbie to Phoenix as well. Yes, I understood that it was last-minute and would cost extra. Yes, I understood that the same flight might be booked.

"Give me ten minutes and I'll see what I can do," Renée told me.

I hung up, groaned my distaste over doing what I'd just done, then leaned back in my chair and closed my eyes.

When, two minutes later, the phone rang, I snatched up the receiver, assuming it was Renée. "Vanessa Cain."

"Hey, baby."

I was momentarily caught off guard, then realized that Lewis was on the other end of my line. "Hi."

"What are you doing for lunch?" he asked.

He certainly was acting like a doting fiancé, with his constant calls and offers of dinner. If only I could be more excited about that.

"I don't know if lunch will work today," I told him. "I've got a lot of work to do."

"Oh. I was hoping you could meet with me and Neil Gorman. To go over some preliminaries before next week's meeting with Tassie."

"Neil wants to meet with me?" I asked excitedly.

"Yes. And with your meeting coming next week—"

"Say no more. Of course I'll meet with you both. Where?"

"I'll make it easy," Lewis said. "We'll come to you. I'll even bring the lunch."

"That would be great, thank you."

"Twelve sharp?"

"Works for me," I said. "I'll see you then."

"And Vanessa?"

"Yes?"

"Stay in your office for the next few minutes, okay."

I narrowed my eyes. "Why?"

"You'll find out why."

Lewis hung up, leaving me very curious about his cryptic words.

Not more than thirty seconds later, my phone rang. It was Nora.

"Um, Ms. Cain?"

"Yes."

"Do you think you can come out to reception for a minute? Someone's here to see you."

"I'm on my way."

Is Lewis already here? I wondered as I rose from my seat. Had he called me while outside the doors to the agency?

I totally expected to see him when I got to the reception area. Instead, the first thing I saw was a huge bouquet of red roses on the corner of the reception desk.

Then another.

And another.

Nora was smiling widely as I approached, one of the few times I'd seen a grin on her face.

"This is Vanessa," Nora said to the man who must have delivered the roses.

"Hello there." The man's eyes lit up as I neared him. "Someone loves you. A lot."

"My God," I uttered, thinking that the reception area now looked like a florist's shop. "These are absolutely beautiful." I gently fingered one of the flowers. "How many roses are there?"

"Each vase has thirty-six long-stemmed roses. One hundred and eight in all."

I gasped. "A hundred and eight."

"My husband gives me roses every year at Valentine's," Nora commented. "But never anything as incredible as this."

Anything Lewis did, he did big. I surveyed the roses. "I don't see a card."

The deliveryman handed me a full-sized card, not the small ones that typically come with a delivery of flowers. "A special delivery like this needed a special card."

Turning my back for some privacy, I opened the envelope and read the card.

Vanessa,
How do I love thee? I cannot count the ways.
I hope these flowers brighten your day and go a long way in proving that you're the only woman in my

heart. One bouquet represents our past. One represents our present. The other represents our future.

I love you,

Lewis

"I hope these flowers are from Chaz."

At the sound of Debbie's voice, I promptly closed the card and turned around. She was eyeing me curiously.

"No," I said slowly. "They're not from Chaz."

Now her eyebrows shot up. "Then who?"

"Lewis."

"Lewis?" Her eyes bulged in disbelief. "That big-time player you used to date?"

"Yes, that Lewis," I said.

I hadn't told Debbie about my renewed relationship with Lewis. I suddenly realized that I was a little pissed with her for her affair, and didn't want to share this aspect of my life with her. Of course, I also hadn't mentioned Lewis because of the fact that I still wasn't exactly sure what I was going to do about our engagement.

Should I marry him, or let him down gently? With each day that passed, the decision became more complicated. One thing was certain, it wouldn't be easy.

11

Five minutes to twelve, Lewis and Neil Gorman arrived in my office. Neil was a short, balding man with a bit of a gut, and from appearances did not look like what I expected of a "shark" attorney.

But once he started talking, it was clear he meant business.

I explained the whole sordid tale with Tassie. How I'd been engaged to her estranged husband, but hadn't known that at the time. That she alleged she had a legal claim to half of my condo as the widow of my late fiancé. How, in the beginning she had wanted me to buy out her half of the condo. My name was on the deed as well as Eli's, so she couldn't stake claim to 100 percent of the property.

"However," I said sourly, "I don't think she expected that I would be able to come up with the cash to buy her out. She figured I would have to sell the property. Now I'm convinced that that's what she wanted from the beginning— to have me out of the condo. Because the moment I came up with a way to pay her off, she changed her demand. Suddenly she wants to relocate to South Beach and wants to move into *my* home?" I made a skeptical face and shook my head. "Yeah, right."

The lawyer nodded and jotted notes. "What you're dealing with is a thorn," Neil said. "A thorn in your side. The kind of person who takes pleasure from being a legal headache. But I'll take care of this."

"Oh, I'm so glad to hear that," I said, grinning. "But I've got to warn you, Tassie is a fighter. She's determined to make me suffer."

"I've dealt with many a fighter. And won."

I nodded. "Do you think it'll be easy?"

"Maybe not easy, but I believe in playing hardball," Neil said. "With this evidence of her affair and abortion that Lewis mentioned, she'll be offering to give you a cash settlement for pain and suffering as well."

My face exploded in a grin. I knew that Neil was joking about the last part, but I was encouraged by his completely positive outlook.

"Now," Neil began, "tell me more about this evidence the reporter uncovered about Tassie."

So I told him, taking pure pleasure in every detail. And when I finished my tale, Neil was nodding vigorously.

"I take back what I said before," Neil said. "This'll be easier than I thought."

I felt hugely relieved. This was a problem that Neil could deal with. A thorn in my side he could make go away. The only issue left to be resolved was Mr. Gorman's fee.

"I haven't asked what you charge," I began. "And I'm not sure—"

Lewis immediately threw up a hand, cutting me off. "I've already told Neil to send me the bill."

Lewis had mentioned this, but I was still willing to pay for Neil's services myself. "Lewis, you don't have to do that."

"You're my future wife. Of course I have to."

I didn't bother to argue. I knew there would be no changing Lewis's mind. So I said, "All right. Thank you, Lewis."

"Babe, there's no need to thank me."

We spent the next few minutes going over some basic details. Neil said he would make contact with Tassie's lawyer and get back to me with the time and location of the meeting.

Then Neil left, and Lewis stayed behind.

The moment Neil was out of my office, Lewis closed the door and looped his arms around my waist. "We're finally alone."

"Lewis…"

"What?" he asked.

"You remember what I said about…messing around."

"Is kissing out of line until we get married, too?"

"No," I said slowly. "It's just that I'm at work."

Lewis ignored me, burrowing his nose in my neck and inhaling deeply. "Baby, you smell incredible."

"Lewis…"

"You have no clue how much I'm dying to sink my teeth into your flesh," he whispered hotly. "To do that thing with my tongue on your earlobe that makes you crazy."

I felt a flash of lust remembering exactly what Lewis used to do with his tongue. And then I stepped backward, out of his arms.

He had a devilish smirk on his lips.

"I hate that you know all my weak spots."

"Why? It'll make our wedding night oh-so-good."

Oh, boy, I thought, inhaling a slow, even breath. Lewis truly was tempting. But I was all too aware that even with the sexual chemistry between us, my heart wasn't in it.

"I guess I do owe you a kiss though," I said. "The roses are simply stunning."

I stepped toward him and gave him a soft kiss on the cheek. Lewis took the opportunity to slip his arms around my waist once again.

He kissed my jaw, then moved his mouth to my lips. I didn't protest as he gave me a gentle and sensual kiss.

When I was breathless, I pulled away. "Thank you for lunch," I said. "And thank you for setting up the meeting with Neil."

"Does that mean you're kicking me out?" Lewis asked.

"I do need to get back to work, yes."

He nodded his understanding. "Dinner tonight?"

"Actually—"

"Don't turn me down, babe."

"Rayna broke her elbow last night," I explained. "I'm going to go home and give her some TLC."

"Oh, no. What happened?"

I took a few minutes to fill Lewis in on how Rayna had gotten injured. "She's okay, but she'll have the cast on for four weeks."

He pecked me on the forehead. "Of course you want to spend time with your baby."

"Thank you for understanding. But we'll talk, okay?"

Lewis gave me a quick peck on the lips. Then he was gone.

When my sister breezed into my office at quarter to five, the first thought I had was that something was terribly wrong. She'd kicked Morris out. Or he'd decided to leave her. My sister wasn't getting married again—she was heading to divorce court.

And if something *wasn't* wrong, I was going to throttle her.

Nikki smiled brightly, as though she didn't have a care in the world. I actually balled my right hand into a fist.

"Hey, sis." Nikki's smile instantly disappeared. "Why don't you look happy to see me?"

I eased backward in my chair and folded my arms over my chest. "Are you kidding?"

"No." Nikki looked dumbfounded. "What'd I do?"

"Uh, remember the phone call to me on Sunday? The one where you and Morris sounded like you were about to kill each other over renewing your wedding vows? You were extremely upset and told me you were coming over to my place. Ring any bells?"

"Oh. Right. Well, I didn't bother because you said you had plans."

"What are you talking about? The very last thing you said to me was that you needed me. You said you were on your way. Hell, I thought you were going to have a couple suit-cases with you."

My sister shrugged nonchalantly. "I thought you'd realize I wasn't coming."

"Through what—mental telepathy?"

"You're not mad at me, are you?"

"Why should I be mad?" I asked sarcastically. "It's not like I didn't change my plans for the day because you said you were coming over."

"I guess I should have called. But that was days ago. There's no reason to have pent-up anger over that."

I said nothing. But I did feel like shaking some common courtesy into my sister.

My sister's eyes moved around the room, noticing the roses for the first time. "Whoa. What's with all the flowers?"

"Oh," I began, scrambling for something appropriate to say. I hadn't told her about Lewis, because I knew she'd give me a hard time about being involved with him again. "Secret admirer."

"Really?" She moved to the bouquet closest to her, the one on the left side of my desk, and sniffed. "They're beautiful. Who do you think sent them to you?"

"I have no clue," I lied.

Nikki's eyes lit up. "Chaz?"

Wouldn't it be nice... "Maybe. A girl can hope, right?"

"Ooh, I bet they are from Chaz! You told me how romantic he was in the Bahamas. Which means what I heard is definitely not true."

"What?" I asked, suddenly panicked. "What did you hear?"

"There was something on one of those celebrity gossip shows about that singer, Maria Lopez, having hired Chaz for a private session before her upcoming tour. Something about needing to mentally prepare before her first world tour—which sounds like it's only going to be ten cities in the U.S. and a couple in Canada. Hardly a world tour."

"Wait a second," I said, holding up a hand to stop my sister. My heart was suddenly pounding. I'd heard of Maria Lopez, and only knew that she was an up-and-coming Latina singer. And that she was stunningly beautiful. "She hired Chaz?"

"Private session," Nikki said, making air quotes and rolling her eyes. "Sounded totally suspicious to me. But, if Chaz sent you all these flowers—and I'm sure he did—then I don't think he and Maria are involved in anything except business."

Lots of people hired Chaz. Mostly, he did group seminars, but I'm sure he did private ones as well for those who could afford him. It was a leap to assume that just because a beautiful singer had hired him for some "private" motivational coaching that he was now involved with her.

But still I asked, "Did they say that Chaz and Maria Lopez are romantically involved?"

"They didn't say that exactly, but I figured that's what they were implying."

I drew in a deep breath, relaxing somewhat.

"Anyway, I'm sure you're wondering why I'm here." Nikki beamed as she took a seat opposite me at my desk. "I was hoping we could go wedding-gown shopping. There are a couple boutiques near here I want to check out."

"Gee, Nikki, I'd love to, but I can't," I said, my tone acerbic. Forcing my thoughts from Chaz, I concentrated on the disappointment I'd felt at my sister not even calling me back after last Sunday's dramatic episode.

Anything to avoid the nauseating thought that Chaz and Maria Lopez were dating.

"No, no, you have to."

"Any other time I would," I said, growing serious. "But Rayna broke her elbow last night and—"

"What!" My sister slapped the armrests on her chair. "Why didn't you tell me?"

"I figured you were in Thailand."

She scowled at me. "Very funny." A beat passed. "Is she okay?"

"Yeah, she's all right." I explained how Rayna had broken her elbow. "I'm sure the cast is weird for her, but she'll be fine."

"I'm so glad." Nikki's lips turned in a frown. "Well, I can see why you want to get home. I guess I should have called first."

"It's all right," I said. "I can spare an hour or so. I called Carla half an hour ago and she said that Rayna was fine. I'll call to make sure she can watch Rayna for a bit longer."

"Thank you. And also tell Carla to keep a better eye on Rayna. I need my little niece to be in top form if she's going to be the flower girl at my wedding."

Somehow, I refrained from rolling my eyes. My sister was already worried about Rayna performing at her wedding. "Rayna will be fine," I assured Nikki. "These things happen."

"Yes, but it can't happen again."

I didn't respond. The last thing I was going to do was relay my sister's message to Carla. I wondered if Nikki had any clue how insulting she could be at times.

I was used to it, however. She never approved of the men I dated, which made her endorsement of Chaz a bit baffling. Whenever I told her about a guy I was involved with, she found ways to cut the guy down. It wouldn't last. He was a player. He wasn't good enough for me. Yes, she'd been right about Lewis when I'd first dated him. And she'd been right about Eli. But a woman has to figure these things out for herself. She relies on her sister for support, not for I-told-you-sos.

My sister got up and made her way around the desk to me. She linked arms with mine and urged me out of my seat.

"Come on, sis," she said, grinning from ear to ear. "Let's go find me the perfect wedding dress. And maybe we need to shop for one for you, too."

If only my sister knew how right she was.

12

I missed Alaina. Missed her office gossip. Missed seeing her behind the reception desk with the phone glued to her ear. Yes, I'd been checking in on her practically every day, but I still missed her presence in the office, and couldn't wait for her to get back.

So I called her Saturday afternoon, hoping she'd be up for a visit. "Hey, Ally."

"Vanessa," she said cheerfully. She almost sounded like her old self. Almost, but not quite. How could she be her old self when her ex-husband had beaten her almost to death? At least the bastard—one of Miami's "finest"—was now rotting in jail and would likely spend the rest of his days there.

"What's up, girl?" Alaina continued.

"Don't worry about me. How are you feeling?"

"Not so bad. It hurts to walk, but I'm trying. I ain't gonna let Jorge keep me down. That's what the asshole wanted. Any day now, I'm gonna be back to normal."

"That's my girl," I said, warmed by Alaina's fighting spirit.

"Hey, Vanessa?" Alaina asked. "Everything okay?"

I was surprised at the question, though I shouldn't have been. Alaina and I were close, and she could often pick up on my mood just from my tone.

"I just miss you, that's all," I told her.

"No, it's more than that. What aren't you telling me?"

I sighed then. I'd watched all the gossip shows I could in the last couple days, hoping to hear news about Chaz and Maria Lopez, but also fearing hearing news about Chaz and Maria Lopez. There'd been nothing about their private session, which had left me feeling hopeful. I was also feeling pretty hopeful about the upcoming meeting with Tassie, but my nerves were getting the best of me just thinking about being in the same room with Tassie and her lawyer in just three days.

"A lot," I admitted. "There's so much I would have talked to you about if you were in the office. I miss you, girl."

"Then why don't you come over?"

"Now?"

"If you can swing it. We can have a glass of wine—just like old times."

"Are you allowed to drink?" I asked. "With your pain medication?"

"One glass of wine won't hurt," she said. "I'm recovering, not dead."

"Then girl, you're on." The idea of finally hanging out with Alaina again outside of a hospital room was exactly what I needed. "You don't mind if I bring Rayna, do you?"

"Of course not. The boys will love playing with her.

And my sister's here, so she can help to watch out for them while we chat."

"That's good. By the way, I didn't get to tell you that Rayna broke her elbow."

"What?" Alaina asked, shocked.

"Yeah, a few nights ago. I should have called sooner, but there's been a lot going on."

"I'll make sure the boys take it easy with her," Alaina said. "They'll be used to that. They've had to take it easy with me since I came home from the hospital."

"No doubt."

"You can tell me all about how Rayna broke her arm— and everything else—when you get here."

"I'll see you soon," I told her, smiling.

Soon turned out to be an hour and twenty minutes later, by the time I got Rayna and myself ready and drove to Kendall. Alaina's sister, Melissa, answered the door.

She greeted me with a warm smile. "Hi, Vanessa. Hi, Rayna." She ran a knuckle over Rayna's cheek. Then she noticed Rayna's arm and her eyes widened. "Oh, no. What happened to your arm, sweetie?"

Rayna curled her head shyly into my shoulder.

"She broke her elbow," I explained.

"Poor baby," Melissa cooed.

"Yeah." I tucked a strand of Rayna's curly hair behind her ear. "She's taking it like a trooper, though."

"Did you know your Auntie Alaina has a cast, too?"

Rayna shook her head.

Melissa stepped backward. "Please, come in."

I stepped into the foyer, then asked, "How are you doing, Melissa?"

"Good," she replied. "Now that Alaina's home." She turned her attention back to Rayna. "You want to see the boys? They're playing in the backyard."

Rayna nodded.

Melissa reached for her. "Then come with me. I'll take you to play with them."

Rayna hesitated, but only for a moment. Then, she went happily into Melissa's arms.

"That a girl," Melissa said, turning back to me. "Alaina's in the sunroom. She wouldn't listen when I told her to stay in bed."

I walked with Melissa to the sunroom, which looked out onto the backyard. Then Melissa continued on with Rayna and out the kitchen's patio doors.

Looking over her shoulder at me, Alaina grinned brightly. "Vanessa!"

"No, don't get up," I told her when she made a move to get up from her leather recliner. "Let me come to you."

I leaned down to envelop her in a hug. "Look at you. The bruises are pretty much gone."

"Each day, I look better and better."

I was extremely pleased at the sight of my friend looking more like herself than she had when in the hospital. The cast on her arm was the only real evidence that she was hurt, though I knew she was suffering from internal and back pain. Jorge's attack on her had caused some damage to one of her vertebrae, in addition to taking anti-inflammatory medication, she was getting massage therapy to cope with the pain.

But she was well on her road to recovery, and just seeing her looking so much better than that first terrible day when she'd been hospitalized completely lifted my spirits.

"Did you bring some wine?" Alaina whispered.

"No. I thought you had some."

"My sister made sure to empty the fridge. Said alcohol's gonna interfere with my medication."

Alaina flashed me a disdainful look, and I couldn't help but smile. "Hey, she's only looking out for you," I said. "Besides, we don't need wine to have a good time."

I took a seat on the sofa beside her recliner. A knit blanket was draped casually over Alaina's upper body and lap. The air-conditioning was on high, which was normally necessary in the sunroom. But because it was overcast outside, the sun wasn't making the room extra hot.

I looked out the window to the backyard. Rayna and the boys were kicking a soccer ball.

"So," Alaina said. "Tell me."

I told her about Rayna's accident at Carla's, and how at the hospital, I'd felt the doctor was judging me. "Of course, maybe I'm just being paranoid," I said. "In the last few months since Eli died, I've felt like a big failure."

"Nonsense," Alaina protested. "You're not a failure!"

"I know, but…"

"But what?"

"I just wish things were different," I said.

"What—that you had that *perfect* man, the *perfect* father for your daughter?" Alaina asked, picking up on exactly what I'd been thinking. "Well, I had a husband, a father for

my kids. And look what he did to me. You're doing fine on
your own. Don't beat up on yourself."

"Thanks," I said softly. And because I didn't want to think
about my complicated love life, I changed the subject. "I do
have some good news I haven't told you."

"Oh?"

I told Alaina about my meeting with Cynthia Martin and
what she'd learned about the "grieving" Tassie. "Quite
frankly, with Eli dead, life is probably a helluva lot better
for Tassie than if he were still alive," I surmised after filling
Alaina in on the details. "She got to keep everything because
she was legally still his wife. No wonder she kept stalling
on the divorce despite having a boyfriend. She wanted to
have her cake and eat it, too."

"Which is exactly what she got. Cars, houses, money…"

"So what the hell does she want to take my place for?"

"It doesn't sound like that's gonna happen," Alaina said.
"Not with what Cynthia discovered."

"I hope not."

Alaina shot me a curious gaze. "What do you mean you
hope not?"

"What if everything Cynthia discovered means diddly?"
I asked. "What if I confront Tassie with her dirty laundry
and she basically tells me to go ahead and air it—that she's
still gonna take my home anyway?"

"Don't worry. An abortion? A boyfriend on the side?
Tassie's not gonna want anyone to know that."

I nodded, feeling better about the whole situation. "No,
I guess not."

"Hey, you want me to go to the meeting with you?"

"Lewis is going with me. And the lawyer, of course."

"I'd be happy to go, too."

"I couldn't ask you to do that. Not while you're recovering."

"Ask me? Girl, I'd pay top dollar to see that woman's face when you present her with the evidence you have."

"Thanks, sweetie, but that's not necessary. However, maybe I'll sneak a tape recorder in so you can hear the whole meeting, play by play."

"Ooh, I love it!" Alaina laughed. "You're gonna kick some Tassie ass."

"Oh, I sure hope so. I'm just glad Lewis put me in touch with this lawyer. Says he's a real fighter."

"So things are going well with Lewis?" she asked.

I hesitated a moment, then said, "Yeah. Sure."

"I notice you're not wearing your ring."

"Oh. Well, I don't like wearing it around the house. And I forgot to put it on before I left."

"Mmm-hmm," Alaina said in a tone I didn't like.

"What?"

"I'm just wondering."

"Wondering what?"

"If *Chaz* had given you that ring, would you *forget* to put it on?"

"Don't do that," I said.

"Why not?"

"Because I don't want to talk about Chaz."

"Mmm-hmm."

I scowled at my friend. "I wish you wouldn't do this, Alaina."

"Talk about Chaz—or Lewis?"

"Chaz," I told her.

"Because I'm right?"

I exhaled sharply. "Because I'm confused."

"Why are you confused? *I* know exactly how you feel."

"If only it were so simple."

"You're in love with Chaz. Seems simple enough to me."

"He doesn't want me, remember?"

"I think he does. You have to keep fighting for him, let him know how much you love him."

I leaned forward, my stomach tightening. "Maybe I am still in love with Chaz."

"Aha!" Alaina grinned, victorious in my admission.

"But…" I said, and Alaina's grin vanished. "First of all, he's not calling, so it's clear he doesn't want me. And," I quickly went on when Alaina opened her mouth to protest, "I also realized something." I paused for a moment. "That day that Jorge beat you and I went to the hospital to see you? Well, when I was driving home, I had a kind of epiphany. I realized that marriages based on hot, driving passion can end in disaster. With lots of jealousy and rage. And that helped me make a crucial decision. To marry someone who's my friend—someone I can count on to support me, make me laugh. Someone who complements me."

"And that's Lewis?" Alaina said doubtfully.

I rolled my eyes. "You liked him before."

"That was before he cheated on you."

"He's changed."

"Has he?"

"Yes."

"Or do you care?"

"What does that mean?" I asked.

"You were hurt when Lewis betrayed you, yeah. But then you got over him, and I don't believe for a second you'll ever feel the same kind of love for him you once did. Maybe it won't matter to you if he cheats this time because your heart isn't in it."

I said nothing.

"Don't get me wrong. If that's your decision, that's fine."

"So why bring it up?"

"Because I know you, Vanessa. You can't live without passion."

I frowned. "Now I'm confused. You know better than anyone how passionate I was about Lewis."

"Exactly. *Was.* Are you gonna tell me you feel the same kind of passion for him now?"

My friend was recovering, and I didn't want to get mad at her, but I didn't appreciate her harping on the situation. I'd had this conversation with Carla, and I didn't care to have it again. "Lewis is here," I told her simply. "Where is Chaz?" When Alaina didn't answer, I went on. "I know this isn't the most ideal, or even the most romantic situation. But I believe that Lewis has changed. You should have seen the gorgeous roses he sent me at work this week. More than one hundred. With a wonderfully sweet note about how much he loves me. He swears I'm the one for him and that he's given up chasing women. And as for me…I know that one day I'll love him with all the passion I once used to."

Alaina didn't speak.

"And when I told him that Rayna broke her elbow, he sent her this huge teddy bear and helium balloons. The bear's so big, I could hardly carry it from the lobby to my apartment. Rayna was thrilled."

Again, Alaina didn't speak. Several seconds of silence passed between us. I felt uncomfortable, and assumed that Alaina did, too.

"You know I only want what's best for you," she said, breaking the silence. "Same as you want for me."

"I do. And on that note, you and Michael are still talking?" Alaina had met Michael, a local on-air reporter, when the media had come to my office to interview me after Eli's murder. She and Michael had just started dating when Jorge attacked them both, doing the most physical damage to Alaina.

Alaina's face lit up, answering my question without words. "Yes. I was so worried that what Jorge did to us would scare him off, but he still wants a relationship with me."

I squeezed Alaina's hand. "That's wonderful. And I'm sure it helps ease Michael's mind that Jorge's in jail."

"He's going to visit me tomorrow," Alaina went on. "I know we weren't dating long, but I really have a good feeling about him."

"Good," I said. "I'm happy for you."

Alaina's expression suddenly soured, and alarm shot through me. "What's the matter?" I asked. "Are you in pain? Do you need some pills?"

Alaina shook her head. "No. But I have some news to share."

"What?" I asked, already fearing the worst. Had her ex-husband been bonded out of jail? Surely no one in his right mind would release a screwed-up cop from custody…would he?

"I found out yesterday that Jorge changed his plea."

My eyes widened. "The man wouldn't be stupid enough—"

"Not guilty by reason of insanity."

"After he already pled guilty?"

"He's apparently talking to psychiatrists—the whole nine yards. Trying to do anything he has to in order to stay out of jail."

"You think he'll actually get away with what he did to you?" The thought was too horrifying to even contemplate.

Alaina shook her head. "I don't believe that. But the jerk is gonna try."

I seethed as I mulled over what she'd told me, but then I said, "You know what—maybe this is better. Let Jorge dig his own grave by not accepting responsibility for what he did. I don't think any judge will look too kindly on that. He'd be better off saying he's sorry and hoping for the court's mercy."

"That's what the prosecutor said, and I feel the same way. But you know what—if in the end, Jorge gets a longer sentence because of this new tactic, even better for me."

Alaina gazed outside, and I followed her line of sight. Her twin boys were pushing trucks around on the grass, and Rayna was doing the same with a red fire truck.

Several moments passed with neither of us speaking. I sensed, however, where her thoughts had ventured. How her boys were dealing with the sudden lack of a father in their lives.

It was all fine and dandy to talk about Jorge spending the rest of his days in jail. It was no less than he deserved. But I couldn't help feeling for Alaina's sons. They'd be hurt in all this, even if never seeing their father again was for the best.

"How are the boys dealing with this?" I asked.

Alaina shrugged. "As well as can be expected. They don't really understand what's going on, just that their father did something bad and they won't be seeing him for a while. They seem to be dealing with it, but you know kids—they can be affected by something and not show it."

"Don't I know it," I agreed. I had no clue how Rayna had been affected by Eli's sudden disappearance, but all I could do was give her love and talk as openly as possible about Eli should she ever decide to ask questions about him. She seemed to be doing fine, but who knew what issues might surface down the road? I hoped there were none, but I had to be prepared for the worst-case scenario.

"They'll be fine," Alaina said softly. "We'll all be."

"Absolutely," I told her, though I hardly dared believe it.

13

The next day, I came to the conclusion that Byron had lost his mind.

He *called* me. Actually had the nerve to dial my cell phone number, expecting me to pick up.

The caller ID told me exactly who it was, so I *didn't* pick up. After the confrontation at my office, I didn't even want to think of what he wanted to say to me, because I knew it was going to be about Rayna.

I turned back to the kitchen counter, where I was preparing sandwiches and snacks to take to the zoo with Rayna. It was shortly after noon, and I hoped to be on the road within an hour. I didn't bother to ask Carla and Amani to accompany us, deciding that I would spend some fun mommy-daughter time with Rayna.

The phone rang again, not five minutes after the first time. I dusted bread crumbs off on my sweatpants and turned around to answer the phone. This time the caller ID showed Private Name, Private Number.

"Nice try, Byron," I muttered, and didn't bother to pick up the receiver.

But I was disturbed. Very disturbed. In two and a half years, I hadn't heard from Byron twice in two weeks. Maybe he really had had an attack of conscience and was ready to be Daddy.

Well, too bad. Not my problem. He'd walked away from his daughter, his responsibility—all his own choice. I didn't owe him anything now.

About a minute after the phone had rung from the private caller, the red message light began to flash. I finished making the peanut butter sandwich I was putting together for Rayna, wiped my hands off on a dish towel, then walked over to the wall phone and picked up the receiver.

Rayna suddenly appeared. "Mommy, are we going to zoo?"

"Yes, sweetheart. In a couple minutes, okay?"

Rayna nodded, then hopped back out to the living room. I took a few steps to the right, past the kitchen wall, so I could watch her go. She climbed onto the sofa and snuggled up with the giant brown teddy bear Lewis had sent her.

I couldn't help thinking that Rayna's speech had matured. She'd asked about going to the zoo in an almost perfect sentence. Had she done that last week? I couldn't remember.

It also struck me that my baby looked noticeably taller. It's weird how you don't notice a child's day-to-day growth, and then one day, bam! It hits you that your child is walking taller, speaking more clearly. And you start to get sentimental about how fast your baby is growing into a little girl.

Before I knew it, Rayna would be graduating high school. Going to college. Getting married.

And I'd be that much older. Would I still be single?

"Don't get ahead of yourself, Vanessa," I told myself. "Just make sure you enjoy every moment."

That was something Byron hadn't done. Now, however, it seemed he'd had a change of heart.

At least for the moment.

I punched in the code to receive my messages. As I did, I realized that my back was stiff from apprehension. I didn't want to hear Byron's voice. Didn't want to hear what he had to say.

"Okay fine," came the male voice, definitely Byron's. "Obviously I made a mistake by not blocking my number before I called." He sighed wearily. "Look, you can't avoid me forever. And I don't know why you're freaking out about the idea of talking to me. You act like I used to abuse you or something."

"No," I muttered. "You just stole from me, lied to me. Not to mention that you abandoned me and your child."

"My mother's in town," Byron went on. "She wants to see Rayna. She's the only grandparent Rayna's got. Call me back. Let me know when we can arrange a time to meet. Because if you keep avoiding me..."

The message ended, and I quickly deleted it. I finally understood what was going on—but I didn't feel better about it.

Byron's mother was in town. I knew she lived in St. Louis

and didn't like to travel by plane. I could only assume she'd taken a road trip to Miami. And if she'd come all this way by car, she didn't want to leave without seeing her grandchild.

In the time I'd dated Byron, I'd never met his mother, but I had talked to her on the phone. She'd even called me to commiserate over the fact that Byron wasn't standing by me during the pregnancy. She'd lent a supportive ear, encouraging me to hang in there, saying that Byron would come around once the baby was born.

Of course, he never had.

Well, until now.

But what had shocked me was that when Rayna was born, I hadn't heard from his mother. Not a word. Perhaps she'd felt awkward about contacting me because Byron wasn't involved in Rayna's life. Or she might ultimately have believed Byron's lies. He'd accused me of having sex with someone else and had suggested—very strongly—that Rayna might not be his child. After that—and after he'd told me I should have an abortion—I'd decided that trying to force him to be a part of Rayna's life would be a wasted effort. To think I'd been willing to try and forgive him his gambling habit, *if* he was truly over it, for Rayna's sake. How foolish I had been.

Based on Byron's message, time had clearly gotten to his mother, and with her being in town, she had to be pressing him to see her grandchild.

Well, it would be a cold day in hell before I called Byron back.

"Mommy!" Rayna called. "I want to see zebras!"

"Coming, sweetheart."

As I bagged the sandwiches and crackers I'd prepared, a terrible thought struck me. A premonition, really.

Byron hadn't completed his statement, but I suddenly feared that I knew what he'd been about to say.

Because if you keep avoiding me…

If I kept avoiding him, he was going to show up at my door.

With his mother in tow.

I quickly put the sandwiches, juice boxes and snacks into a knapsack, then hurried to the living room to get Rayna. But I hesitated, something making me turn toward the window.

I made my way to the living room window and peered down to the street. My God. There was a black car parked on the street in front of my building, a dark car with tinted windows.

Last night when I'd left Alaina's place, I'd noticed a black car several times when I'd looked in my rearview mirror. I'd had the odd feeling that I was being followed, but had dismissed the feeling as paranoia.

But now…

I spun around and rushed to Rayna. "All right, sweetheart. Mommy's ready to go." I tried to keep any anxiety out of my voice, though I was suddenly worried that Byron was going to show up any second. "Ready to see the zebras?"

"Yes!" she trilled, her eyes lighting up with excitement.

I hurried with Rayna down to the car. Minutes later, I was turning right out of the parking garage and heading toward Fifth Avenue. It didn't take more than a couple minutes for me to realize that the black car I'd seen outside my building was now following me. A nondescript sedan with tinted windows. I wouldn't have been so certain if not for the fact that I saw a similar car following me at a distance when I left Alaina's place yesterday.

Byron's new car? What was he going to do—stalk me until I agreed to meet with him?

When I turned left onto Fifth at the light, so did the sedan. I stayed in the left lane, making it look as though I would head straight onto the causeway, but at the last moment, jerked into the right lane and turned right onto Alton Road. My heart slammed against my rib cage when I saw that the sedan, two cars behind mine, also turned right onto Alton Road.

"Damn you, Byron," I muttered. I couldn't see who was in the car, but after the two phone calls, it made sense that it was Byron. Who else would it be?

And then the race was on. The race to give Byron the slip. Did he think that chasing me around South Beach was going to warm me to the idea of letting him see Rayna?

I sped up. Turned right the first moment I could, then raced down that street and turned left onto Washington. Then it was left on 11th, followed by a quick right. I continued my erratic driving, speeding and cutting people off, glancing periodically in the rearview mirror.

I let out a relieved breath when, after a few minutes of erratic driving, I no longer saw the black sedan. And then nearly had heart failure as I thought I saw the nose of the black car rounding the corner several car lengths behind me.

I sped up. Made a hasty right turn. But I was going too fast. I lost control of the wheel, and my car veered sideways as it spun out.

I screamed, fearing the worst. I didn't even know if traffic was coming, and if I was going to collide with anyone. All I could do was grip my steering wheel and hold on as tightly as possible.

Seemingly in slow motion, my car made a 360-degree turn. I felt a bump, my airbag exploded and then the car came to a stop.

I'm not sure how long I sat there, the airbag in my face, but it seemed like minutes passed. I'm sure it was only seconds. I was numb and terrified at the same time. I kept my eyes closed, afraid to open them. Afraid I'd hit something. Someone.

Rayna's cries forced me to open my eyes. I spun around and looked at her, reassured myself that she hadn't been hurt in the impact. She was securely strapped in her car seat, but no doubt terribly frightened.

My breathing ragged, I pressed the button to unlock my car doors. I wasn't sure if I opened it, or if someone else did, but I do know that a man was standing outside my door, looking concerned, asking me if I was okay.

I'm not sure if I said anything. I only knew that the man helped me out of the car. That's when I saw that my car had mounted the curb and plowed into some shrubs. But other than that, there didn't seem to be any damage.

"My baby." I scrambled around the car to Rayna's door and pulled it open. A couple cars had stopped. People standing on the street stopped strolling and stared. Others drove past slowly, looking for damage.

I pulled my crying daughter into my arms. "Oh, my baby." I shook her, cooing softly. "Mommy's sorry."

Rayna's crying ceased. I was certain that she wasn't hurt, just scared.

"It doesn't really look like there's any damage," the stranger said while he rounded my car and bent down, continuing to inspect it. He fingered the side of my Accord. "A couple scratches, but nothing major. This can be buffed out." Rising, he met my gaze. "What happened?"

"I…I don't know. I just lost control."

As I spoke, I saw the car. The black sedan. My body froze. In a nanosecond, I understood my fear. Yes, it could be Byron. But what if it wasn't? What if someone else was following me, someone who meant me harm.

Tassie?

Did she want me out of the condo so badly she'd resort to scare tactics, or worse, violence?

The sedan door began to open. And then the wail of a siren sounded as a Miami Beach cruiser went through the intersection. The sedan's door closed, and a moment later, the car turned left, driving off.

That only heightened my suspicion. Someone had been about to come out of that car. Had it been Byron, wouldn't he at least have come over to make sure his daughter was okay?

A male police officer exited the cruiser and approached me. "Are you all right, ma'am?"

I nodded jerkily. "Yes. I'm okay. Just a little shaken up."

The cop surveyed my car. "What happened here?"

"I'm not sure," I said.

Even with his dark sunglasses on, I could see the surprised expression on his face. "You're not sure?"

"What I mean is I lost control. I was trying to make that corner over there and…and…" I let my voice trail off, hoping that was enough of an explanation for the officer.

"Have you had any alcohol to drink, ma'am?"

"No." Was he serious? "Of course not."

He stood staring at me, as though he didn't believe me. "I haven't," I insisted.

"If you were turning from that corner—" he pointed across the street "—and ended up over here…" He gestured to the bushes my car had run into. "You had to be going pretty fast."

I hadn't wanted to admit to speeding, because I didn't want to get a ticket. But now it seemed the only thing that made sense. "I probably was going a bit fast."

"And you've got precious cargo there," the officer said, indicating Rayna with a jerk of his head. "You need to be careful."

I nodded. Pressed a kiss to Rayna's cheek.

"I know who you are," the officer said slowly. "You're that woman who was dating Eli Johnson."

"Yeah, that's me," I said sheepishly.

"There's no real damage here," the cop said. "I'll let you off with a warning."

"Thank you," I said. "I really appreciate it. I promise, I'll slow down."

Now the officer slipped his sunglasses off. "Some men I just don't understand. They've got a gorgeous woman like you, and yet they screw around." He paused a beat. "You still single?"

I wasn't quite sure what to say. Was this cop *hitting* on me?

I noticed the bright yellow Lamborghini then, and knew before it pulled up to the curb who it was.

Lewis.

The officer looked over his shoulder, following my line of sight, just as Lewis got out of the car. He hurried toward me, sweeping me into his arms when he got to me.

"Lewis," I said. "What are you doing here?"

"I was in the area. I realized that was you from down the street. What happened?"

I glanced at the cop. He slipped his sunglasses back on. "Ma'am, you have a good day. And slow down."

"Thank you, officer."

"What happened?" Lewis asked again when the cop was out of earshot.

"Someone was following me. At first I thought it was Byron—he called again—but then I wondered if maybe it was someone hired by Tassie. She might be trying to scare me out of my condo before the meeting on Tuesday."

Lewis nodded thoughtfully. He rubbed my arms, then ran a hand over Rayna's hair. "Hey, sweetie," he said to her. "Are you okay?"

Rayna didn't respond. Just angled her head into my neck.

"Don't you worry about Tassie," Lewis said to me. "She won't be a problem after Tuesday. I promise you that."

I wanted to believe that, but wasn't sure I could.

14

Neil Gorman, Attorney at Law.

I stared at the large sign over the door on the building in Coral Gables, my nerves making my stomach tighten. I was really here. Really about to meet with the wretched Tassie Johnson.

Lewis placed his hand around my waist and pulled me close. "You all right?"

He must have sensed my hesitation. I glanced up at him, nodding. "Yes, I'm fine."

"You have nothing to worry about, sweetheart," Lewis assured me. "We're gonna kick some ass in there."

Minutes later, we were inside, and Neil Gorman's secretary, an older, portly lady, led us to the conference room. The building didn't appear much bigger than a house from the outside, so I was shocked to see such a huge conference room inside. A large mahogany table sat in the middle of the room, and I guessed that it could seat around thirty people. The dark leather chairs were overstuffed and screamed of pomposity.

They also looked extremely comfortable.

I wondered if my lawyer and I would be seated at one end of the table, and Tassie and her lawyer at the other. I could almost envision us taking turns sliding envelopes down the length of the smooth tabletop the way hockey players shoot pucks down the ice. Better yet, maybe we could all play shuffleboard on the table and forget the talks altogether.

"Are you nervous?"

At the sound of my lawyer's voice, I glanced toward the conference room door. He stood smiling.

"Hello, Neil," I greeted him. I was taller than him by about two inches. "Yes, I am nervous. I'm not really looking forward to seeing Tassie—even though there's no way around it."

Neil patted my shoulder. "There's no need to worry. I assure you."

Neil greeted Lewis with a handshake.

"Are they here yet?" I asked.

Neil flicked his wrist forward and looked at his watch. "They're due in ten minutes."

Ten minutes. I wasn't emotionally ready for this. Then again, I wasn't sure I ever would be.

"Would you like some water, coffee?" Neil asked. "I'll tell Rosemary to get whatever you want."

I contemplated asking for a shot of tequila. "Coffee would be nice."

"I'll have water," Lewis said.

"All right. You two have a seat wherever you want."

When Neil was gone, I said to Lewis, "If Tassie and her lawyer will be here in ten minutes, that doesn't leave any time to go over preliminaries."

"I think we discussed everything we needed to discuss in your office last week," Lewis said. "Neil's formulated a game plan, and you just have to trust him to run with it."

"I suppose you're right." There was no need for me to worry about Neil's competence. "It's not like I've ever done anything like this before, so I don't know what to expect."

"Expect results. Neil always delivers."

Rosemary entered the room with a bottle of water and a large cup of coffee. Lewis and I accepted the drinks, then went to the conference table. I took a seat closest to the window, about four chairs down from the end. Lewis sat beside me on the right, leaving the space on my left for Neil.

Two minutes later, Neil entered the room. "They've arrived," he announced.

"Are you going out to greet them?" I asked.

"Rosemary will bring them in," Neil said.

I nodded, then pressed a palm to my forehead. Clearly sensing my tension, Lewis gave my hand a reassuring squeeze. "I know you're nervous."

"Understatement of the century."

"Relax, babe."

I did anything but relax when I saw the brass door handle begin to turn. My heart pounded furiously, and tension made the back of my neck go stiff.

But when the door opened and Tassie strutted into the

room like a runway model, my tension ebbed away, replaced by disgust.

Tassie had had the nerve to wear black, as though she were still grieving.

Well, this wasn't the court of public opinion. Her pretense of being a grieving wife would score her no points here.

Especially not when a very different truth was revealed.

My eyes narrowed in anger as she did her catwalk to the table. She was wearing a simple black dress, black Chanel sunglasses…and my hat.

The hat I'd worn to Eli's funeral…but had also left at Eli's funeral in my rush to get out of the room.

The nerve!

Neil, who'd been standing near the door awaiting Tassie and her lawyer's arrival, shook hands with Bradley. The two exchanged casual greetings. For them, this was business.

It certainly wasn't for me and Tassie.

"Shall we sit anywhere?" Bradley asked. Unlike Neil, Bradley was tall, lean and very attractive. Fleetingly, I wondered if the blond-haired, blue-eyed lawyer was working so doggedly for his client because she was paying him—or because he hoped to get into her pants.

If he hadn't already.

"Wherever you like," Neil told Bradley.

Bradley sat first, directly opposite me at the table. Tassie sat to his right, opposite the chair Neil would occupy. She didn't look directly at me, but I could tell she was staring at me through her dark sunglasses.

While Neil sat, Bradley opened a briefcase and extracted

three folders. For the life of me, I couldn't imagine what the heck he had pertaining to my disagreement with Tassie that fit in three folders. Maybe he was simply trying to intimidate me.

Neil waited patiently while Bradley leafed through various sheets of paper, getting himself organized. When he was finished, Bradley closed the briefcase, looked across the table and smiled.

"Are you ready?" Neil asked.

"Yes," Bradley replied.

Tassie finally slipped off her sunglasses, then whispered something in Bradley's ear. He nodded, and she took my hat off of her head.

"Before we start," Bradley said, "Tassie wanted to return this to your client."

Bradley passed the hat across the table, and Neil shrugged before lifting it. "This is yours?" he asked me.

"Yes," I replied through clenched teeth. Though as a matter of principle, I wouldn't wear it again. Not when Tassie had deliberately donned it to piss me off.

"And if you don't mind me asking, who is this?" Bradley gestured to Lewis.

"He's a friend of my client's," Neil responded.

Bradley nodded, but didn't seem pleased. "No disrespect, but I'd prefer if we kept the meeting to only those directly involved in the matter."

I was about to protest, but Lewis rolled his chair back and stood. "All right. I'll wait outside."

I shot him a frantic look, and he gave my shoulder a squeeze. "You'll be fine."

Tassie kept her eyes on Lewis as he strode to the door, scrutinizing him, and no doubt wondering what his relation was to me.

When Lewis had closed the conference room door behind him, Bradley spoke. "Okay. Let's get down to business. Do you mind if I begin by stating what my client would like?"

"Please," Neil told him.

Bradley nodded. "We all know that we're here regarding the joint property shared by Eli and your client. With Eli's death, my client inherited his share of the property. Now, at one time, my client thought she simply wanted a monetary settlement, but having had time to think about this, she has changed her mind. Instead, she now wants to buy out Ms. Cain's share of the property so she can move in."

"Why now?" I couldn't help asking. "Why now when I came up with the money to buy her out?"

Neil shot me a look, one I took to mean I should let him do the talking. Then he turned back to Bradley and Tassie. "Can you shed some light on why your client had this change of heart? I understand she was originally quite persistent in having my client buy out her share of the condo."

"Certainly," Bradley said, sounding conciliatory and professional. "This property meant something to Eli. My client, being Eli's widow, expressed an interest in living there so she can feel closer to her deceased husband."

Tassie nodded, and she even dabbed at an eye with her finger.

I snorted in derision.

"Tassie is prepared to pay above market share," Bradley said. "A very nice six-figure sum."

Neil nodded, and I wanted to scream. I didn't want him playing nice. I wanted him to play hardball, damn it!

When Neil spoke, his voice was even and calm. "That offer is not acceptable to us."

"My client is being more than reasonable," Bradley said. "She's prepared to offer four hundred thousand."

"That won't buy me another condo on South Beach," I interjected. "Not one like I have right now."

Neil looked at me and said, "I've got this."

After a moment, I nodded.

Neil turned back to Tassie and her lawyer. "As you've just heard, your offer, no matter how generous, won't buy my client another condo like the one she has right now."

"It'll be more than she had before she met Eli," Tassie spat out.

"What?" I asked, my eyes widening.

In reply, she met my gaze with a hard expression.

"Eli was in love with me," I told her. "And you can't deal with that, so you want to make me suffer."

"Vanessa…" Neil said.

Huffing, I looked away. But what I really wanted to do was ask Neil if I could have five minutes alone with Tassie to beat the crap out of her.

"I was his *wife,*" Tassie pointed out.

"A wife Eli never mentioned to my client," Neil said. "Vanessa is an innocent victim in this, and she shouldn't have to suffer because of Eli's mistakes."

"I don't believe that," Tassie said.

"This meeting will go a lot more smoothly without your client's outbursts," Neil said. "We all want a resolution that will work for everyone."

Bradley instructed Tassie to let him do the talking, and while she didn't look pleased, she shut up.

"As you've mentioned," Neil began, "your client was Eli Johnson's widow. Even though they hadn't been together for many years, as his widow, she's still entitled to their matrimonial property, vacation homes, cars. I've looked in to this, and the value is in the fifteen-million range, not to mention the money left for Eli's sons. Come on, Bradley— you know as well as I do that your client does not need this condo on South Beach. If she does want to relocate, she has more than enough money to buy her own property."

"Legally, the property is half hers," Bradley pointed out.

"That remains to be seen in a court of law. If Ms. Cain knew of your client's existence, that would be one thing. But she was engaged to Eli, fully expecting to spend her life with him. They bought a condo together. This isn't as black and white as you might like to believe."

"I beg to differ," Bradley said. "Tassie is Eli's legal widow, and the law is very clear. Besides, my client is offering to buy her out for more than market value."

"That's not acceptable to my client," Neil said. "She has a young daughter, and this is their home. Why should they have to be uprooted because of Eli's lies? We respectfully ask that your client waive her rights to this property in the interest of reaching an agreement that is fair to both the injured parties."

Tassie rolled her eyes, then leaned toward her lawyer. "Tell her," she said, in what I figured she thought was a low tone. "Tell her that the courts don't look favorably on 'the other woman' and she'd be wise to resolve this before it gets worse."

"How, exactly, can it get worse for me, Tassie? You crucified me in the press." My lawyer placed his hand on my arm, I guess to stop me from speaking. "You humiliated me at Eli's funeral. And for what? Because you were angry with Eli…or because you couldn't accept the fact that he was in love with me?"

"You were a plaything," Tassie said, her eyes shooting venom at me.

"I was his *fiancée*."

"A gold digger."

I balled my hands into fists. I literally wanted to lunge across the table and pound Tassie's face to a pulp. Instead, I took a deep breath and turned to my lawyer. "End this charade," I told him. "Let her know what we found out."

Tassie's eyes widened ever so slightly, registering her surprise at my words. Then the smug look was back, as if to say, "Show me what you got."

I shot a smug look back at her, thinking to myself, *The fun is about to begin.*

"Bradley," my lawyer began, "it's time for a reality check for your client. You and I both know that her wanting my client's home isn't about what she feels she's legally entitled to. It's about her wanting to lash out at Ms. Cain. She never knew my client before Eli's death, and yet she just accused her of being a gold digger." Neil paused. "Tassie knows she's in the financial position to bully my client, but that's all going to change."

Bradley opened his mouth to speak, but Neil held up a hand to keep his comment at bay.

"Until now," Neil went on, "your client has been acting as though she has a right to Eli's half of the South Beach condo because he was having an adulterous affair. That Vanessa had deliberately destroyed her marriage."

"It's true," Tassie blurted. "I don't believe for a second that Vanessa didn't know about me."

My lawyer turned his attention to Tassie. "Before the funeral, when was the last time you saw your husband?"

Tassie's eyes widened, and when she spoke, her tone was indignant. "Excuse me?"

"When was the last time you saw your husband?"

"I—I saw him all the time," Tassie said.

"Really?" Neil sounded intrigued. "In Miami, or in Atlanta?"

"In Atlanta."

"How many days a week. Seven? Five? One?"

Tassie's eyes flitted to her attorney's. He nodded, silently telling her to answer the question. She huffed, but said, "On average two days a week. He spent a lot of time in Miami."

"So, if we were to talk to your boys," Neil continued, "they would concur that they saw their father on average two days a week?"

I couldn't help smiling. Why hadn't I thought of that? I'd learned from Eli's teammate, Leroy, that Tassie had kept her sons from Eli. If they were brought into this mess in court, they would be able to say that they hadn't seen their father in years.

"I will not let you bring my children into this," Tassie said, the venomous look on her face saying she wished she could rip my lawyer in two.

"Is that because they won't be able to verify your version of the story?"

"How dare you!" Tassie yelled.

"Tassie," her lawyer said, the tone of his voice saying she needed to keep it together.

"Mrs. Johnson, it's time to stop the charade," my lawyer said. "The only reason that you don't want your children involved is because they'll confirm that you and your husband hadn't been in touch in a long, long time. Yes, you were still legally married, but you were living separate lives."

Now Tassie's lawyer spoke up. "Still legally married. That's the key point, here."

Neil didn't respond, just opened his briefcase and withdrew a manila folder. He opened the folder and pulled out two pieces of paper, one of which he slid across the table to Bradley.

"What's that?" Tassie asked, sounding nervous.

"Mrs. Johnson, despite being married to your husband, you were involved in an ongoing affair with a Mr. Ray Carlton. Isn't that true?"

Tassie's eyes grew as wide as saucers. A couple beats passed, then she said, "No. That is absolutely not true."

"You don't know a Ray Carlton?" Neil asked.

"No. I do not know anyone named Ray Carlton."

"Hmm." Neil frowned. "How very odd."

Tassie was panicking. I could see it in her eyes, even if she were trying to maintain her cool.

Neil glanced at me, and I saw the hint of a smile on his face. Then he turned back to Tassie.

"Because I know for a fact that while you were still married—while Eli was still living with you in Atlanta—you aborted Ray Carlton's child. It's all in that report I just passed to your attorney."

15

Bradley Harris quickly read the document before him. Tassie's pale brown skin grew paler. Her expression was one of pure mortification.

Bradley turned to Tassie. "Is this true?"

"N-no!" she stammered, outraged.

"So, yes, you were officially married to Eli," my lawyer went on. "But for you to act as though my client was the demise of your marriage—"

Tassie snatched up the report and crumpled it into a ball. "This is garbage. Obviously fabricated."

Watching her sweat, I grinned.

"My client gets to keep her condo," Neil said. "She was prepared to offer your client a cash sum that represented Eli's share of the property, but let's face it. Your client is simply being vindictive in going after Ms. Cain, who is a hard-working single mother. The condo is her home, her child's home. With the mansion in Atlanta, the waterfront home in Myrtle Beach and the time-share in Aruba, what more does your client want?"

"Unacceptable," Tassie said, looking first at my lawyer, then at me. Finally, she turned to her attorney. "Tell them that the law is on my side. I was *married* to Eli."

"The law may be on your side," Neil said calmly, "but what about the court of public opinion?"

As the implication of what my lawyer said settled over Tassie, her eyes widened. "You wouldn't."

"You did," I pointed out. "Blamed the downfall of your marriage on me to anyone who would listen. When all along, you were still having sex with your high-school boyfriend."

"Shut up!" Tassie snapped. "You dumb whore."

I actually started to rise from my seat. Instinct took over, and I'm not sure what I was going to do, though I really was ready to hurl myself across the expensive tabletop and wrap my hands around Tassie's narrow throat. But my lawyer put a hand on my shoulder to keep me in my seat, and fuming, I did just that.

Then he withdrew two eight-by-ten photos from an envelope. I hadn't seen any photos before, and tried to get a good look as he passed them across the table. I could make out images of a couple embracing and kissing, but couldn't see the faces.

Had Lewis's investigator been able to get photos of Tassie and her lover? If so, why hadn't Lewis told me about that?

It was one thing to go to the media with allegations that Tassie had had an abortion. But pictures of her in another man's arms…that would be priceless.

"What is this?" Tassie asked.

I leaned in to my lawyer and whispered, "Can I see them?"

He passed me another folder, and I opened it. Then I narrowed my eyes, examining the photo. That was Tassie—no doubt about it. But was the man with her...I shook my head slowly. That wasn't the man I'd seen her with at the funeral.

Oh, my God. It was Christian Blake!

Christian Blake, former Miami Dolphins star, who was a notorious womanizer. I'd seen him a couple times. In fact, I'd first seen him at the fund-raiser the night I met Eli. I knew he had more than his fair share of women, but he'd had Tassie as well?

I threw my gaze across the table, disgust filling every part of me as I stared at Tassie. "My, my, my. You sure do get around, don't you?"

"This—" Tassie stabbed her finger against the photo "—is bullshit."

"Pictures don't lie, Tassie," Neil said. "Unlike people."

"That's not me," she insisted.

"Deny, deny, deny," I mumbled. "You accused me of being a gold digger, but that's exactly what you are, aren't you? That's why you married Eli and continued to keep Ray on the side."

"That isn't me," Tassie repeated.

"Mrs. Johnson," my lawyer began, his tone pitiful. He lifted the photo and scrutinized it. It was most certainly Tassie Johnson. "You're saying this isn't you?"

"It's not."

"I think CNN would beg to differ."

"I've never even met Christian Blake!"

"Funny, you know who he is," I said softly—but loudly enough for her to hear.

"If you continue to pursue your malicious attempts to take my client's home," Neil said, addressing Tassie directly, "then we'll be forced to go public with these photos and the fact that you aborted another man's baby while you were married."

My lawyer let that news settle over Tassie and her lawyer. Tassie was whispering furiously and gesturing angrily. I heard her saying, "I've never met the man before. This photo's been forged."

"It's okay, it's okay," Bradley soothed. Then, to us he said, "Will you excuse us for a moment?"

"Certainly," Neil responded.

Bradley pushed his chair back and stood, and Tassie clumsily did the same. Then she stalked out of the conference room, her lawyer behind her.

"My God," I said the moment they were out of the room. "Tassie was involved with Christian Blake?" I spoke to myself more than to the lawyer. "How did you get those pictures?"

"The investigator Lewis hired," Neil explained. Then he patted my hand and smiled. "We've got this. With this kind of evidence, Tassie's going to let you keep the condo."

The words were music to my ears.

A couple minutes later, Bradley entered the room, followed closely by Tassie. The moment they were seated, Neil spoke. "I've taken the liberty of drawing up an agreement," he announced. "Once you sign this, Mrs. Johnson, you'll never have to see or hear from my client again." Neil passed it to Bradley.

Bradley's eyes volleyed back and forth over the paper as he read. Tassie looked on as well, her expression none too pleased.

"What does it mean?" Tassie asked.

"This says you sign away your rights to the condo," her lawyer explained.

"What!" she shrieked. "I won't sign it. They can't make me."

"If you sign it, you get all the copies of the photos currently printed, as well as the negatives."

Tassie snorted. "Negatives? No one uses film anymore."

"This photographer does. You have our word that if you sign this agreement, Ms. Cain won't go public with the truth."

"The truth? This isn't the truth." Tassie ripped one of the eight-by-ten photos into pieces. "You are living in my husband's property. *That's the truth.* I won't sign this."

She lifted the agreement and held it as though to rip it as well, but the lawyer put his hands on both of hers, preventing her from doing just that.

"What are you doing?" Tassie demanded.

"Let's take a moment to discuss this," her lawyer suggested.

"Why—so she wins?"

There it was, right out of her own mouth. This was about Tassie winning. Playing with my life was just a game to her—a game designed to punish me because her husband had been engaged to me.

I already knew that, of course—but now her lawyer knew it, too.

"We need to discuss this," Bradley repeated.

"We'll give you a moment," Neil announced, and pushed his chair back. "Vanessa and I don't mind waiting in the hallway."

The moment I stepped into the hallway with my lawyer, I burst into a grin. Then came the laughter. I put my hand over my mouth to muffle the sound.

Lewis ambled over to us from across the room. "What's happening? Tassie looked pissed when she came out here."

Neil grinned widely, but I suspected he wanted to laugh, too. However, he wanted to appear as professional as possible. He gave Lewis the condensed version of the story, and then Lewis high-fived me.

"You must have known about her and Christian Blake," I said to him. "Why didn't you tell me?"

"I wanted it to be a nice surprise if she wasn't cooperating," Lewis said. "Didn't I tell you you have nothing to worry about?"

"You did. And Lewis, thank you so much for all your help." Then I turned to Neil. "Tassie's making a big fuss, but she'll sign the agreement. Right? I mean, she wouldn't be that crazy to say no. Not with the evidence we have of her own indiscretions."

"It's a great deal," Neil said. "It doesn't make sense for her to turn it down. She's already got two homes and a ton of cash. If she's desperate to live in Miami, she can buy her own condo here."

"*Exactly.* But I wouldn't put it past her to turn it down.

She's got money, so she figures she can slug it out." I shook my head disdainfully. "What I'd like is a bat and five minutes in a room with her. I'd have her changing her mind in no time."

"Don't worry," Neil said. "She might be stubborn, but no one wants that kind of information about them leaked to the press."

I nodded, Neil's words reassuring me. What a great lawyer this guy was. Lewis really had picked the perfect person for the job.

One more thing for which I have to be grateful to Lewis, I couldn't help thinking, and the thought made my stomach tense slightly.

The door opened suddenly, startling me. I turned to see Bradley standing there. "You can come back in," he said.

I made my way into the room, making a point of not looking at Tassie. But I could feel her gaze on me, her hate burning my skin.

"Do we have a deal?" my lawyer asked as he sat.

"No," Bradley said.

My stomach sank. Now I looked at Tassie. This time, she didn't meet my eyes.

"No?" Neil asked. "This is an incredible deal. If this goes to court, Mrs. Johnson's children will have to be involved, and the evidence of her adulterous affairs won't remain a secret. The media will have a field day."

"Let me clarify," Bradley went on. "We don't have a deal…yet. My client wants more time to think about this."

Now I understood. She would sign the deal, but only after making me sweat some more first. What she didn't understand was that she no longer intimidated me. If she wanted a fight, she'd get one—and it'd be dirty.

"You have until Friday," my lawyer said. "And that's generous. If we don't hear from you by Friday, I can't guarantee that Ms. Cain won't go public with every major media outlet in the country. I assume, Mrs. Johnson, you don't want that to happen."

Tassie's mouth was set in a firm line, but I saw her jaw flinch. She was trying to act tough in the face of a potential disaster for her. But she was worried.

Real worried.

Take that, bitch.

"You'll have my client's decision by Friday," Bradley said.

Tassie pushed her chair back, jumped to her feet and fled the room.

"I look forward to hearing from you," Neil said, as though nothing unusual had just happened.

We stayed seated while Bradley gathered his things and left the room. When I was finally alone with Neil, I placed my hand on his arm and gently squeezed. "Thank you," I said. "You were incredible."

"She'll sign the deal. It's obvious her lawyer wants her to, and after a night's reflection, Tassie will realize what's best for her."

I believed it. I no longer had any doubts.

Finally, I was getting rid of the one major headache in my life.

Thank the Lord.

16

I was on an emotional high all evening. I'd called both Carla and Alaina and given them the update, and would have shared the story with Debbie if she'd been in the office when I'd returned.

I thought that absolutely nothing would kill my mood. Until my sister called.

I was in the kitchen, cooking dinner for me and Rayna when the telephone rang. Leaving the pot of alfredo sauce on the stove, I went to the wall phone and picked up the receiver.

"Hello?" I said.

"Forget what I said about Chaz the other day," my sister began without preamble. "Turns out he's as big a player as they come."

"Excuse me?"

"He sends you all those beautiful roses, and it turns out he *is* dating Maria Lopez."

My stomach sank. "Wh-what?"

"You haven't seen *Entertainment Now* yet?"

"N–no. I'm not watching television. I'm over the stove, actually." Chaz was seeing someone else?

"I'd tell you to turn the television on, but the story about him and Maria Lopez is already over. It's big news. It was the lead story."

"Are you sure?" I asked.

"Yep. They're definitely an item. He might be a dog, but I guess no one can accuse him of having bad taste. Maria is gorgeous."

Yes, Maria Lopez was extremely gorgeous. There was no denying that. My throat was suddenly clogged. I found it hard to breathe.

"I hear Maria used to work as a singing stripper—until some music producer discovered her in Cancún."

"Hmm." I started to feel light-headed.

"She's beautiful, but she certainly has no class. But guys always fall for those gorgeous, curvy types. Especially the ones who flaunt their sex appeal."

I didn't say anything. I could hardly swallow, much less speak.

"It's better you found out now that Chaz was a dog," my sister said. "The last thing you need is more heartache."

I wanted to tell Nikki to shut up, but I couldn't form any words.

"Seriously, Vanessa. You need to let me fix you up with someone. I can find you a very nice man. Maybe he won't have six-pack abs, but he'll be loyal."

I said nothing.

"Vanessa, are you listening to me?"

"Yeah. Yeah, I'm hearing you."

"Ohh." My sister suddenly sounded surprised. "You're upset."

I said nothing.

"I just figured…you two are no longer a couple…."

"Exactly," I said. "It's over." And if Chaz was now dating some Latina singer, I couldn't deny the truth anymore. He'd moved on.

It was time I move on as well.

A hissing sound drew my attention to the stove. "Oh, crap!" I grabbed my oven mitt from the counter and wrapped it around the pot's handle. "Nikki, I just burned my dinner. I've got to go."

The alfredo sauce had bubbled over the side of the pot, spilling onto the stove. I quickly moved the pot from the stove to the sink, placing it inside. Then I dropped the receiver onto the counter, grumbling as I did. I turned on the cold water faucet, letting it fill the pot, which caused a plume of smoke to rise out of my sink.

"Damn it!" I yelled.

"Mommy, what's wrong?"

I spun around to see Rayna standing at the entrance to the kitchen, concern etched on her little face.

"Nothing, sweetheart. Nothing's wrong. I just ruined something on the stove, but it's okay."

"I hungry."

"I know. I know, me, too." And I was no longer in the mood to eat fettucine alfredo. I wanted a juicy burger loaded with calories. And maybe a hot chocolate brownie smothered with ice cream.

Or two.

Only on a rare occasion when I was stressed did I feel the urge to overload on junk food.

But if finding out that the man you loved was no longer into you wasn't reason for a junk-food bender, then what was?

I ate a huge burger smothered with Swiss cheese and mushrooms, an order of onion rings, and I even splurged on two chocolate desserts. A brownie with ice cream and chocolate bits, smothered with chocolate and caramel sauce, and a piece of caramel cheesecake, though I only got through half of it before I had to give up the junk-food fight. I couldn't eat another bite.

The next morning, I paid the price for my junk-food blitz. I had a huge zit in the middle of my forehead, the kind that not even makeup helped to hide.

"What happened to your face?" Carla asked when I dropped off Rayna.

"A pimple," I said, touching it self-consciously.

"You never get pimples," she said.

"I guess I can't be lucky all the time," I pointed out.

At the office, I tried the best I could to surreptitiously cover the ugly zit as I entered the building and when I walked past Nora to my office. I opened my compact the moment I was behind my desk, checking to see if it had gone down any.

It had gotten worse. Honestly, I don't think I'd ever seen a pimple so massive.

I applied a dollop of foundation to the spot, trying unsuccessfully to cover it. At least it didn't look quite as grotesque.

There was a quick rap on my door, then it opened and Debbie stepped into my office. The smile on her face disappeared, her eyes widening as she checked out my face. "Is that a zit on your forehead?"

Consciously, I touched a hand to my forehead. "Yeah," I answered.

"Wow. I've never seen you with a pimple before."

I tried to laugh off my misfortune. I'd learned my lesson the hard way and would not overdose on junk food again. "Was there something you needed?"

"Yes," Debbie said, taking a seat behind my desk. "I wanted to apologize for last week. For snapping at you about my relationship with Jason. I know you had only my best interests in mind."

"That's true," I pointed out. "I don't want to see you lose your marriage."

"I know. I guess I'm just conflicted over the whole issue. On one hand, it's like I'm addicted to Jason. I know he's not good for me, and I don't want anything long-term with him, but in the meantime, he's so darn exciting. He gives me something Ben doesn't...and I'm weak."

I nodded, not wanting to give the same advice I'd given Debbie before. She knew where I stood.

"I'm going to end it," she told me. "Soon."

"Should I ask you how the trip to Phoenix went?"

"The seminars were fabulous. Lori drew a huge crowd." Debbie paused, saw my raised eyebrows. "And the sex with Jason was great. But I do think he's become too clingy, or too needy. I haven't talked to him since we got back."

"It's not me this matters to," I offered. "It's your marriage."

"I know." Debbie stood. "I guess I just wanted you to know that I thought a lot about what you said, and I'm moving in the direction I need to be going." She paused. "But in the meantime, I hope this doesn't affect our friendship."

I got up, rounded my desk and hugged Debbie. "We're always going to be friends, okay? Even if I'm mad at you from time to time."

Debbie was the first to break the hug. "Everything okay with you?" she asked. "Other than the zit?"

I filled her in on the meeting with Tassie and her lawyer.

"Then you should be smiling from ear to ear," she pointed out. "Why aren't you?"

My stomach twisted as I remembered my sister's words from last night. "It turns out Chaz is dating someone. That Latina singer, Maria Lopez."

"Maria Lopez!" Debbie exclaimed. "I heard she used to be a stripper."

"So my sister says."

"I can't imagine Chaz liking her type if he was interested in you."

I shrugged nonchalantly, though I felt anything but nonchalant over the matter. "I guess some men like variety."

"I know you were really into him, but if he's not the one for you…" Debbie gave me a faint smile. "You're a fabulous woman, gorgeous, with a lot to offer. You'll find the man worthy of you."

So my friends kept telling me.

The rest of the week passed slowly, with me being anxious as hell over what Tassie would decide. With each day that passed, I was more and more worried that she would say no to the offer my lawyer had proposed.

On Friday at 3:00 p.m., my phone rang.

"Vanessa Cain."

"Vanessa, it's Neil."

"Hello, Neil," I said, my heart speeding up. "What's happening?"

"I heard from Tassie's lawyer."

My heart filled with hope. "She signed the agreement?"

A beat. Then he said, "No."

The hope in my heart began to slowly seep out, but I refused to think the worst. "You mean, not yet."

"She's requesting another five days to think about it," Neil informed me. "Personally, I think she's just stalling—"

"And testing to see whether I go public with the pictures of her and Christian Blake. Damn."

"It's your call," Neil said.

I was silent as I considered my next move. If I leaked the story to the media, Tassie would most likely *not* sign the agreement. Oh, in the end she might give up the fight, but it'd be a long, dirty fight. One she could afford and I couldn't.

The media would scrutinize her, certainly—but what if they scrutinized me as well? Started following me around again, and worst—my little girl?

I wanted Tassie to sign the damn agreement already and let us both get on with our lives. Why did she have to be so evil?

"Vanessa?"

"Fine. Let's give her five more days. She damn well knows

I won't leak the story, because then she'll get even nastier than she's been."

"And in five days, if she doesn't sign the agreement then?"

I didn't respond. I didn't know the best answer.

"Word of advice, Vanessa?"

"Sure."

"We set out the terms for Tassie. Very specific terms. If she realizes that we won't call her bluff, then this game will go on endlessly. My opinion is that you stick to the terms we set out for her. Which means that if, by next Wednesday, she hasn't signed the agreement, we play dirty. I guarantee you, once she sees those pictures of her and Christian Blake on CNN, she'll be signing whatever we want her to. Sometimes, playing dirty is the only way to fight some people."

"Okay," I agreed. But I wasn't so sure.

17

Tassie's stalling over signing the agreement put me in a bad mood all weekend. I'd called Lewis with the news after speaking with Neil. Then I'd called Alaina to bitch about the turn of events, and then I'd called Carla.

On Sunday, I was still bitching.

"I just don't understand her," I was saying to Carla as I sat beside her on her living room sofa. "She knows she was involved with another man. She knows she had an abortion. And she damn well knows that I did not have any clue Eli was married to her at the time I was engaged to him."

"Uh-huh," Carla said.

I got the feeling that she was bored with my complaining, but I couldn't stop myself. Bitching about my situation was the only thing within my control.

"So what do you think I should do?" I asked. "Go to the media on Wednesday if she asks for more time?"

"I already told you," Carla said. "Go to the media. At this point, you have nothing to lose."

"But what if they make my life hell again? And poor Rayna? She doesn't deserve that."

Carla sighed softly. "You have to decide what's most important to you."

"I know." I reached for the glass of wine I was drinking, which sat on the coffee table. As I did, my eyes ventured to the television. It was tuned to CNN, but the volume was down.

My eyes widened as I thought I caught a brief glimpse of Tassie's picture on the corner of the screen. Now the screen showed a person on a gurney being taken to a waiting ambulance. The caption on the bottom of the television said Breaking News.

"Oh, my God," I said to Carla. "I think I just saw Tassie's picture on the television. Where's the remote?"

"Here," Carla responded, lifting the remote from beside her on the sofa. She turned up the volume as the screen filled with an image of a swollen and bruised face, eyes closed.

My God. It *was* Tassie.

"…the vicious attack," the brunette newscaster was saying, "but we do know that the injuries Tassie Johnson sustained were serious. Possibly life-threatening. Tassie Johnson is the widow of the late Atlanta Braves player, Eli Johnson, who was murdered earlier this year in Miami, after his lover's husband found them in bed together."

I held my breath. Waited for my name and some of the unflattering images of me to fill the screen, but neither of those things happened.

"We'll continue to monitor this story and bring you updates as they come in."

The newscaster went on to talk about another story, and only then did I turn to Carla. "Oh. My. God. Someone assaulted Tassie!"

"That wasn't just an assault. Someone seriously beat her ass. Probably another one of Eli's girlfriends she was harassing."

"I can't believe it. Yeah, people get assaulted every day, but it's still a shock."

"Why? People with personalities like hers piss off the wrong person eventually."

"I guess," I said softly.

Carla's eyes narrowed. "Don't tell me you feel sorry for her."

Did I? "I…I don't know." I shrugged. "Maybe," I said, surprised at myself. I'd actually daydreamed about having five minutes alone in a room readjusting her attitude with one of Eli's bats. But seeing her on that gurney, her face swollen and bruised… It reminded me of how Alaina had looked after her ex-husband had beaten her badly enough to land her in hospital.

"I don't believe you," Carla said. "That woman has been nothing but an awful bitch to you, and you feel sorry for her?"

"I don't like her," I said. "Never will. But no one deserves that kind of beating."

Carla tsked. "Turning soft in your old age, are you?"

"No. But seeing Tassie like that reminds me of Alaina in the hospital. Tassie might be a bitch, but I can't be happy about seeing her in pain like that."

Carla looked stunned. Trust me, I was stunned to hear the words coming from my mouth as well. I'd never expected to feel that kind of empathy for Tassie.

I'd also never expected to see her beaten to a pulp.

"The newscaster said she might die," I said softly.

"At least then your problem will go away."

"Carla!" I was glad our children were playing in Amani's bedroom, so they wouldn't have to hear this conversation.

"Okay, I didn't mean that. But you know, perhaps a near-death experience will soften her attitude. Remind her of what's important in life." Carla paused. "You still want her to sign the agreement, don't you?"

"Of course I do."

"Then let's hope she does, and she's out of your life forever."

The very next day, I heard from my lawyer at the office.

"Tassie signed the agreement," he began without preamble.

"What?" I asked, shocked. "But she's in hospital. I saw that on the news."

"Yes, but she had her sister call her lawyer. Insisted he head to the hospital with the papers. He brought in a notary public to witness her signing of the agreement. The condo's yours. And you don't have to pay her a red cent."

I swallowed, not sure what I was hearing was real.

"You should be happy," Neil said. "It's over."

"I am happy," I said, but I spoke in a monotone voice, my relief not at all evident in my tone.

"It's what you wanted."

"It's what's right."

Just last night, Carla had wondered if Tassie being viciously beaten would bring about a change of heart in her the way people who'd come close to death often did a one-eighty in terms of their attitude and behavior. A near-death experience often brought home to people what was important in life.

It turned out Carla was right.

Tassie clearly had realized that in the grand scheme of things, her battle with me was petty and unimportant. It was consuming negative energy on her part and mine.

"So if Tassie signed the agreement, does that mean she's going to be okay?" I asked.

"I admire your concern for a woman who has done nothing but give you grief. And yes, she's apparently going to be okay. I asked Bradley that question when he called me this morning."

"That's good to know."

"Bradley is couriering the agreement today. We'll have it by tomorrow."

"So it's really over?" I asked.

"It's really over."

Finally, I felt relief. It flowed through my veins like a burst of energy. "My baby and I get to keep our home. Thank God."

A few beats passed. Then my lawyer said, "I want you to know that what you said that day when we met with Tassie and her lawyer—you're protected by attorney-client privilege."

For a moment, I said nothing. I didn't understand what the lawyer was getting at. "I'm not sure what you mean."

"When we were in the hallway," he prompted, his tone lower, as though he thought someone might be listening to him.

"I still don't understand."

"What you said about having five minutes alone in a room with her?"

"Oh," I said. Then understanding hit me like a bat to the stomach. "Wait a second—you think I beat up Tassie?"

"If you did, I'd understand your frustration."

"No!" I exclaimed. "I'd never do that to her. To anyone." Short of someone attacking my daughter—or me—I wouldn't beat anyone to a pulp.

"Sorry," the lawyer said. "I've seen worse in my business. I couldn't help wondering."

"I had nothing to do with what happened to her," I stressed, in case he was harboring any doubt.

"Forget I even mentioned it," Neil said.

But how could I forget it? Because if Neil was wondering if I had anything to do with what had happened to Tassie, wouldn't she be wondering the same thing?

18

The next day, I was sitting behind my desk when a familiar face poked through my door.

Alaina.

She grinned from ear to ear. "I'm *baaack!*"

I sprung from my chair and ran toward her. I hugged her hard—then loosened my grip, remembering she might still be feeling some pain.

"Alaina, I didn't know you were coming back to work!"

"I wanted to surprise you," she said.

"Oh, my God, this is the best surprise." And the serious boost I needed after speaking to Neil the day before. His suspicion of me and my possible involvement in the attack on Tassie had me worried.

Had Tassie signed the agreement because she'd had a life-altering change of heart…or because she thought I'd had her assaulted to force her hand?

I wondered if she really believed the latter, and if she did…

I concentrated on checking out Alaina. She'd lost a good ten pounds since Jorge's assault, mostly because she hadn't felt like eating solids. She also still wore her cast, but other than that, she looked absolutely radiant, and I couldn't have been more pleased.

"How are you feeling?" I asked.

"My ribs are still a little sore, and I've still got this cast on, but I'm okay. I was going crazy staying at home. My doctor said as long as I'm not doing anything strenuous, that I could come back to work."

"I'm so excited." I gave Alaina another hug, this time more gentle. "I wondered why I didn't see Nora when I arrived. Girl, that woman was so dull, it was painful." I grinned. "But now I've got my Ally back!"

Alaina returned my grin. Then she looked over her shoulder toward the door. "Well, I'm gonna head back to the reception desk. I don't want Debbie firing me on my first day back."

I was still grinning when Alaina left the office and I settled behind my desk. Her being back at work meant she had pretty much recovered.

I took that good news as a sign that everything was finally going to go well in my world as well.

Shortly before eleven, Alaina popped her head into my office again. I erupted in a smile, feeling like things had definitely returned to normal. I'd missed so much Alaina coming into my office at different times during the day to talk about office gossip. I couldn't wait to hear what she had to say this time.

"What piece of juicy gossip do you have for me today?"
I asked her.

Alaina didn't return my smile. In fact, she looked grim.

"Alaina—"

"Vanessa, there's a detective here to see you."

My heart thundered in my chest. "A detective?"

A man now stepped into the doorway. "Detective
Coleman, ma'am. With Miami-Dade Police Department."

My eyes flitted between Alaina's and the detective's.
Alaina shrugged as if to say she didn't know what was going
on, and then she silently slipped away.

I remained seated as the detective stepped fully into my
office and closed the door. Suddenly, I felt guilty. But guilty
of what?

The detective was about six feet tall and quite attractive.
I figured his heritage to be African-American and Cuban,
if his warm dark skin and black wavy hair were any indication.

"How can I help you?"

"I'm here to ask you a few questions."

"Oh?"

"I understand that you were affiliated with Tassie
Johnson."

My mouth fell open. My fear was coming to fruition.
The police actually thought I was behind what had
happened to Tassie!

"I know her, yes. But I didn't hurt her."

He looked at me oddly then. I couldn't help it—I started
to sweat. What was it about cops staring at you that made
a person start to feel guilty even when they weren't?

"I'm sure that's why you're here," I went on. "I saw what happened on the news, and anyone who's paid attention to the news in the past few months knows that Tassie and I weren't exactly on good terms. I was engaged to her husband—but I didn't know he was married. I swear. We don't get along, but it's not like I wanted her dead or anything."

What the heck was I doing? Rambling like a bloody moron. Giving the detective several reasons to think I'd have cause to hurt Tassie.

Good going, Vanessa.

"Where were you last Saturday night?" he asked me. "June twenty-seventh?"

The night Tassie had been assaulted. "I was home with my daughter. I didn't even go out that day, it was so hot and humid."

"Anyone who can corroborate that?"

My unease was slowly being replaced by annoyance. "You can ask my daughter. But she's two and a half. She won't be the best witness."

"Anyone else?" the detective asked.

"A couple friends I spoke to." Oh, shit. I couldn't give this man Carla or Alaina's names. He'd ask them what I talked about, and they'd say I had bitched nonstop about Tassie Johnson.

This was bad.

"Your friends' names?"

"Sarah and Rachel," I lied, aware that that wasn't the right course of action. But I didn't want to tell him the truth in case he came to the wrong conclusion:

"Do Sarah and Rachel have last names?" he asked.

"Of course they do."

"I'd like to contact them."

"Why is that important?" I asked. "Do you think I'm lying?"

"Calm down, Miss Cain. I wouldn't be doing my job if I didn't question you."

"You'd be wise to question everyone who ever came into contact with Tassie," I said sourly. "She leaves a great impression."

"You really don't like her," the detective pointed out.

"Maybe not. But I didn't assault her."

"Tassie says that the day after the assault, she signed over a condo that belonged to her husband to you."

I rolled my eyes. "Tassie is a liar. Actually, I suspect the woman's crazy. She's living in her own fantasy world and couldn't figure out reality if it hit her in the face."

"Is that what you did—hit her with a little 'reality'?"

"That's not what I meant. I already told you, I was home with my daughter. Yes, she signed an agreement that said she'd stop harassing me for *my* condo. I bought it with her estranged husband. And again, I had no clue he was married. He lied to us both."

I couldn't tell if Coleman believed me. In fact, I was certain he didn't, as he continued to eye me with suspicion.

"You can call my lawyer, Neil Gorman, who will tell you about the terms of the agreement and why she signed it. But the gist of it is that she didn't want the media to learn about her affairs." I took a few minutes to explain the story to Coleman. He only nodded and jotted down notes, but gave no indication that he believed me or didn't believe me.

"Like I said, call my lawyer. He'll be happy to explain the circumstances."

"I'll call," Coleman said. "But it's only fair to tell you that I'm here because Tassie has said that you need to be investigated. She said that whoever beat her up whispered in her ear, 'sign the deal.'"

"What?" I gasped.

"That's what she said. She said she signed the agreement under duress. Her lawyer indicated she might want to contest it in court."

I slammed my hands on my desk. "That fucking *bitch*."

"Calm down, Miss Cain."

"Don't tell me to calm down. You want to charge someone with assault, charge her. That woman is trying to make me die of heart failure!"

"Did you hire someone to assault her?"

I glared at him, wondering how I'd ever, even for a moment, thought of him as cute.

"Miss Cain?"

"I'm a single mother on a fixed income," I answered angrily. "I don't have the cash to hire hitmen." *Even if I'd like to,* I added silently, knowing Coleman wouldn't understand my pissed-off humor if I'd dared to express my thought aloud.

Coleman jotted down more notes.

"You know what I think? I told you Tassie's crazy. I think she's crazy enough to have had someone beat the crap out of her, or at least beat her so it looked good, all so she could get out of the agreement she signed. Then, with the whole world seeing her as a victim once again, she'd take her chances with my leaking the story of her affairs, hoping the media would choose to show the world images of her in a hospital bed, rather than photos of her in another man's arms."

Coleman said nothing. My words might not have registered with him, but they suddenly struck a very loud chord with me. I'd rambled out a crazy theory, but suddenly I was wondering just how crazy it was.

Not so crazy at all, actually.

I chuckled mirthlessly. "Oh, she's good."

"Excuse me?"

"I didn't hurt her. Trust me, I'm not about to risk my freedom for the likes of her." Even if I did have to move out of my condo, my freedom still wouldn't be worth the satisfaction of smashing her face in. "I have a daughter. I'm her only caregiver. I'm not about to do anything to get arrested."

"The surnames of your friends, Ms. Cain," Coleman said. He referred to his notes. "Sarah and Rachel."

My face flamed. "Um, well. I kind of lied about that part."

"You lied?"

"Yes," I admitted. "But that doesn't make me a criminal. If you want to know who I was speaking to on the weekend, Alaina Rivera, the woman who brought you to my office, is one of them. Also my babysitter, Carla. I can give you her number if you like."

"Please," Detective Coleman said.

I rattled off Carla's number. Then I said, "And so you know, yeah, I complained to them about Tassie this weekend. But I did not have anything to do with what happened to Tassie. That's the truth."

Detective Coleman nodded and closed his notebook. "That's all for now, Miss Cain."

"Do you even believe me?" I asked.

"The investigation is ongoing, but my gut says you didn't have anything to do with what happened to Tassie. You certainly don't like the woman—but that's not a crime."

The corners of his lips curled in a slight smile, reminding me of the reason I'd thought him cute. I almost wanted to say, "You're a lot more attractive when you're not being a jerk."

But common sense made me refrain.

"If there's anything else," he said, "I'll be in touch."

"Of course." I forced a smile on my face as I got to my feet. I walked the detective to the door. "You have a good day now."

"Thank you," he said.

The moment he stepped into the hallway, I closed the door behind him.

Ten minutes later, there was a knock at my door. I cringed, thinking it was Detective Coleman returning after his talk with Alaina. But when it opened, I saw Alaina's face.

"Girl," she said. "What is going on?"

"Come in," I told her. "And close the door behind you."

19

The week had started off badly, and it only got worse. On Thursday, FedEx delivered me a package from Byron McLean.

I opened the package. Found an envelope inside. I tore open the envelope and pulled out a letter. It bore nice letterhead, with Byron's name and address in a cursive font. It looked like it had been printed on a laser printer.

Kinkos, perhaps?

I began reading the letter.

July 1

   To Vanessa Cain,

   This letter will inform you of my sincere intent to become the father that my daughter desperately needs. Make no mistake—just because I have not always been there for Rayna doesn't mean I don't love her. I sincerely regret the time I have missed spending with her over the last three years.

"Three years?" I said aloud, huffing. "Three years? She's two and a half, jerk."

I continued to read.

I am getting my life on track, which means becoming more financially stable and I am able to offer my daughter the kind of stability she needs.

I am very disappointed that you would not agree to meet with me and my mother so she could spend some time with her granddaughter. However, I am willing to put that behind me. It's time that we meet, sit down and discuss our daughter's future. She deserves no less than two parents in her life who love her. Let's do what's best for our child.

Sincerely,

Byron McLean

"What the heck?" I asked aloud. My office offered me no answers.

I reread the letter, feeling as if I were in the twilight zone. Was this for real?

First of all, the wording of the letter didn't sound like Byron. At all. And what the hell was the purpose of a letter anyway? Anytime he'd tried to talk to me about Rayna— which hadn't been very many times—he'd shown up or called and had been demanding rather than polite.

Now he was sending some sort of formal-sounding letter? I didn't get it.

I read the letter yet another time, hoping to make sense

of it this time around. But as I reread it, I only became furious.

Was this some sort of threat? Some sort of written demand that I share custody of Rayna?

It had been sent via courier, my signature required. What the hell was Byron up to?

I needed to talk about this. Needed to vent was more like it. I picked up the receiver and dialed reception.

"Believe The Dream, Change Your Life," Alaina said in her cheery, reception voice.

"Ally, you got a minute?"

"To chat or to see you?"

"You know what? I'll come right out." Debbie didn't like the reception desk to be unmanned. I wanted to talk to Alaina, but I wanted her to read the letter first.

I went out to the reception desk as though I was on official business and passed Alaina the letter, including the envelope. "Read that," I said. "Then call me."

I was back in my office no more than two minutes before the telephone rang. I picked it up, knowing it was Alaina, but in case it wasn't, I gave my standard greeting.

"Vanessa Cain."

"What is this shit?" came Alaina's question.

"I was hoping you could tell me."

"'We need to arrange a meeting,'" Alaina read in a mock-deep voice. "'We need to do what's best for our daughter?'"

"I especially love the part where he talks about 'for the last three years.' For God's sake, he doesn't even know how old his daughter is."

"I'd tell Byron to stick it where the sun don't shine."

"Why do you think he wrote me a letter? That's so not his style."

"Maybe he was drunk at a bar somewhere," Alaina suggested.

"Or a casino." I snorted.

"Exactly."

"It doesn't even sound like him," I said. I worried my bottom lip for a moment, finally understanding what bothered me so much about the letter. "You think he had someone help him write the letter? Like a lawyer or something?"

Alaina emitted a low gasp. "You think so?"

"I don't know. But he's been bugging me about becoming a part of Rayna's life. Out of the friggin' blue." My heart was beating faster, and I was definitely feeling sick. "But a letter? Byron has never written me a letter before."

"I didn't even know he was literate," Alaina scoffed.

"What do I do?" I asked. "Do I bother to respond, or just file that under *T* for trash?"

"Well," Alaina said, "I'd be tempted to burn it. But, maybe you ought to hold on to it. Just to keep a paper trail if Byron tries anything stupid."

My heart spasmed. "Stupid like what?"

"I don't know. Stupid like try and get custody of Rayna."

My stomach wretched suddenly and painfully. "My God, Ally. Is that what you think this is all about?"

"I don't know. I just wouldn't trust him."

I stewed on Alaina's comment long after I hung up with her. Was it possible that Byron actually wanted joint custody of his daughter? After all this time of being a nonexistent dad?

It was all I could think about as I headed home. So much so that the moment Carla opened her door, I held the letter out to her face and began without preamble, "What do you make of this?"

Carla took the letter from my hand. "What is it?"

"Read it," I told her as I walked into her apartment.

"Mommy!" Rayna jumped up from the living room floor, raced to me and vaulted into my arms. I caught her, giggling as she wrapped her good arm around my neck and squeezed.

For a kid who wasn't yet three—unlike Byron thought— she had an amazingly strong grip. "How's my baby?" I asked her.

"I missed you."

"Oh, sweetie. Mommy missed you, too."

"Come, Mommy." She wormed her way out of my arms, immediately took me by the hand and led me into the living room. On the coffee table were various shapes made with Play-Doh. The stuff was everywhere, and Carla had had the foresight to lay a vinyl tablecloth over the table first.

"Lots of ponies!" Rayna exclaimed, gesturing with both hands. She had adjusted to the cast without much effort, it seemed, not at all letting it hold her back.

"I see that." What I really saw were globs of various colors, none of which looked particularly like a pony.

"These are the ponies from Ponyville," Amani explained.

"Very nice," I told her. And rubbed an affectionate hand over her head.

"What the—" Carla stopped short, and I suspect she'd been about to utter something profane. "Did Byron bring this to your office?"

"No. He sent it via *courier*. I even had to sign for it."

"Help us," Rayna said, offering me a ball of purple Play-Doh.

"What do you make of it?" I asked as I took the ball Rayna offered me. I eased down onto my butt on the floor. Absently, I squeezed the ball, my eyes on Carla for her reaction.

"It sounds like he wants to be part of Rayna's life."

I squished the piece of Play-Doh until it oozed through my fingers. "Please don't tell me you really believe that."

"What else could the letter be about?"

Carla was right, of course. I had hoped, however, that she'd give me a different spin on the letter. Like the opinion that Bryon was simply trying to be an asshole.

"He doesn't even know how old Rayna is," I pointed out. "The last *three* years?"

Carla was silent as her eyes scanned the letter once more. "I don't mean to make you any more upset," she said after a moment. "But I don't like that he put this down on paper. If he thought he wasn't getting through to you in person, he could have just called. Left a voice mail. But to send a letter via a courier…"

"What? What does it mean?"

"Maybe that he's trying to set up some sort of paper trail."

I drew in a sharp breath. "Like for court or something?"

"Mommy." Rayna tugged on my hand. "Make a pony."

I remolded the blob of Play-Doh in my hands, rolling it into a ball. "I'm making a beautiful pony," I told Rayna. As I squished and shaped the ball into something resembling a horse, I met Carla's gaze once more. "Is that what you think this about? Court?"

"I'd be concerned about that, yeah."

"Damn it," I muttered, and slammed the blob of Play-Doh onto the coffee table. Rayna immediately looked at me with alarm. Remembering what I was supposed to be doing, I quickly picked up the Play-Doh and began reshaping it. I made a rectangular-shaped body, then took some green pieces from the table to use to make legs.

It was by no means a masterpiece, but Rayna grinned from ear to ear nonetheless.

"What if he really has changed?" Carla said softly. "Maybe you could introduce him to Rayna slowly, in your own way, on your own terms."

I gaped at my friend. I couldn't believe the words coming from her mouth.

Then again, I hadn't known her when I'd been with Byron, when he used to lie and steal from me and gamble our cash away. When he'd bring his shady friends to our apartment.

"Carla, I'm not sure I ever told you the whole story about Byron. More than his being a deadbeat dad who abandoned me when I got pregnant." I hadn't seen the point in telling her every dirty detail, because the truth was, I was embarrassed for staying with Byron for so long, even after he'd stolen from me. I had wanted to believe he could overcome his gambling habit, but it was clear he couldn't. Carla was happily married, and maybe she wouldn't understand staying with a guy who'd lied, stolen and gambled. But now, she needed to know.

"Go on," Carla said.

So I told her about Byron's compulsive gambling, how he'd gambled away not only his money, but also the money in the joint account we'd opened. Thank God I still had my own account he hadn't been able to touch. But when he hadn't been able to get his hands on more cash, he'd stolen jewelry—jewelry that had sentimental value and could never be replaced. I told her how he'd lied about everything, about how involved he was with a bookie, how one of his gambling buddies assaulted a stranger and ended up going to jail.

"And the worst thing, Carla—although the timing was probably a clue from the universe because it was at a time when I kept hoping that Byron would turn his life around for Rayna's sake—was this awful story I saw on the news. Rayna had just turned three months old. It was about a man in New Jersey who was like Byron, a compulsive gambler, up to his eyeballs in debt to bookies and even a loan shark. He'd stolen from the family funds, owed a hell of a lot of money with no way to pay it back. You know what this loser did? Gave his daughter to his loan shark as collateral when the man was demanding the money be paid. I don't know how this guy expected to come up with over a hundred grand. He didn't, and the daughter's body was found at the side of a road a week later. She'd been murdered." I drew a shaky breath.

"I watched the news footage of the mother, absolutely devastated, and I cried and cried. And I had the most horrible thought. If something so awful could happen to that mother, couldn't it happen to me? When your husband or boyfriend is in so deep, maybe they'll do things out of desperation even they didn't think they'd be capable of. And I resolved, right then and there, as I was holding my baby in my arms and crying my eyes out at the loss of this young girl, that I would never let Byron get close to Rayna. He'd already walked away, and I realized it was a blessing. I didn't want Rayna involved in Byron's world in the least."

"Oh, sweetie." Carla put her arm around me. "I get it. I understand."

"When I met Lewis, a man who was confident, successful, and didn't gamble, I felt relieved. I realized that dating a man who was more financially secure would spare me from any of the ugliness I'd dealt with with Byron. He wasn't someone who had to gamble in hopes of earning easy cash." I was surprised at my last statement to Carla, because I'd never connected the dots before. But now it made so much sense.

"I understand," Carla repeated.

As if Rayna sensed the seriousness of our conversation, she came over to me, rested her face on my knees and looked at me. After a moment, she smiled.

I got misty-eyed as I stared at my daughter then. She really was the most adorable little girl in the world.

A girl who deserved a father, but had been abandoned by hers.

She deserved better than Byron.

I had vowed to protect her heart, to spare her pain as much as I possibly could.

Unfortunately, that meant sparing her from Byron. Because as far as I was concerned, he had hurt her most of all, before she'd even been born.

20

"All right," Alaina said the next day over lunch. We were at a restaurant in Bayside, close to the office, but where we'd have some privacy. "This is what you're going to give to Byron."

"What?" I watched as Alaina reached into her purse.

She withdrew a folded piece of paper, opened it and passed it to me. "I worked on that this morning."

"A letter?" I asked, seeing the multiple lines of text.

"Byron wrote you a letter. Now you're going to write him one. Feel free to change the words if you like, but that's what I thought of."

Holding up the letter, I started to read out loud. "'Dear Byron. I read the letter you gave me and was completely surprised. Never in your life have you shown any interest in our daughter. You don't even know how old she is. She is two and a half, not three—something you would know if you were even remotely involved in her life. I still remember the day you demanded I get an abortion. When

I refused, you said you didn't believe Rayna was your child. I was absolutely crushed, but I was not afraid to raise a child on my own and I decided I'd be a wonderful mother even without you around. In fact, I was better off without you because of your gambling problems. I'm not sure what you really want now. To ease your conscience? To please your mother? Rest assured, Rayna is very well cared for. She doesn't know you, and she doesn't need you. Please stop harassing me, or I'll call the police.'"

As I finished, Alaina was looking expectantly at me. "So? You like?"

"It's a good letter," I told her. "I might change a bit of it."

"If you don't like the part about calling the cops, you can take that out."

I nodded. "But why do you think I need to write him a letter? I've watched shows where cops talk about not engaging crazy people in conversations or any crazy interaction. And I think Byron's acting crazy."

"You're going to write a letter to show that you're not intimidated by him. To mess with his mind a bit because he's trying to mess with yours."

"Carla thinks the letter is about Byron trying to go to court or something," I told Alaina. "That he wants to set up some sort of paper trail to make it look like he's been trying to contact me regarding our daughter."

"Well, you're going to set up a paper trail right back!" Alaina said.

"Maybe I should," I agreed. "And I can mention dates— the few times he ever saw Rayna, how he behaved recently when trying to get me to meet him." I paused, munching on a nacho. "Ally, if this is about going to court…I don't know if I can deal with that. Damn it, haven't I dealt with enough drama to last a lifetime?"

"I hear you," Alaina said. "But you know what, I've discovered that you never know what someone is capable of—especially not someone who used to love you."

"Ain't that the truth." Jorge had supposedly loved Alaina but then nearly killed her with his vicious attack. Byron had loved me, but rejected his own child right from the moment I announced I was pregnant.

Was there even one decent man in the world who wouldn't betray you or hurt you?

Well, there was Chaz.

But of course, he didn't want me.

Since the day I'd plowed into the bushes with my car, I hadn't noticed the black sedan following me again.

But I noticed it today when I was heading north on I-95. Noticed it, and immediately felt fear.

"Don't freak out," I told myself. "It can't be the same car." How many black sedans were there in the world? And in South Florida?

Far too many to count.

When the car fell several car lengths behind, I dismissed the idea that the same person was in the car now as the one who'd followed me before. I merged into the right lane, getting ready for my exit onto the MacArthur Causeway that would take me to South Beach.

The black sedan quickly got into the right lane as well.

And that's when I got worried. Yes, hundreds of people traveled to South Beach each day, but was it coincidence that another black sedan appeared to be tailing me?

I didn't think so.

I stayed to the right, continually checking my rearview mirror. The sedan stayed in the right lane, a few cars behind me.

I kept up my pace, merging left, then right, and watching what the sedan did. It didn't move around, and I started to relax. I turned right the moment I exited the causeway, hoping the sedan would continue to go straight.

When it didn't, that's when my heart began to beat out of control.

"Shit," I muttered, convinced now that whoever was in the black car *was* following me. The question was why.

Did someone want me dead? Just to scare me? Was it Byron? Or was it Tassie? Or was it someone else altogether?

I didn't know what to do. There was a steady stream of traffic, and it wasn't like I could lose this guy. I couldn't start driving in and out of traffic the way they did in the movies, because unlike in the movies, I wouldn't be able to skillfully escape oncoming traffic without risking certain death.

And I didn't want to get into another accident, even a small one, like I had before.

I did the only thing I could think of. Pulled into the parking lot of Monty's, a popular seafood restaurant by a marina, and waited. If someone was about to confront me, at least there'd be a lot of people around.

The car kept driving.

Gripping my hands on the steering wheel, I let out a sigh of relief. But then I wasn't sure I *should* be relieved.

If someone was following me, it meant they knew where I worked. Likely knew where I lived.

And that was something I couldn't escape.

"Mommy, I sleep with you."

At the sound of Rayna's voice, my eyes opened. I hadn't been sleeping, just lying in the dark, hoping sleep would come. I was stressed about everything that was going on in my life.

My first instinct was to say no, follow my sister's advice and put Rayna back into her own bed. But the thought of her little body snuggled up to mine was just what I needed.

She was already at my bed, and I said, "It's okay. Come up."

The pale moonlight filtering into the room allowed me to see the smile on Rayna's face. I pulled her beside me and adjusted the sheets over her small frame. Then I snuggled her close, careful not to put any weight on her broken arm.

For about ten seconds, we lay still, and I was hopeful that Rayna would fall asleep. Then she said, "TV."

What the hell. I didn't have to work the next morning. And maybe a little TV, even if it was the twenty-four-hour cartoon channel, would take my mind off of my own problems.

I turned on the television and began flipping through the channels.

I stopped when I saw Chaz's face fill the frame.

It was a rebroadcast of *Entertainment Now,* the show I'd

definitely avoided watching after my sister had told me about Chaz and Maria Lopez.

But a video clip of Chaz was playing on the screen now. He and Maria were strolling a tree-lined street somewhere.

"Oh, Chaz," I whispered. It was painful to see him. To see him and know that he'd moved on, despite how much we'd once meant to each other.

Our time in the Bahamas had been a whirlwind romance. A time when, despite all reason and illogical timing, I'd fallen in love. We both had. Despite his rejection of me only a couple of weeks later, I didn't doubt that he'd fallen for me just as hard as I'd fallen for him.

"*My Little Pony,*" Rayna protested.

"Not right now, honey."

I needed to watch this, to hear what the gossip was about Chaz and Maria.

"Chaz Anderson was spotted out on the town in L.A. with up and coming singing star, Maria Lopez, fueling rumors of a budding romance. Chaz is arguably the hottest motivational speaker in the country, and he and Maria met when she attended one of his seminars."

"Want to watch *My Little Pony!*" Rayna demanded.

"Not right now!" I snapped, then caught myself. I wasn't angry with Rayna. I was angry with Chaz for being with some bombshell after cutting me out of his life like a cancer. "I'm sorry, sweetheart. Mommy isn't mad at you."

Rayna's mouth quivered as she tried not to cry. "I'm sorry," I repeated, sitting up. I pulled her into my arms and cradled her. "You know how sometimes you just don't feel good? Well, Mommy just doesn't feel good right now. But I shouldn't have gotten mad at you. And I'm sorry. Okay?"

Rayna nodded.

When I turned my attention back to the television, Chaz's picture was no longer there. Instead, Brad and Angelina graced the screen on a red carpet in London.

I channel-surfed until I found the twenty-four-hour cartoon station for Rayna. She smiled, content.

As Rayna watched and laughed, my thoughts were all over the place. Was Chaz really involved with Maria Lopez? Maybe it was simply speculation, something gossip shows did best.

But she was extremely beautiful, the kind of woman any guy would fall for.

Even Chaz.

And yet I couldn't reconcile the Chaz who had been so down-to-earth and not at all superficial falling for a woman like Maria, especially if she'd once been a stripper.

One couldn't believe the reports on entertainment television. They were always exaggerated. The moment two stars were seen together, even for a friendly lunch, the entertainment reporters started speculating that love—or at least lust—was in bloom.

That had to be what was happening with Chaz. He'd been in love with me, hadn't he? He wouldn't be involved with another woman so quickly.

The hypocrisy of my statement hit me as I stroked Rayna's hair. Who was I to talk? I was engaged, for goodness' sake. To a man I liked a lot, but one I wasn't in love with. If Chaz were to learn of my engagement to Lewis, what would he think?

The circumstances were different, of course. Lewis had offered a way to help me out of a problem. Unable to see another answer, I'd taken it.

But Chaz wouldn't know that, would he?

I was surprised when my phone rang, considering it was shortly after midnight. Easing Rayna out of my arms, I moved across the bed to answer the phone. "Hello?"

"Hey, baby."

Lewis.

"Hi, Lewis. Why are you calling me so late?"

"I just happened to catch a bit of *Entertainment Now.*" He paused. "Thought you should know that Chaz Anderson is involved with someone else."

I swallowed painfully. "Coincidentally, I just saw that myself."

"I'm not stupid," Lewis went on. "I know you've been holding off giving me your heart because of Chaz."

He paused again, as if he expected me to either confirm or deny what he was saying. When I said nothing, he continued. "Didn't I take care of your problem with Tassie?"

"Yes."

"And don't you believe that I love you, that I've changed?"

"Yes," I admitted. I did believe that.

"You've got to admit, I've been patient in this whole deal."

"I know," I said.

"And I've certainly supported you. You can't deny that."

"I know." Because of the investigator he'd put me in touch with, I'd gotten those pictures of Tassie with Chris-

tian Blake. It was still a little mind-boggling to believe that
Tassie had been involved with him, though I shouldn't have
been too surprised. Tassie had had the nerve to make me
out to be a gold digger, but she was the one who'd had an
agenda. She had married Eli only for his cash, and had still
been involved with a high-school boyfriend the entire time.
The fact that she'd slept with Christian Blake had been icing
on the cake, and going to the media with the sordid pictures
would have humiliated her.

I still contemplated secretly sending them to the *Atlanta
Journal-Constitution*. And the *Miami Herald*. And CNN. And
Fox News. All the media outlets that had made Tassie out
to be a saint and me the ultimate sinner.

The thought made me smile.

All this had come about because of Lewis.

"Hey," Lewis said, and I realized that I'd gotten lost in my
fantasy of revenge.

"Sorry. My mind drifted for a moment."

"Tassie has backed down. Signed away her rights to the
condo. You don't even have to pay her out."

I grinned at that fortunate twist in this whole saga. "It
worked out better than I ever imagined."

"Exactly," Lewis said. "And yet we haven't celebrated."

He was right. We hadn't.

"I think it's time we celebrate, sweetheart."

"What do you have in mind?"

"I have to go out of town, and I want you to go with
me."

"Where?"

"The Cayman Islands."

"You want me to go to the Cayman Islands with you?"

"Yes. It's the July fourth weekend, so I know you don't have to work. Come on this trip with me, baby. Let's spend three sun-drenched days on Grand Cayman and celebrate in style."

My heart faltered. If I went on this trip with Lewis, that would be closing the door on the past.

But as the seconds went by, I wondered why was I holding off. Chaz hadn't called. In fact, if I were to believe the report I'd seen on that show and what my sister had said, he'd moved on to another woman. Lewis, however, had come through for me in every way that mattered—including respecting my request to hold off on making love.

Lewis was being everything I needed him to be. He was here for me.

Chaz wasn't. For all I knew, some other woman had snagged his heart.

It was high time I let go of the fantasy that I'd reunite with Chaz. Clearly, that wasn't going to happen.

"All right," I said to Lewis, my decision made. "When do we leave?"

21

The trip to Grand Cayman took only an hour. We flew on Lewis's private plane, which was luxurious beyond anything that I could have ever imagined. Beige leather seats. Polished mahogany walls. And the plane didn't just have a toilet bowl and a sink. It had a shower stall made of marble—the kind you'd expect to find in a posh hotel.

No doubt about it, Lewis would give me an incredible life.

But far more important to me than glitz and financial security was a stable relationship and a secure future. Lewis was first and foremost a friend, the best basis for any marriage.

We checked in to the Ritz-Carlton. We had our own private pool, an ocean view and miles of pristine white beach just steps from our ground-floor suite.

"I hate to do this," Lewis said once our luggage had been delivered to our room. "But I have to go tend to some business. Do you think you'll be all right alone here?"

"Oh, I think I feel safe," I said. I stared out at the Caribbean Sea, a gorgeous turquoise blue. A few yachts were floating in the distance. "I'm going to sit here and enjoy the million-dollar view."

"Feel free to order whatever you want. Wine, food. A massage."

"Thanks."

Lewis gave me a quick peck on the lips. Then he was gone.

I sat staring out at the view of the sea for several minutes after Lewis had left. The place was idyllic, romantic, and I couldn't help thinking of another time in the not too distant past when I'd been on a different Caribbean island with another man. My time in the Bahamas with Chaz had been out-of-this-world; a whirlwind, once-in-a-lifetime experience.

My heart filled with angst at the memory, and I had to remind myself why I'd decided to come on this trip with Lewis. Because I was closing the door on my past with Chaz. Trying to get over him once and for all.

Sighing wearily, I headed back inside, away from the enigmatic view. There was no time like the present to call home and check on Rayna. I didn't like leaving her, but I did believe I needed some time to just be Vanessa, and not Mom.

Thankfully Carla was able to watch Rayna for the days I'd be gone. When her husband returned from Iraq, she might not be as available as she was now.

"Hey, Carla," I said when she picked up the phone.

"Vanessa, hi. I guess this means you arrived safely."

"Yeah, we did." A beat. "How's Rayna?"

"She's fine. Don't you worry about her. The person I'm worried about is you."

"I'm perfectly fine," I lied. My heart still hurt, but I was trying to keep my emotions in check. "Lewis had to run out for a bit, and he told me to order whatever I want. I think I might get a spa treatment."

"It's not too late to tell him you want to only be his friend," Carla suddenly said.

"What?" I asked.

"Just tell him and get it over with already."

"Someone's at the door," I lied. I didn't want to hear this—not right now. "Room service. I'll call you later."

I hung up the phone before Carla had a chance to protest.

I dialed my home number next to check for new voice mail messages. Not because I really expected there'd be important new calls since the time I'd left, but for something to do.

The robotic female voice told me that I had two new messages. I wrapped my fingers around the handle to the full-size fridge, ready to open it and survey its contents. But as the first message began to play, my fingers froze, then grew slack. They fell from the fridge's door handle and went to my stomach, which had just bottomed out.

I was certain that somehow, I was imagining the voice I was hearing. So much so that when the message ended, I had to hit the key to play it again.

"Vanessa." Pause. "I know you'll be surprised when you hear this message. Maybe you don't even remember my voice."

My hand holding the receiver grew sweaty.

"It's Chaz, Vanessa. Look, I've had a long time to think. A long time to try to get over you. And you know what— I can't. I thought I'd be able to, but no matter what I do, I can't erase you from my mind. From my heart.

"And I've also had a lot of time to reflect. You lied to me, and yeah, that was bad. But you know what was worse? The way I turned my back on you. Turned my back on someone I loved. It made me think real hard, Vanessa. And I realized that I let the hurt and betrayal I'd felt at my wife's lies affect how I dealt with you. So your daughter's father isn't dead? Does that change what we found? God, I'm rambling. I don't even know if you feel the same way about me anymore. But maybe you can call me…let me know where I stand. And if there's a chance for us?

"I've been meaning to call for a while," Chaz went on. "Thinking about it, at least. But I was featured on an entertainment show recently, something you might have seen. Bottom line, if you saw the reports supposedly linking me romantically to Maria Lopez…well, I wanted you to know that there's nothing between us. There's nothing between me and her because you're the one in my heart." Pause. "I hope you'll call me."

I stood stupidly, holding the receiver to my ear. When the voice mail prompted me to either save the message or delete it, I hung up the receiver.

My head was spinning like debris in a tornado. So much so that it was hard for me to really process what had just happened.

Chaz still loved me. He regretted the way he'd ended things.

He wanted another chance.

My heart kick-started into action, pounding out of control.

Talk about the worst timing possible! Here I was on an island with Lewis, having finally decided to put my heart into my relationship with him, and *now* Chaz called?

The timing might have sucked, but I was suddenly sure about one thing.

I had to end my engagement to Lewis.

I turned at the sound of the door. Lewis stood there with a bouquet of red hibiscus, grinning at me like a fool in love.

God help me, I thought. *This can't be happening.*

Slowly, Lewis moved toward me. "For you," he said, presenting me with the beautiful bouquet.

My hands shook as I took the flowers from him. "Th-thank you."

Concern suddenly flashed in Lewis's eyes. "You okay?"

"Yeah. Sure. Of course I'm okay."

He placed his hands on my shoulders, and I tensed. "Then why do you look upset?"

"I'm not," I lied. *Just do it. Tell him you can't marry him.*

"I know what's wrong," Lewis said after a moment.

My eyes widened. "You do?"

He nodded as he ran his hands over my upper arms. "Yeah. You're tense because of that whole 'no sex before marriage' thing. Here you are with me, the sexual chemistry between us as intense as ever...and you're figuring we're going to end up in bed."

"Right," I said slowly. "Yes. I guess you're right."

"Which brings me to my surprise," Lewis said, his eyes brightening.

"Surprise?" I echoed.

"Uh-huh."

"Well, don't keep me in suspense."

"You don't have to worry, sweetheart. I won't compromise your virtue."

I blew out a relieved breath. "Oh. Well, that's good to hear—"

"Tonight," Lewis said, cutting me off.

I angled my head and looked at him quizzically. "Tonight?"

"But tomorrow night, that's a different story."

My eyes narrowed in confusion. "I don't understand."

"Marry me, baby," he said.

"I…" My voice trailed off. I didn't understand what Lewis was getting at. Why he was proposing again.

Though this would be a good time to tell him that I'd had a change of heart.

"Tomorrow morning," he went on. "Marry me tomorrow morning."

I stared at him, my mouth falling open, but I couldn't think of a word to say.

"That's the business I had to take care of," he said. "And now it's all been arranged. The minister, the witnesses. Everything. All you have to do is say yes, and we can get married in this Caribbean paradise."

I couldn't speak. Couldn't form one single word.

Then Lewis drew me into his arms and lifted me off the ground as he hugged me, clearly taking my silence as agreement.

"Lewis," I said when he lowered me to the ground.

"This is the way it should be." He framed my face. "A

simple, romantic wedding. Your parents are gone. So are mine. There's no reason to have some monstrosity of a wedding just so we'll get written up in the *Miami Herald*." He softly kissed my forehead. "Besides, I've been waiting a long time to get you naked. I can't wait anymore."

"Ha." My attempt at a laugh sounded like a strangled cry.

"What?" Lewis asked. "You don't think we'll be good in bed anymore?"

"I don't think we'd have a problem there," I replied honestly.

"Neither do I," Lewis agreed, grinning. Then he kissed me on the lips.

I let the kiss last a few seconds before I eased away from him.

"What?" he asked, his voice husky.

"It's just…" How could I let him down easily? After all Lewis had done for me, I didn't want to hurt him.

His eyes searched mine as his fingers curled around my hands. "What?"

"Rayna," I finally said. "I'd like her to be a part of my big day. And…and she's not here. So, as much as getting married tomorrow is a nice idea—"

I stopped speaking as Lewis chuckled. It was a warm sound, not at all condescending. "Rayna is two and a half. Her missing the wedding isn't going to matter to her." Lewis trailed his palms up my arms. "Baby, I want to marry you. How long have we known each other? Let's just do this."

He kissed me again, a deep, meaningful kiss. I let him kiss me, hoping to feel my heart was in it.

I'd loved Lewis once. How much effort would it take to love him again?

But as we pulled apart, all I could think of was Chaz.

Chaz still loved me.

More important, I still loved him.

But damn, Lewis was grinning at me like a fool in love. How could I destroy his happiness right now? He'd been so good to me and, despite everything, I cared about him a lot. He deserved better.

Tomorrow, I told myself. I would let Lewis have tonight, and break the news to him in the morning.

And since Lewis wasn't pressuring me to make love to him tonight, there really was no particular sense of urgency.

No real reason to crush his dreams *right now.*

"Wine?" Lewis asked.

I smiled at him. "Wine would be lovely."

As he went to the phone to order, I felt good about my decision. I'd enjoy one last pleasant evening with Lewis. Tomorrow, I would let him down gently.

And then I'd be on the first plane back to Miami.

Back to Chaz.

22

The smell of coffee awoke my senses. Then I slowly became conscious, and opened my eyes.

I saw the romantic netting hanging from the oversized bed posts, and in a nanosecond, remembered where I was.

In Grand Cayman. With Lewis.

Panic washed over me as I remembered the conversation I'd had with him last night.

This was going to be our wedding day.

I bolted upright in the bed, quickly throwing off the covers. I had to tell Lewis that I couldn't marry him. Before he got the wedding plans in motion.

I found Lewis on the terrace, which was quite large and had a table for two as well as a couple loungers. There was a gentle breeze filling the suite through the open terrace doors, making the sheer curtains billow.

It was all very romantic.

I made my way to the terrace. Lewis saw me before I reached the doors, and stood.

"Morning, sweetheart," he greeted me. He pulled out the wicker chair directly opposite his, and I sat at the table.

"Coffee?" he asked.

"Yes, please." Coffee was the first order of business—before I broke his heart.

The coffee was in a glazed white teapot, and he poured some into my delicate white cup. Cream and sugar were also in little cream and sugar bowls. The table was set, complete with properly folded napkins and a tray of fresh fruit. Had someone been here and put this together…or did Lewis have domestic skills I wasn't aware of?

"This is quite an elaborate spread," I commented, lifting the bowl of sugar. "Did you do all this…or did you pay someone?" I smiled sweetly.

"I spent an hour cutting pineapples and honeydew melon."

My hand stilled on the spoon I'd put into the sugar bowl. "You're kidding."

Lewis smiled. "Yeah, I am kidding. Room service set it up. They're going to come back and make breakfast here, too. I just have to call and say when."

I gazed out at the stretch of beach, the palm and coconut trees, and the turquoise blue ocean, taking in the beauty of the island. I knew Lewis loved to travel, and with him, trips to the Caymans or Hawaii or even Paris would be frequent. It was a nice life, I couldn't deny that.

But when I traveled the world, I wanted to do it with the man I trusted with my heart completely.

Maybe that was it, what was bothering me about being with Lewis. Yes, he seemed to have changed, but there was a part of me that couldn't one hundred percent let go of the past. Lewis had been the consummate player. And while we were able to remain friends after our relationship ended, I just didn't know if I'd have his heart forever—even if I had it now.

And of course, there was the fact that Chaz still loved me. Always Chaz.

"Eat," Lewis said. "The pineapple is the sweetest I've ever tasted."

I put some pineapple on my plate, then lifted the heavy silver knife and fork. I cut the pineapple into bite-sized pieces and ate one.

Lewis was right. It was sweet and delicious.

"Isn't this beautiful?" he asked, gesturing to the beach, ocean and lushly landscaped grounds.

"It is."

"I want to travel the world with you, baby. Maybe head to Paris next? Have you ever been?"

Was Lewis reading my mind? "No."

"It's an incredible city. I know some Americans don't like to go there these days because they think the French hate us, but you know what—there's no place more romantic than Paris."

I couldn't do this. Couldn't let him continue to envision the fantasy of our life together when it wouldn't happen.

"Have you been to Mexico?" he asked.

"No."

"Then we'll plan a trip to Cabo. Though personally, I like the Mexican Caribbean better. The sand is beautiful, the water amazing—"

"Lewis," I said, cutting him off.

"Yes, baby." He reached across the table and took my hand, looking at me with such love, it broke my heart.

"Lewis, I…" I inhaled a deep breath, preparing myself to tell him what I needed to say.

There was a loud crash. So loud I knew someone was in our unit. I jumped up, spinning my head around. I saw a flash of movement, white and black, at the same moment that I heard the yelling.

"Down, down! Get down!"

Fear shot through my body when I saw the nose of a gun, and my heart thundered out of control. Someone had broken in to our suite! My God, we were going to die.

I threw a quick glance at Lewis, saw his hands in the air and the mortified look on his face. He began to go down, and I followed suit, dropping to the concrete floor like a sack of potatoes.

"Faces down! Hands up!"

I shot my hands up while keeping my head down—not a very comfortable position.

Beside me, Lewis cursed.

"Okay, now link your hands behind your head."

Trying to hold my tears in, I did just that. Sneaking a glance at Lewis, I saw that he was doing the same. But I couldn't help wondering why he wasn't saying anything. He was the man here. He needed to ask these hoodlums what they wanted. Maybe he could offer them a large sum of money that would appease them.

"Lewis Carter?" one of the men said. He had an island accent.

A beat. Then Lewis said, "Yeah."

There were at least three of them, because I could see three pairs of polished black boots.

The feet began to move, at which point I realized there were more than three of them. At least five, based on the army of boots that began to surround us.

"Lewis Carter, you're under arrest."

What?

Thick hands encircled my wrists and I was jerkily hauled to my feet. I took a look at the men, all wearing uniforms that consisted of black pants, while shirts and police hats.

Yes, I'd heard correctly. The men—six of them—were police officers.

"What on earth is going on here?" I demanded. I shot a frantic glance at Lewis. He didn't look outraged, nor in complete shock. In fact, he looked...sort of resigned.

"Lewis," I said, my voice a whisper now. Surely he had no idea what this was about. And I didn't believe it had anything to do with Tassie, since the police had mentioned Lewis's name, not mine.

One of the officers pulled Lewis's arms from behind his head and began to cuff him behind his back. "Lewis Carter, you have the right to remain silent."

I widened my eyes as I stared at Lewis, silently imploring him to *do something.*

"What the hell's going on?" Lewis asked. "Why are you arresting me?"

Finally.

An officer began to cuff me as well.

"Money laundering, Mr. Carter."

"Money laundering?" I exclaimed, though I was at least relieved. "Obviously, there's been some mistake. We're here to get married. We only got here yesterday."

"Ma'am, there's been an ongoing investigation between the United States and the Cayman Islands," one officer explained. "We've been watching Lewis and his associates for a long time."

I stared at Lewis, waiting once again for his indignant reaction. Surely it would come. But he wouldn't meet my eyes.

Oh, my God…

"Vanessa Cain, you are also being detained."

"Detained?" I repeated, aghast. "You mean you're arresting me?"

"Yes, ma'am."

"What on earth for? And how do you know my name?"

"Like I said, Lewis Carter and his associates have been under investigation for quite some time."

"What's really going on here?" I asked. There had to be another explanation, because this one simply didn't make sense. "Is it money you want?" I knew that there were many people in positions of power who were corrupt. Perhaps someone had been watching Lewis for a long time, knew that he was worth a lot of money. Now they were coming up with some trumped-up charge in order to blackmail Lewis for a ton of his cash.

That explanation certainly made more sense than money laundering…didn't it?

The officer holding me turned me toward the terrace door. I noticed then the small crowd on the grounds, staring at our balcony. All that screaming and hollering as the cops had busted down our door had attracted serious attention.

At least I wasn't in Miami, and no one here would give a rat's behind who I was.

My momentary relief was immediately squashed when the officer holding me gave me a shove. I stumbled, then caught my footing, and began walking in the direction I was being guided—back through the suite.

Only the man didn't stop. He continued on toward the door.

"Wait a second," I said. "What are you doing?"

"Taking you to the police station."

"Like this?" I shrieked. I was only wearing the hotel's fluffy white robe.

The officers in the room exchanged glances. Lewis was also wearing the hotel's white robe. We'd make a funny pair at the police station, or worse, side by side in a jail cell.

The officers conferred. Then one of them spoke. "You'll both be allowed to change. One at a time."

My cuffs were loosened, and I was allowed to go into the bedroom. I quickly found a skirt and blouse in my luggage.

As I changed, something awful suddenly struck me, and I stumbled backward as if I'd been zapped with a stun gun.

We were in Grand Cayman.

A lot of criminals chose the Cayman Islands to have offshore bank accounts.

It was a coincidence, wasn't it? Surely Lewis wasn't involved in illegal business.

He was a real estate developer. A successful one.

I bet if Donald Trump showed up on Grand Cayman, no one would arrest him.

But still, something niggled at the back of my neck. I was suddenly no longer sure of anything.

When I exited the bedroom, an officer loosened Lewis's cuffs and told him it was his turn.

Once Lewis had changed, we were both taken outside. The walk to the front of the resort was unending—and I felt as if I were heading toward my execution. People lined the paths, getting a good look at me and Lewis. I couldn't have been more embarrassed.

When we neared the small police cars, I whispered to Lewis, "Tell me you didn't do what they're saying you did. Please, Lewis. Tell me you didn't."

A pause. Then he said, "Of course not."

"So why are we being carted off in handcuffs?"

That was all I got to ask before being urged into the backseat of a car. I gazed out the window helplessly, my eyes meeting Lewis's in the other police car.

He mouthed something. I didn't understand what he was saying.

He repeated it, and I finally figured out what he was trying to tell me.

"It'll be okay."

That remained to be seen.

23

To my dismay, once we reached the police station, Lewis and I were put into different rooms. I don't know about Lewis, but I was left in the hot, stale room without a clock for what seemed like at least an hour.

I think they were trying to make me sweat, and they succeeded—literally. Sweat beaded out on my forehead and pooled under my arms. And my God, couldn't they give a person a drink of water?

I was starting to wonder if I'd die of dehydration when the door finally opened. In walked a man who was about five foot eight and two hundred pounds. I didn't understand how he could be dressed in a suit in this weather.

"Hello, Ms. Cain," the man said.

"Why have I been in here so long?" I asked.

"Sorry about the wait. But you'll be leaving shortly."

"What?" I asked, panic rising in my throat. "Where are you taking me?" Somewhere where they'd beat me until I was ready to confess to anything?

"The U.S. Marshals are on their way to retrieve you."

U.S. Marshals? *Retrieve* me? This man may as well have been speaking another language. "Why are the U.S. Marshals coming?"

"They are escorting you back to the United States."

This couldn't be happening. "But my suitcase, my passport—"

"You needn't worry. Your belongings have been collected."

I needn't worry. *Yeah, right.* As if that were possible.

"Are you going to at least tell me what's going on?"

"You have been detained for alleged illegal money laundering of drug money. You are being deported back to the United States by federal marshals, who will take you into official custody when you arrive in Miami."

Take me into custody... I almost burst into tears, but somehow I kept control.

So much for spending an amazing July 4th weekend on a beautiful island.

The man started for the door, and frantic, I called out to him. "Wait!"

He slowly turned, no discernable emotion on his face.

"I need to make a phone call."

No reaction.

"Please. I have a daughter. I need to call my sister so she can pick her up." God only knew how long it might be before I was out of custody. Days? A week? "A quick phone call to Miami. Isn't every person arrested entitled to that?"

"This is not America," the man said.

"I'm asking you out of the goodness of your heart.

You've got a cell phone right in your jacket. It'll be a quick call."

The man made a face as he considered what to do. Then he pulled the phone from his front jacket pocket. "I've always had a soft spot for pretty ladies," he said. "What is the number?"

I told him, and he placed the call. Then he walked around the table and put the phone at my ear.

My sister picked up the phone. "Hello?"

"Hi, Nikki."

"Vanessa! Where are you? I called earlier—"

"I'm in jail," I blurted. There was no easy way to say what I needed to say, no way to sugarcoat it. And I needed to speak quickly so that I'd get to tell Nikki everything.

"You're *what?*"

"You heard me," I said. "I'm in police custody."

"I don't understand. What did you do?"

"I didn't do anything. And I don't have long. But I need you to pick up Rayna, okay? I'm not sure when I'll be back in the States."

"Wait a minute. Where are you?"

"Grand Cayman."

"What on earth for? And with whom?"

I hesitated. Braced myself for my sister's reaction. "With Lewis."

"*Lewis?* You're seeing him again?"

"Look, I can't get in to all of this right now. I just need you to please, please pick up Rayna for me. Because I don't know how long it'll be before this is sorted out."

"Vanessa..."

"That's all I can say right now," I told her, emotion clogging my throat. "Please."

"All right. I'll do it."

"Thank you," I said. Then I moved my head away from the phone. I looked up at the detective and said, "Thank you."

"You're welcome," he told me.

He was starting to walk away when I said, "Do I have to stay in here—handcuffed?"

"Yes."

"I'm dying of thirst here. Can you please bring me some water?" I spoke sweetly, trying to appeal to his soft side for pretty women.

"I've already let you use my phone."

"I've been in here a long time. And the room is extremely hot. Please."

The man slipped through the door. I didn't know if he was going to get me water, or if he couldn't care less. But he was back a couple minutes later with a bottle of water. He uncapped it and put the mouth to my lips, and the cool liquid was the best thing I'd ever tasted.

"I'll be back shortly," the man said when I'd had my fill.

I nodded. I didn't know if shortly was another hour, or even longer. All I could hope was that once I was with the U.S. authorities, they'd see reason and I'd be released.

At the door, the man turned and faced me. "Such a shame," he said. "A pretty woman like you, mixed up in a crazy mess like this. But sadly, I see it all too often. Women attracted to bad men. Is it the excitement?"

I didn't dignify his question with an answer.

"Unfortunately, you're going to learn the hard way that crime doesn't pay."

The man disappeared. Unfortunately, I couldn't kick his ass.

The nerve. I hadn't been found guilty of anything—something he should have kept in mind.

At least the U.S. Marshals were coming, a thought I never expected to ever think in my entire life. They'd straighten this mess out.

My trip back to Florida could only be described as terrifying. The U.S. Marshals hauled me and Lewis off in a dark SUV with tinted windows, the kind of vehicle you imagine is used to abduct people.

And that's how the experience felt to me—like I was being *abducted,* rather than *escorted.*

Still in handcuffs, Lewis and I were put in the back of the vehicle. There were four marshals, three white, one black. Two of the white ones had crew cuts, while the third one and the black marshal were bald. Neither cracked a smile nor made any small talk, making me wonder if they'd been taught that in the U.S. Marshal handbook.

We were taken to the airport and led onto a small plane. Private. Well, thank God for that. At least I wouldn't have to face hundreds of tourists while I was in handcuffs. The shame alone could have a person dying of humiliation.

Lewis didn't speak, and neither did I. We didn't have any privacy, for one thing. But even if we had, I wasn't sure I wanted to say anything to Lewis.

Hell, I wasn't sure I ever wanted to see him again.

Though I'd originally been outraged and convinced some awful mistake had been made, the more I thought about it, the more likely it seemed that Lewis had his hands in something dirty. It wasn't just the accusation—I know many an innocent person is accused of something he or she didn't do—but it was Lewis's expression. He didn't look baffled. He didn't look mad as hell. I'm sure I did…because I didn't know what the heck was going on.

And Lewis was abnormally quiet, avoiding eye contact with me most of the time.

The bloody moron!

My humiliation was only intensified when we arrived at the airport in Miami. Even if I wasn't handcuffed, I don't think anyone for a second wouldn't have figured out that I was in police custody. The two men "escorting" me looked like cookie-cutter undercover federal agents.

And the press was there. My God, how did they know about this! They snapped photos voraciously and shoved a microphone in my face. I did my best to hide my face with my hands cuffed behind my back, and I didn't dare say a word.

I thought the media intrusion after Eli's death had been unbearable. But this was one hundred times worse.

Because this time, I might be spending the rest of my days in jail—if this whole situation wasn't cleared up.

I stifled a cry as that thought hit me. What the hell had Lewis gotten me into? And what if the worst-case scenario happened and I was sentenced to jail time?

No, I told myself as I was helped into the back of an unmarked cruiser. *I won't go to jail. That simply isn't an option.*

I was my daughter's only parent. I couldn't go to jail on a bogus charge and leave her all alone.

No way in hell.

The American way is innocent until proven guilty, but that was impossible to tell by the way I was treated when I reached police headquarters.

I was in a room with Good Cop and Bad Cop. That much I knew from watching movies and television. Good Cop was sitting at the table across from me, a sympathetic look on his face, while Bad Cop was wearing a hole in the floor, looking like he wanted to tear me to pieces.

"I get it," Good Cop said, his voice kind. "You didn't mean for this to happen. You fell for Lewis Carter, and basically got caught up in a dangerous game."

"No," I said. "That's not true. I was involved with him, yes. But he told me he was a legitimate business man. A real estate investor. How was I to know otherwise?"

Bad Cop whirled around and pinned me with the kind of stare that could make a person with a bad heart drop dead. "Stop the fucking games, all right? You were caught red-handed. You flew to the Cayman Islands on Lewis's private plane, and don't try to pretend that you didn't know what was going on. You want to spend the next thirty years in jail? Do you?"

The man slammed his hands down on the table, and I flinched. "N-no."

"Then you better start telling us the truth, lady."

I started to cry. I couldn't help it. I wanted to remain

strong, but in the face of odds that seemed insurmountable, that was harder to do as each moment passed by.

"Forster," Good Cop said. "Chill out." Then he turned to me. "I don't believe for a second that you're some cold-hearted, seasoned criminal."

"I'm not."

"But do you know more about what happened than you're letting on?" Good Cop shrugged. "My bet is yes. And I get that. You've got to be terrified. You have a daughter, right?"

I sniffled. "Yes. And I'm her only parent."

"What—is her father dead or something?" Good Cop asked.

"He may as well be," I replied. "He's still alive. But he's not a father to her. I'm all she has."

"Which is why you'd better start talking," Bad Cop bellowed. "You talk, that'll go a long way in court. Maybe you'll walk away with three to five years instead of thirty."

Three to five years? This couldn't be happening. I couldn't do any time—not when I wasn't guilty of anything.

"I don't know anything about any money laundering," I stressed. "How many times can I say that?"

"Ever heard of RICO?" Bad Cop asked me.

I stared at him dumbly. "I don't know anyone named Rico."

He chuckled. "It's not a person. It's a federal statute. Designed to bring down those involved in organized crime."

"Organized crime! Is that what you think? That I'm involved in organized crime?"

"You handle your agency's finances, right? Believe The

Dream, yada yada," he added, making air quotes, implying the agency wasn't on the up-and-up.

How did he know where I worked? "Yes," I responded. "But—but that's not a crime."

"It is if you use the agency account to launder money."

"Me? Launder money? I can barely keep on top of laundering my clothes. When would I have time to launder money?"

Now both Good Cop and Bad Cop chuckled. I wondered if they'd be laughing if they were the ones sitting in my position.

From a folder, Bad Cop produced a photo of me, Neil Gorman and Lewis. For a moment, I was confused as to how he would have gotten such a picture. Then I realized it had been taken while I was in the parking lot outside of Neil's law offices, about to leave after the meeting with Tassie.

"What is your relationship to Neil Gorman?"

"He was my lawyer. I had to deal with him regarding a property issue."

"A property issue?" Bad Cop asked. "What kind of *property* issue?"

"My home," I told him. "I was involved with someone, who turns out was still married, and his wife wanted to take my home.... Look, it's a long, convoluted story that has nothing to do with any money laundering."

"Do you know what kind of lawyer Neil Gorman is?" Good Cop asked.

"I don't know. Civil?"

"The kind of lawyer criminals use," Good Cop explained. "He's as dirty as they come."

"And don't pretend you didn't fucking know that!" Bad

Cop yelled. "You think you can waste our time, lying about what you know?" Bad Cop came close to me, lowering his face to mine. "You think that'll help you when you're facing thirty years in jail?"

"I want a lawyer," I said. The talk about Neil Gorman had reminded me that I was back in the U.S., and entitled to a lawyer. Clearly, neither of these cops were going to see reason, and with the chance of me going to jail sounding extremely likely, I needed someone to represent me.

Like yesterday.

"You refuse to answer any more questions without a lawyer present?" Bad Cop asked.

He wasn't going to intimidate me out of my decision. "That's right," I told him.

Bad Cop threw his hands in the air and marched out of the room. Good Cop stood and followed him, giving me a sympathetic look before he disappeared through the door.

That's when I burst into tears. I bawled like a baby.

One minute, I'd been trying to find a way to end my relationship with Lewis. The next, I was in federal custody.

Why didn't you have the guts to tell Lewis before we headed to Grand Cayman? I chastised myself. *If only you had…*

If only… If only wasn't going to help me now.

I'd continued my relationship with Lewis, even though my heart wasn't in it, because I hoped that he would help me out of my predicament with Tassie. But now I was facing a problem far, far greater.

Good Cop came back about ten minutes later, and told me that a lawyer couldn't make it out to see me until the morning. He seemed to genuinely care that I'd have to remain in custody until the morning. But of course, it could have been an act.

I was put in a cell with a narrow, hard bed. I curled into a fetal position and prayed for sleep. I was far too stressed to sleep, but at some point, I finally drifted off.

In the morning, a female officer came to my cell to tell me that a lawyer had arrived. I was then taken to a room where I was allowed to speak with her.

My lawyer was a middle-aged black woman in a sharp business suit. Everything about her screamed professional and efficient—except her short, red afro.

"Vanessa?" she asked as she walked toward the table. "I'm Laura Steele, a state appointed attorney."

"I didn't do what they said. The only thing I'm guilty of is falling for the wrong guy."

She sat opposite me at the table and pulled out a notepad. "Tell me everything that happened. From the beginning."

"The beginning when we went to Grand Cayman…or before that?"

"Tell me about your relationship with Lewis Carter."

So I did. I told her how I'd met Lewis a couple years earlier at a nightclub, and how over time what had started as lust had turned into love. I told her about finding the red thong in his pocket, and how that had reminded me that Lewis, though charming, would always be a player. Then I went on to talk about Eli, and how love had sparked and tragically ended, then my relationship with Chaz, and how that had led me back to Lewis.

Laura was silent as she scribbled notes. "What are you thinking?" I asked.

"Other than the fact that you need Dr. Phil?" She smiled to soften the blow. "Lewis lied to you. It wasn't your job to question the validity of what he'd told you. It wasn't your job to have a private investigator investigate him. If you'd known about his illegal activities, would you have continued your relationship with him?"

"No," I said adamantly. "Absolutely not. I didn't want to lose my condo, but it would hardly be the worst thing in the world. I…" My voice cracked. "I have a daughter. She's all that matters."

I started crying again.

"I'll get you out of this," Laura assured me. "The police have nothing on you. I figure they think you know more than you're saying, and they can use you to testify against Lewis."

I wiped at my tears. "What does that mean?"

"That they're trying to make your life hell so you'll give them what they want."

"I have nothing to give them."

"I believe you," Laura said. "And I'm betting that they're believing you, too."

"I don't know. That cop, Forster, seemed pretty convinced I'm lying."

Laura pushed her chair back and stood. "I've seen cases like this a million times. Good girl falls for bad boy. I'll straighten it out."

As Laura left the room, I allowed myself to hope. In fact, I closed my eyes and muttered a prayer that this would all be sorted out in short order.

I'm not sure how long it took for Laura to come back to the room. It seemed like forever, but it was likely around forty minutes. But when she did, she was smiling from ear to ear.

I sat up straight.

"You're free to go."

For a moment, I sat in shock. "What?"

"You're free to go."

"Oh, my God."

"Lewis told the police that you had nothing to do with any of this. And without any evidence against you, the police can't hold you here."

I got to my feet. I started crying again, but this time, happy tears.

"Go home and be with your baby."

"Thank you," I said. I pumped Laura's hand with both of mine. "Thank you so much."

"You're welcome." She reached into her briefcase and gave me a card. "Here's my card. If you have any questions, or if the police want to question you, call me."

"You think they'll want to question me again?" I asked, alarmed. If I didn't see Forster again, it would be too soon.

"It's possible. But considering Lewis has made a statement that completely absolves you, I doubt it."

"Thank you, again," I said. The past thirty hours had seemed like a bizarre dream. A nightmare, really.

Laura grinned. "No problem."

At the reception desk, an officer returned my belongings to me. Then she said an agent would take me wherever I needed to go.

With my luck, Bad Cop would be that agent. "No, thanks," I said. "Can you please just call me a cab?"

I went directly to my sister's house, and the moment I saw Rayna, I scooped her into my arms and hugged her, never wanting to let her go.

24

Half an hour later, I'd filled my sister and Morris in on all that had transpired over the last couple days.

"My God," Nikki said. "What were you *thinking?*"

"Not that I'd end up arrested," I said testily.

My sister tsked. "I could have told you Lewis was bad news. In fact, I think I *did* tell you that the first time you dated him."

"Nikki, this isn't the time for I-told-you-sos. I've been through enough."

"I'm just saying—"

"Enough," Morris said to Nikki, and I was surprised. He didn't typically stand up to my sister, and I was grateful for his speaking up on my behalf. "Vanessa's right. She didn't know what Lewis was up to. She can't be blamed for what happened."

"She might not have known what he was up to, but after the way their relationship ended the first time, I'm surprised she started dating him again. Good Lord, she was about to get *married* to him."

"I wasn't going to go through with it," I said softly. "I was about to end it. That's when all hell broke loose."

My sister shook her head. "I've said it once, I've said it a thousand times. With the kind of men you get involved with, it's no surprise that you get hurt over and over again."

"You know, Nikki," I said, getting to my feet, "this is not what I need from you right now. My God, when will you ever get off of your high horse?"

"I'm only saying—"

"You're rubbing salt in my wound, that's what you're doing. And if I remember correctly, it was *you* who burned Morris's clothes, assaulted a cop and ended up arrested! If I hadn't pulled some strings for you, you might be rotting in a Miami jail. So don't talk to me about getting into trouble 'over and over again.'"

My sister's mouth fell open, aghast, as though she couldn't believe I'd dared to speak to her the way I had.

"Fine," she said after a minute. "I'll keep my opinion to myself."

"Wonders never cease," Morris muttered.

My eyes flew to his in surprise.

"What did you say?" Nikki asked.

For several seconds, Morris didn't speak. In fact, he didn't meet Nikki's eyes.

Then he slowly looked at her, his gaze unwavering. "Your sister's right," he said. "You're giving her a lecture when she needs your support. At least her arrest was a mistake."

Nikki shot to her feet. "Meaning my arrest wasn't?"

"Exactly," Morris said, and I swear, my jaw hit the floor. I'd never seen Morris stand up to my sister like this. In fact, I hadn't known he was capable of it. "You were arrested for acting incredibly stupid."

Nikki looked mortified, and on the verge of tears. "You're the one who cheated on me."

"I know. And I'm sorry. The point is, you're not perfect, so you really have no right to get on Vanessa's case. For God's sake, what's it going to take for you to stop being so damn judgmental?"

Nikki looked more wounded than angry. "I guess I'm just an awful person," she said, and then she stalked off.

My guess is that she expected Morris to go after her, but he didn't. I wanted to stand up and cheer.

My sister retreated to her bedroom like a spoiled child, even slamming the door behind her.

"I love her," Morris said after about a minute had passed. "But sometimes, I don't know why. She can be so impossible."

"I know." For as long as I could remember, she had always been that way. Overbearing and self-righteous. She was my sister, so I had to put up with her, but I'd wondered more times than I could count what was wrong with her.

"I know I screwed up. Trust me, I know. But sometimes I wonder if she'll ever let me forget it. Anything she wants for our second wedding, she has to get—and if I say no, she throws in my face the fact that I had an affair."

"Well, lucky you." At the sound of Nikki's voice, both Morris and I looked to the entrance of the living room. Neither of us had heard Nikki approach. "You don't have to worry about the expense of marrying me again, because our second wedding is off!"

"Nikki," I said, getting to my feet.

"Oh, don't try to make nice after you were clearly talking about me behind my back."

I walked toward my sister, debating pussyfooting around the issue. But I realized that that was exactly the problem where she was concerned—she was so damn overbearing that everyone else always backed down around her, encouraging her to continue her boorish behavior.

"Yeah, we were talking about you, but I'm just as happy to say to your face what I said behind your back. What is wrong with you?" I asked, the question serious. "You have a sister who loves you, and it seems like you're not happy unless you're pointing out my flaws. Making me feel bad about every mistake I've made. And Morris—my God, the man is a saint to put up with you. Surely you must know that."

Nikki's eyes flew to Morris's. "Is that what you said to her?"

"No." I spoke before Morris could. "That's what *I'm* saying. I'm not blind. For years, I've witnessed how you've treated your husband. You have a good man. A man who will do anything for you. And you nitpick him to death. You boss him around. You don't let him be a man." I paused. "Honestly, is it any wonder he cheated on you?"

"I can't believe you're condoning what he did!"

"I don't condone it. But you can't push a person away all the time and expect them to not leave. You want a strong marriage with your husband? You've got to learn how to treat him with respect."

Nikki's mouth opened, and I thought she was going to protest. Instead, she said nothing. Just looked weary.

"You weren't always like this, sis," I said softly.

I stared at Nikki, and she at me. Again, she didn't speak, but I knew my words were getting through to her.

It was time for a heart-to-heart that was a long time coming. Turning to Morris, I asked, "Do you mind giving me a few minutes alone with my sister?"

Morris nodded, then walked out of the room. I watched him disappear, then faced my sister once more.

Nikki spoke before I could. "You wanna tell me off some more? This time without a witness?"

"No," I said softly, shaking my head. "Why don't you sit down with me? I think we need to have a serious talk."

Nikki sighed, and I expected her to protest. Instead, she walked past me to the sofa and sat down. I sat beside her.

I took her hand in mine. Gave it the kind of sisterly squeeze I hadn't in forever. "I mean it when I say you weren't always like this, Nikki. Controlling, and sometimes overbearing. You know you weren't."

Nikki didn't say anything. Just listened.

"You know what I always loved about you?" I asked. "The way you loved to laugh and didn't take yourself too seriously. I looked up to you, my big sis, who seemed to have everything going for her." I smiled at her, my eyes already misting. "But then you changed."

I saw tears in my sister's eyes, too. She turned away.

"I know I'm not perfect," I said. "But sometimes...sometimes you get on my case so much, it's like you feel I'm a bad person or something."

"I've never said that."

"Maybe not, but that's how I feel. You see all my flaws, point them out over and over again. Sometimes—no, a lot of the time—I just want you to listen to me. To hear the kind of crappy day I've had, or bad experience, and just say you're sorry. Not find reasons why I brought on whatever bad thing myself."

Nikki opened her mouth, but then she didn't speak. Perhaps for the first time, she was realizing how much truth there was to my words.

"Morris is a good man," I went on. "He loves you. And I'm sure you love him. But you talk down to him, like he's your child, not your equal. Was he wrong to cheat on you? Absolutely. But you treat a man like a child, nitpick him over everything and try to control him, he's bound to start noticing the woman who smiles genuinely at him, tells him how nice he looks…"

"Stop," Nikki said. "Not another word."

I stopped. I thought she was going to tell me off, but instead, she began to softly sob. I squeezed her hand harder, showing her that I was there for her.

"I hope you know that everything I'm saying, I say in love," I told her.

"Morris said I pushed him away, but I didn't want to hear it. Didn't want to believe it. But in my heart…"

Nikki's voice trailed off, but I didn't need to hear her complete her statement to know what she was going to say.

"And you. I want us to be close. I really do. I see how you are with your friends, and I wish we had that kind of relationship."

"We did, once. What happened?" I asked slowly. "How did you change from the happy person you were to a controlling person it's sometimes hard for me to be around?"

Nikki wiped at her tears with her free hand. "After Mom and Dad died, I was so lost. I had to grow up pretty much over night. I know we were with Aunt Lola, but I became a mom to you. I wanted to do everything to protect you from all the bad things in the world."

"And you did a good job," I said.

"I know. But you were devastated when we lost Mom and Dad. I was, too, but all I remember is wishing I could take your pain away. I couldn't—but I could try to protect you. Keep you safe."

"Unfortunately, we both learned the hard way that bad things happen." My voice cracked slightly as I remembered the day I'd learned my parents would never be coming back. "Often when you least expect it."

"Do you remember that about a month before Mom and Dad died, I went to a modeling agency?"

I hadn't, but Nikki's words caused a memory to stir. I was in middle school, while she'd been a senior about to graduate from high school. "I have a vague memory about it."

"What you don't know is that the week after Mom and Dad died, I got a call from an agency I'd sent the pictures to. They loved the shots, and wanted to represent me."

"They did?"

Nikki nodded.

"So what happened?"

"Nothing," she said. "Nothing."

"You didn't pursue it?"

"Our parents had just died. Suddenly, it didn't matter anymore. And you needed me."

"So that was your dream? And you gave it up?"

Nikki nodded again. "I don't know if I would have ever made it as a model, but I wanted to try. And yeah, I gave it up."

"For me?"

"After our parents died, all that really mattered was making sure you had as much security as possible. I knew that being a model meant traveling all over the place. We'd already lost our parents. I didn't want you to lose me as well."

I took in what my sister was saying. She'd missed out on her dream because of the sacrifices she'd made for me. I suddenly felt guilty, though I knew it wasn't my fault. And I also know that if our roles had been reverse, I would have done the same thing, too.

"Maybe it's not too late," I said. "To pursue your dream."

Nikki waved off the suggestion. "It's way too late."

A beat passed. Then I said, "I'm sorry. You gave up your dream for me. I'm sorry."

"It wasn't just you. I didn't want to be flying all over the place. Risking my life for a dream. What if a plane I was on crashed because I was heading somewhere to take pictures or walk a runway?" Nikki shook her head. "It was a risk that suddenly wasn't worth it. So I went to college, met Morris. Got married, got pregnant. All that mattered was family. Protecting my family."

"In other words—and I'm not a shrink or anything— you felt that if you could control everything, nothing bad would ever happen again."

Slowly, Nikki nodded. "I didn't really think of it that way, but I guess…that makes a lot of sense."

"Unfortunately, as much as we try, we can't stop bad things from happening. We just don't have that power. Look at what happened to Eli. And yes," I said, holding up a hand. "You were ultimately right about him, but that's not the point. The point is, I have to figure out my life on my own. Make my own mistakes. And you—you can't spend the rest of your life waiting for the other shoe to drop."

Nikki drew in a deep breath. "I know you're right. And I'll try. I promise."

"You better do more than try. Because, girl, you know how to get on a person's nerve." I chuckled softly, then put my arm around her shoulder and drew her close. "I love you, sis," I went on. "And I want to see you happy. I don't believe for a second that controlling everyone is making you happy. Is it?"

"I didn't even think of my happiness."

"Well, you need to. You need to find enjoyment in life, and that's not going to come when you push people away."

Several moments passed. Then my sister pulled away from me and offered me a smile. "Thank you for this talk. I think."

I smiled back, and squeezed her hand again. I hoped this was a new start for me and my sister. The start of a closer, more genuine relationship.

I didn't expect a one-eighty over night, but as long as she was aware of her issues and tried, that was all I could ask.

"Now," Nikki said, and raised an eyebrow as she looked at me, "what about you?"

I gave her an odd look. "What do you mean?"

"Lewis?" she asked. "You were going to marry him."

"I explained that," I said, not meeting her eyes.

"And I understand. To a degree. But. It's not just that you got involved with Lewis again—and yes, you've learned your lesson, and it was your lesson to learn. I get all that. But before Lewis there was Chaz, and before Chaz, there was Eli. And Lewis. You go through one serious relationship after another one. Why?"

My sister had listened to me as I'd given her my opinion of her. It was my turn to listen—and absorb—what she was saying to me.

"You say you want me to be happy," she continued. "And I want the same for you. And this isn't being judgmental, but I don't see how you'll be happy when you don't even take time between relationships to grieve before going on."

"It's not like I was looking for new relationships," I said. "They kind of just happened."

"Mmm-hmm." My sister sounded doubtful.

"What?"

"I don't believe that. And I don't think you believe it, either."

"I don't know what you expect me to say."

"Maybe that you keep dating because you think you're a failure. That you need a man to validate your existence and be a father figure to Rayna."

I gaped at my sister, her harsh words making my heart pound wildly. "No! That's not true."

"Exactly."

I stared at her, not understanding.

"Vanessa, you're not a failure. You're a great mother, doing your best to raise your child. And you have the ability to bounce back after a crisis like no one I've ever known. So why are you selling yourself short, dating men who aren't good enough for you?"

"Chaz was good enough for me," I said. "Chaz was different."

"Maybe he was. But there are other men, Vanessa. Other men who will treat you with respect and love you with all their heart."

I shrugged. I knew in my heart that if I didn't end up with Chaz, it would be a long time before I'd even think of being with anyone else.

"I admire your spunk," my sister said. "I admire how fearless you are."

"Me? Fearless?"

"And here I am, a stay-at-home mom who's got no adventure whatsoever in her life."

"Are you kidding me? You're happily married. You're president of the P.T.A." As I said the words, I realized that my sister was right about something. As much as she'd gotten on my nerves over the years, I envied the stable marriage she had. The loyal, doting husband.

The father to her children.

"But I don't have any adventure in my life. Why do you think I want to go to Thailand for my second wedding?"

I got it, just like that. Understood what had seemed like an outrageous request. "Have you explained that to Morris? Rather than try to bully him into it?" I added, smiling.

"No."

"Then you should. Tell him why it's important to you. Talk to him, Nikki. He'll understand. And I know I said the trip would be expensive, but you can count on me. I'll be there. If it's really that important to you."

"I appreciate that," Nikki said. "It means a lot. But." She paused. "Enough about me. Back to you. And your relationship drama. If it takes you one month or ten years, I don't want to see you settle for anything less than you deserve. No more dating bigamists and criminals."

"Hey."

"I say it out of love," my sister said, smiling sweetly.

"Touché. And you're right about not settling," I agreed. "One hundred percent. The thing is, I found all that I wanted, all that I could ever want, in Chaz." I paused. Drew in a painful breath. "He called me, you know. He finally called when I was in Grand Cayman with Lewis." I shook my head, silently cursing my luck. "I was already trying to find a way to let Lewis down easy. He'd been so helpful to me, and part of me felt I owed it to him to marry him. But I couldn't do it. Once maybe, but not anymore."

"You talked to Chaz?" my sister asked.

"No. He left me a message. I didn't want to call him back until I was back home. Until I'd resolved the situation with Lewis. And then I got arrested." I dragged a hand over my face. "I already know I was all over the news. I have no doubt that Chaz saw it, or his brother. Or someone he knows who knew we were dating. Word will get back to him. And if he couldn't forgive me for lying about Rayna's father, how can I expect him to forgive me for this? For seeming to move on so quickly."

"You can't know unless you call him."

I shook my head.

"Why not?"

"Because I'm afraid," I admitted.

Morris appeared at the entrance to the living room then. "Is it safe to enter?"

"Yes," I said. "In fact, I think I'll leave you two alone."

Morris stepped toward Nikki as I walked out of the living room. I turned to see Nikki spread her arms wide to her husband.

My life might be screwed up in many ways, but at least my relationship with my sister was back on track.

And at least I wasn't going to jail.

25

It was a good thing I'd decided to stay at my sister's place, because from what Carla told me, the media had returned with a vengeance outside of my condo.

Now that I'd been arrested—even though I'd ultimately been released—the media was practically salivating, excited that there was more news pertaining to the woman who'd dated the married ballplayer. It's one thing to be the subject of media attention once—but to be involved in a second scandalous story… Well, that pretty much made me a media "star."

Of course, I wasn't at all excited at that fact, nor that status.

I stayed with my sister until Tuesday, when I returned to work to find the media lining the streets. I wasn't going to make the mistake I had in the past. I didn't give any statement.

Other than Alaina, whom I'd called while at my sister's place, I didn't want to speak to anyone at work about what happened. I think it must have been clear to everyone that

I just wasn't in the mood to discuss the crazy ordeal. Maybe the next day, but it certainly wasn't the topic of conversation I wanted to engage in the first moment I got back.

Debbie poked her head into my office at five after nine. But she must have seen the same expression on my face that others had seen, because she said, "You know what? I'll come back later."

My phone did ring quite steadily, and this time instead of engaging reporters in any conversation when they called, I simply said, "No comment," and hung up. I didn't want to take any chances that I would end up misquoted, misrepresented, or made to look like a fool in any other way.

It's probably too late for that, I told myself sourly as I sipped my grande Caramel Macchiato from Starbucks.

Pretty much, I tried to keep a low profile. I know I didn't do anything wrong, but there was that whole guilt-by-association thing. I didn't know if people would think I *had* to know about Lewis's criminal activities, but I hoped at least those in the office would be smart enough to realize that my only crime was trusting someone I clearly shouldn't have.

Lewis… I blew out a heavy breath as I thought of him. I didn't know if he was still in custody, or released on bond. A small part of me felt guilty about not even trying to check up on him. But another part—a bigger part—was pissed off as hell that he'd put me in such a predicament to begin with.

Had he tried to call me? I hadn't been home, and I'd deliberately left my cell off, so I didn't know.

"Don't even think about Lewis," I told myself as I booted up my computer. It was better that we didn't speak again.

What had happened had made it clear that we were over—irrevocably—and it was unlikely that we'd ever be friends.

My desk phone rang, interrupting my thoughts. I snatched up the receiver. "Vanessa Cain."

There was a pause, then, "Vanessa."

My chest tightened. "L-Lewis?"

"It's me, babe."

"Hi. Where are you?"

"Out on bail."

"My God, Lewis. What the hell is going on?"

"I'm in a mess of trouble, babe. But with some luck—and some good lawyers—it'll all get straightened out."

A long silence ensued. I didn't know what to say to Lewis. What I wanted from him was an explanation. But would he be honest if I asked him about the charges?

There was only one way to find out.

"Lewis…did you know that you were being investigated for illegal activity?" That seemed the softest way to frame the question.

"I can't talk about that. Not over the phone."

"I think you owe me an explanation."

"And you'll get one. In person. Can you meet me today?"

I shook my head, even though Lewis couldn't see me. "I don't think that's a good idea."

Pause. "What does that mean?"

"Come on, Lewis."

"No, tell me."

"All right." I needed to just be honest. Finally. "It means the engagement is off."

"You're dumping me? After everything I did for you?"

I didn't know how to answer that question, and said nothing for several moments. "I'm grateful, Lewis. Eternally grateful for how you helped me out." I sighed. "Can you honestly tell me that there's no basis for the charges against you?"

Now Lewis was the one who grew silent.

"In all the time you've known me, you know I'm not into…an alternative lifestyle, so to speak. I can't live a life where I'm constantly looking over my shoulder. I'm not trying to judge you, but I know what I can deal with, and what I can't. And that, I can't."

"Do you know how much I love you?" Lewis asked.

"I know you really wanted to marry me," I said. "I believe you were entirely sincere."

"I did everything I could to help you get rid of your Tassie problem. *Everything.*"

Something in Lewis's tone made a bad feeling creep over me. I wasn't sure I wanted to ask what he meant by that.

I didn't have to. He asked, "You know the pictures of Tassie and Christian Blake?"

"Of course. They made all the difference with our negotiations with Tassie."

Lewis began to chuckle.

"What?" I asked.

"Well, let's just say that it's amazing what computers can do."

At first, I didn't understand what he was saying. Rather, I don't think I wanted to understand what he was getting at. But then, I couldn't deny it, and my jaw hit the floor. "Wh-what?"

"It's not like Tassie hadn't been screwing some other guy. Hell, probably a whole baseball team. The photos of her and Christian Blake only helped seal the deal."

"They were *forged?*" I asked. I had to be sure that that's what Lewis was saying. Another thought struck me then. One that made a chill run down my spine. "You didn't have anything to do with…with what…" My voice trailed off. I couldn't say the words.

"With what happened to Tassie?" Lewis supplied.

"Yeah." I swallowed. "That."

"I told you once that I'd do anything in my power to take care of the ones I care about." For the first time, I heard something cold in Lewis's voice. Something I'd never noticed before. "The bitch was fucking with you. She needed…let's call it a wake-up call."

I gasped. Covered my mouth.

"Don't freak out, Vanessa," Lewis said gently. "I'm not an animal. I can count on one hand the amount of times I've had to…*persuade* someone with force. And I never deal with anyone I love that way. *Never.*"

If that was supposed to reassure me, it didn't. No, I'd never seen Lewis get angry. And with me, he'd never raised his voice or handled disagreements in any way but civil. But that he could deal with enemies—even if they deserved it—with force… Well, it was downright unsettling.

"The bottom line is she signed the agreement. The condo is yours."

"The police questioned me about what happened to her!" I exclaimed. Then I remembered that I was in my office and didn't want anyone to overhear what I was saying.

I continued in a lower tone, "What if they figure out you were behind the attack, and think *I* asked you to hurt her? I could go to jail, Lewis!"

"Sweetheart, relax," he said. "First of all, no one will *ever* connect you to what happened. You're not going to jail."

"I didn't want you to do that," I said. "I didn't want you to hurt her."

"I wanted her to stop hurting you. And I was never going to tell you about it, because you didn't need to know. But now… Well, I felt you needed to know just how much I've done to help you. And I also want you to know that when you're with me, you're safe. No one will ever hurt you, take advantage of you. And that includes me."

His words would have put me at ease…if they weren't so scary.

"Don't leave me now, baby," Lewis said. "Not after everything I've done for you. I was there for you when you needed me. Sure, I made some mistakes, but it's not as bad as it sounds."

"Money laundering?"

"I don't want to talk about this on the phone."

"What's the difference? The feds were watching you for God only knows how long. Watching me. Probably listening to every conversation you've had in eons." Oh, my God. The black sedan! Had it been a federal agent in the car tailing me?

"I'm a businessman," Lewis insisted.

"What does that mean?"

"If I'm guilty of anything, it's bad judgment. I guess a couple of my associates are into illegal activities, and because of my dealings with them, suspicion's fallen onto me. Now do you understand?"

I didn't respond.

"This will all get straightened out in court, Vanessa. I assure you that."

Because he was innocent…or because he had good lawyers who could get him off on a technicality or reasonable doubt?

"You believe me, don't you?" he asked.

On one hand, it was inconceivable to me that Lewis was into anything illegal. I never saw him take part in any sly dealings when I was with him on Ocean Drive, never saw any questionable characters give him a pat on the back or some elaborate handshake.

But what did I really know about what he did? He told me he sold real estate. How hard would it be for a real estate investor to launder money?

There was a reason the U.S. Marshals had had him— us—arrested in Grand Cayman. That was the one thing I couldn't get around, no matter how much I wanted to believe he was innocent.

Okay, so perhaps his hands had been dirtied unknowingly by an associate. Maybe he'd even made an error in judgment that was coming back to haunt him.

If it was a one-time thing…I could forgive him, couldn't I?

Perhaps—and that was iffy. But what I couldn't forgive was what he'd done to Tassie. That kind of violence… It was frightening, almost more-so because Lewis had seemed so casual about it. In his mind, it needed to be done, and it was done.

But my God, his actions could still come back to haunt me. *I* could be arrested for Tassie's assault—if the police tied Lewis to that and therefore assumed I'd ordered her beaten to a pulp.

"Vanessa?"

"Lewis, I'm really sorry, but I just can't do this anymore. It's—it's over. I'm sorry."

I quickly hung up the phone, hoping I would never hear from him again.

The rest of the day was business as usual, except I was pretty much hiding out in my office. No one had dared to broach the subject of my arrest when they'd come to see me regarding various business matters, and that was fine with me. My private life was my private life, and I owed no one an explanation.

Near the end of the day, however, Debbie entered my office and took a seat opposite me. Before she even spoke, I was pretty sure the suspense had finally killed her.

"I want to talk to you about something," Debbie said.

My shoulders sagged. Though I hadn't wanted to talk to any of the regular office staff about my crazy long weekend, I was finally ready to give my side to Debbie.

"I have the worst luck in the world," I said. "I honestly had no clue about Lewis and his *business.* If I had even thought for a second that he was into anything shady—"

Debbie held up a hand. "I know that," she said. "And we'll get to that. But first, I want to talk to you about planning a surprise."

Of course. She wanted me to arrange something else with Jason. I folded my hands on my desk and waited for her to speak. Some scandalous rendezvous at a downtown hotel? Me buying Jason an extravagant gift on her behalf?

"I'd like to plan a surprise party for Alaina," Debbie went on, a smile spreading on her face. I immediately felt a tad guilty for assuming the worst. "Some bottles of champagne, trays of food from a local eatery. Some pastries and desserts. It doesn't have to be over-the-top extravagant, but it needs to be nice. And ideally, I'd like it to be this week. Thursday or Friday if at all possible."

"That is a great idea!" I clapped my hands together. "Truly fantastic. And after everything Alaina's been through, a completely appropriate celebration."

"I know. That's why I wanted to do it. Every day I'm reminded of how close we came to losing her." Debbie made a face as she shook her head. "Do you think you can take care of it for this week?"

"Oh, definitely. I'll start making calls."

"And remember—it's supposed to be a surprise."

I made a motion of pulling a zipper across my lips. "She won't hear anything from me. And all the better to plan something sooner rather than later, so no one slips up and says anything to her."

"Excellent. I want Alaina to know exactly how much she means to me. To all of us." Debbie grinned, satisfied, while she crossed her arms over her chest. "Now, there's something else I want to talk to you about."

"Okay."

"It's about Jason."

I held up a hand. "Debbie, we can respectfully agree to disagree on the issue of Jason."

"Hear me out, okay?"

I nodded. "Okay."

"I wanted to tell you that I took to heart what you had to say about me, and him…and…well, I've told him that I want to cool things off."

"You did?" I was surprised.

"Yes. You gave me a lot to ponder, Vanessa. I think I need to seriously reevaluate my life, maybe even get some therapy. But bottom line, I want my marriage. And that means I have to stop doing what I'm doing with Jason."

"Debbie, I'm proud of you." I didn't plan on it, but I found myself rising from my chair and rounding my desk. I wrapped my arms around Debbie as she sat, giving her a long, hard hug. "I know it's your life, but I really do believe this is for the best."

"It is," Debbie agreed as I eased away from her. "Jason is like a toy, but I've lost interest in playing with him. Maybe that's not entirely true, but I know I have to put him in an emotional toy box, one I won't open again."

"Another bit of advice?" I said.

"Sure."

"Go to couples therapy with Ben. I think it will help."

"I plan on it," Debbie told me. "In fact, I plan to broach the subject this weekend. Maybe we can finally work through some issues."

"Good," I said. "That's really good."

"And now," Debbie began, "what the hell happened with you and Lewis? Other than the condensed story I saw on the news."

I rolled my eyes. "Perhaps we should both get a coffee from the kitchen," I suggested. "This could take a while."

26

I was just about ready to head for home when my office door flew open, startling me.

Byron was standing there. My stomach lurched. What was he doing in my office?

"Byron. What are you—"

"Arrested?" he said, cutting me off. "You were *arrested* in Grand Cayman?"

That's why he was here? "All a misunderstanding."

"And that attack on your boyfriend's wife?"

"*Estranged* wife. And I had nothing to do with that!"

"You've got the nerve to throw my gambling in my face when you're exposing Rayna to all kinds of shit? I won't allow you to make some drug dealer her father!"

"Keep your voice down," I said.

"Don't tell me to keep my voice down. Rayna is *my* daughter. You don't think I care about how you raise her?"

"You haven't cared about Rayna since before she was born!" I shot back. "All you cared about was easy cash!"

"But drug dealing is okay in your book?" Byron returned.

"I had no clue about Lewis's business. Now that I do, it's over. He won't get near Rayna again. The same way I keep her from anyone into anything shady." I gave Byron a pointed look.

"I've worked on my issues. I needed some time to do that, okay?"

"I'm supposed to believe you? The same way you expected me to believe some thief had broken in to our apartment and stolen my mother's jewelry?"

"You need to get over the past already, especially since you're clearly not as perfect as you want to pretend. I want to see Rayna. Today."

For a few seconds, I said nothing. I was momentarily stunned. Then my brain kicked in. "No."

"Yes."

"No! You're not going to see Rayna. You have no paternal rights where she's concerned."

Byron's lips twisted in a scowl as he stared at me. "We'll see about that."

Was he delusional? "Get out of my office."

Byron made no move to leave. "You listen to me, and you listen to me good. Things are going to change where Rayna's concerned."

"Get out," I repeated. I put my hand on his arm and gave him a little push.

In a quick motion, Bryon had his fingers wrapped around my upper arm. He squeezed—hard.

"Ow! You're hurting me!"

"Things are going to change," he repeated. His gaze was dark. Alarming.

I jerked my arm away, determined not to let him intimidate me. "Get out now. Before I call security."

He turned then, walking to the door. When he stepped over the threshold, he faced me with a hard expression. "Remember what I said."

I slammed the door shut. I wanted to scream at the top of my lungs, but I knew I couldn't. Not here. Instead, I pounded my fist on the door to release some of my pent-up aggravation.

What the hell had gotten into Byron? How dare he barge into my office and tell me that things were going to change? Was he suddenly so concerned about being a father because his mother was getting on his case? I had hoped he'd go away, but he was being far more persistent that I'd imagined.

I want to see Rayna. Today.

Panic gripped me as I recalled not only his words, but the determined way in which he'd said them. I hustled to my desk, and reached for the receiver. It rang before I could snatch it up.

Putting the receiver to my ear, I said, "Vanessa Cain."

"Girl, what the hell just happened?" It was Alaina. "I saw Byron—"

"Alaina, let me call you back," I said hurriedly. "I need to call my babysitter."

"Oh." She sounded concerned. "All right."

I ended the call with her and immediately punched in

the number to Carla's place. The phone rang twice before she answered.

"Hello?"

"Carla, it's me."

"What's up?"

"Has everything…is everything okay over there?"

"Of course. Why?"

I took a deep breath. Rubbed my arm where Bryon had squeezed it. "Something crazy just happened. *Byron* showed up in my office. Said he wants to see Rayna today. Demanded, really. So, I'm a bit worried that he might try showing up there."

"He doesn't know where I live, right?"

"Right." My panic slowly dissipated. Byron was such a nonexistent part of Rayna's life that I didn't have him on any emergency contact forms. And he sure as hell didn't have Carla's information.

But he did know the building where I lived, thanks to all the press coverage after Eli's death, and what if he hung around, hoping to see Rayna somewhere?

"I just think it's best if you stay inside with the girls. In case Byron starts hanging around trying to cause trouble."

"Okay. I was going to take them to the park for a bit, but we'll stay in instead."

"Thanks."

I felt better after my talk with Carla, and decided that when I got home, I would hang out at Carla's place for a while in case Byron showed up.

I didn't think he would, though. I mean, the guy didn't

really want anything to do with Rayna. He did, however, like making my life difficult.

As I sat and stewed for a minute, I remembered that I hadn't called Alaina back, and she had to be wondering what was going on. So I pressed the button to enable the speaker phone and called the reception desk.

"Vanessa?" Alaina said.

"You got a minute?"

"Tell me what happened."

I filled Alaina in on what had happened with Byron, and ended by saying, "So what do you think? I mean, you think he's trying to make me sweat, or has his paternal urge finally kicked in?"

"I think we should talk about it over some food, because I know you didn't have lunch. It'll be my treat."

Twenty minutes later, Alaina and I were at Bayside, enjoying lattes while we waited for our burgers and fries.

"Do you believe Byron?" I asked. "Showing up like that?"

"I wouldn't worry about him," Alaina said. "He can't honestly expect to be part of Rayna's life now."

"Exactly. He can't expect to get any sort of custody now."

"And that's what the judge will say." Alaina sipped her coffee. "Don't worry."

I frowned. "I don't know… What if it's not as simple as that? The whole thing with the arrest in the Cayman Islands…"

"You were cleared."

"Yeah, but Lewis is going to trial. Byron said something about me exposing Rayna to bad influences. What if a judge—"

"You can count on one hand the amount of times Byron has seen Rayna. Or sent money for her. A judge would have to be on crack to even think of allowing him visitation, much less any kind of custody agreement."

I sipped more coffee. "You're right. I know you're right. I guess it just freaked me out. And not so much because I believe that a judge would give Byron custody. But because I don't want him suddenly showing up, trying to be a part of her life." I paused. "When he walked away from me while I was pregnant, I was devastated. Then, when Rayna was born, he came around a couple times in the first two weeks, and I really wanted to give him the benefit of the doubt. I didn't want to push him out of Rayna's life. I wanted to give him time to get comfortable with the idea of being a father. But then he stopped coming around. And that broke my heart, Alaina. Not because I cared about being with him anymore. But because I knew that if he was a once-in-a-while father, that could destroy Rayna. Then there was that story about the gambler whose daughter was killed by a loan shark..." I'd called Alaina after the news story broke, crying as I relayed it to her. "I realized I had to protect Rayna. Even if that meant protecting her from her own father."

"I know."

"You think I wanted to keep Byron out of Rayna's life? I'm not the kind of person who would ever try to punish an ex by keeping his child from him. But Byron was more interested in gambling."

"Hey, you don't have to convince me."

"If I thought he'd changed—really changed—as much as

I can't stand him, I would try to find a way to reintroduce him to Rayna and help build that relationship. But for him to come into my office acting like a jerk, grabbing my arm with such force…you tell me how he's changed? He's the same ass he always was. And if he tries to be a part of Rayna's life now, I *know* he's going to hurt her."

"Hey," Alaina said softly. "I know you're worried, but try not to be. This is what Byron wanted. To give you a few hours of stress."

I nodded, Alaina's words making sense. "I guess you're right."

"No, I *am* right. And if he gets the bright idea to start showing up at your place or lurking around your building, you call the police. Or get a restraining order. Whatever you have to do."

I nodded again.

"Now, any word from Chaz?"

"Are you kidding? After that story broke about me and Lewis?" I shook my head, wanting to cry. Why was nothing in my life ever simple? Why couldn't Chaz have reached out *before* my trip to Grand Cayman? I never would have gone away with Lewis. Never. But I had, and everything had changed. Now I was too humiliated to call Chaz, knowing he'd have read all about me and Lewis. He would never want me now.

"I don't expect to hear from him ever again," I added sadly.

But with Byron harassing me and the whole crazy situation with Lewis, I was beginning to realize that winning Chaz back was the least of my problems.

"Well, I have news," Alaina said.

"About Jorge?"

"No. No news on the trial date yet."

"Then what?"

"It's about me and Mike." A smile slowly grew on her face. "He told me he loved me last night."

"Oh, Ally," I said, grinning. "That is great news."

Alaina pulled her purse onto her lap and reached into it. She fiddled around, doing something I couldn't see because the table between us obstructed my view.

I eyed her curiously. "What are you doing?"

Her hands stopped moving. Then, her smile getting bigger, she raised her left hand onto the table, showing off a beautiful, cushion-cut engagement ring.

My mouth fell open. "Ally…"

"He proposed!" she exclaimed, so happy she actually bounced around in her seat.

"Oh, my God!"

"I know. I couldn't believe it, but I'm so happy, Vanessa. He's the one."

Despite my happiness for Alaina, a stab of pain pierced my heart. She was getting her happy ending. A well-deserved, long overdue one.

And yet, I couldn't help thinking about the fact that I wasn't as lucky.

27

Thursday bright and early, I got a call from a producer from *20/20*. I was surprised, though I shouldn't have been. It wasn't just my arrest in the Cayman Islands that made me an interesting prospect. It was the whole sordid affair with Eli, the estranged wife and kids he'd never told me about, and the way I'd been the subject of the media after that. Suddenly, people knew my name—but for all the wrong reasons.

"It would be a casual chat about your involvement with Lewis, how your trip to the Cayman Islands turned into something you never expected."

"Right," I said sarcastically. "Casual chat."

The man clearly missed the sarcasm in my tone. "Exactly. We want to hear from you, an ordinary woman…and single mother, right?"

"Yes."

"Your story is the kind that women across the country will relate to. Dating someone who ends up being far different from the person you expect. First, you had that bad luck with Eli Johnson, a story that's still fresh in many women's minds. Now this tragedy in the Cayman Islands… This is the kind of story that is perfect for our show."

"I'm not interested."

"I assure you, we'll handle—"

"I'm not interested," I repeated. "Thank you for your call, though."

I heard the beginning of a protest, but I hung up the phone. I knew all about how sensitively the media handled scandalous topics.

There would be photos taken of me in my grief, voice-overs about my single-mother status and how I'd failed to find a decent man. Perhaps even an interview with Chaz about my failed relationship with him.

The media coverage of me after Eli's death had been bad enough. After *20/20* coverage of the story, I'd have to move to China.

Alaina joked that I had become a "star," and it was such a weird feeling to actually have producers calling to either book me on their shows, or talk about making a TV movie about my life. One day, this would all die down, I was sure.

I just wished that day was today.

When five o'clock rolled around, I told Alaina that I needed her. Needed to have a bitch session over a couple of drinks.

I pretended to be distraught, leading her to believe that I'd heard from Chaz and that he no longer wanted to see me. In reality, I needed to get her out of the office so the caterers could bring in the trays of meat, cheese and pastries for the surprise party we were having for her.

"That's so hard to believe," Alaina said as we walked from Bayside. "Why would he call you, want to see you, only to call you back and say he's not interested in you?"

I tried my best to look devastated. "I don't understand."

"Sounds like he's on the fence about you, not sure what to do." Alaina frowned. "But, you know what—as much as I hate to say it, if he's being so damn wishy-washy, then you've got to move on. Forget about him and move on."

"I know," I said sadly. "I know." Then I quickly said, "Oh, gosh. I forgot something upstairs. Will you head back up with me?"

"If you want," Alaina said, shrugging. I'm sure she was wondering why I needed her to go back up to the office with me when we were both going to be heading home.

"Thanks. By the way, what's the latest with Jorge?"

"Nothing. At some point, a trial date will be set. I only hope it's soon."

We strolled back into the building, where I winked at Edgar, whom I'd asked to call upstairs and alert the office when he saw me and Alaina return. Alaina and I rode the elevator to the agency's floor.

As soon as we walked into the agency, everyone yelled, "Surprise!"

Alaina stopped in her tracks, glancing around in confusion. But it took only a couple more seconds for her to get it. And then her face erupted in a megawatt grin.

"You knew," she said, turning to me.

"Of course I knew." I hugged her. "Welcome back."

"So that whole talk about Chaz—it was all a lie?"

I nodded. "I haven't heard from him."

"No wonder you didn't seem particularly torn up."

I shrugged and smiled sweetly.

The office personnel made the rounds, giving Alaina hugs and telling her how happy they were that she almost entirely recovered from her injuries. We all wandered into the conference room, where the spread of food was laid out on the tables, as well as the bottles of wine and champagne.

"Everyone get some champagne," Debbie instructed us. When we all had some in our glasses, she raised hers in toast. "To Alaina. For having the courage to fight. We love you, girl."

"Hear! Hear!" I exclaimed, adding a hoot before sipping from my glass.

After the toast, the music began. It was a CD of instrumental music that Debbie's secretary had brought in.

My eyes volleyed over the happy crowd. Alaina was truly surprised. That much had been obvious. Thankfully, no one had let the news of the party slip.

Everyone who worked for the agency was there. Ben, Debbie's husband, was also there. He was across the room, standing near a window, near a few people but clearly on his own. I was glad to see him out, because it meant that Debbie was serious about wanting to get her marriage back on track, so much so that she'd invited him to an office function.

I offered Ben a wave. He waved back.

I turned. Mingled through the crowd, making small talk, and laughing. Generally rejoicing in Alaina's recovery. With her cast now off, she looked pretty much as good as new.

When my eyes wandered in Ben's direction again, I noticed that he was looking at me. Staring, really. He didn't turn away once it was clear his gaze had lingered too long.

How odd. And a little unnerving.

I didn't get the sense that he was ogling me. Nothing about his gaze seemed sexual.

I turned away, saw Alaina at my side. "Hey, you." I nudged an arm against hers. "Having fun?"

"Yeah, this is fun. Very nice." She leaned close and whispered, "Okay. Fess up. How'd you get Debbie to agree to have this party for me?"

"Actually, it was Debbie's idea."

Alaina looked doubtful.

"I swear," I said. "She suggested it—but you know I planned it."

"I'm in shock," Alaina said.

"Why?"

"I can't believe she'd want to have a party like this for me."

"Why not? I think we all needed it. The weeks without you here were awful—for everyone."

"Vanessa?"

At the sound of the male voice, I turned. Ben was standing there.

"Hi, Ben," I said pleasantly. "Are you having a good time?"

He nodded absently. "Can I speak with you for a minute? Privately?"

"Sure." I threw a glance across the room at Debbie, who was laughing and speaking with Jack Crawford, one of her

Miami clients. Jack was a fitness guru who produced videos on getting fit and sold them by the thousands.

"Privately," Ben reiterated, placing a hand on my elbow.

"Okay," I told him. "We can go to my office."

I led the way there, Ben walking in step beside me. "What do you want to talk about?" I asked when we reached my office.

Ben closed the door, then exhaled sharply before meeting my eyes. When he did, he gave me a pointed look and asked, "Is my wife having an affair?"

"Wh-what?" I sputtered.

"I know she was. About a month ago. What I want to know is if she's still having the affair."

"Ben, I—I—" I didn't know what to say. And I sure as hell didn't know why he'd decided to ask me this loaded question.

"I need to know, Vanessa."

It really wasn't my place to tell him. Especially not after Debbie's decision to end the affair with Jason. So I did the only thing I could do. I lied. "If she is, I don't know about it." When Ben didn't seem convinced, I went on. "But I know she loves you. She's committed to your marriage and your family."

"You ever see a young guy come around here to see her? Probably twenty, twenty-two?"

Does he know? I wondered, suddenly panicked. *Does he know that Jason went to Phoenix with Debbie?*

"Ben," I began slowly, "I'm not comfortable with this conversation."

He held up a hand. "All right. I'm sorry. It's just… Never mind. I shouldn't have brought you into this."

Thank God. I didn't want to get into the middle of Ben and Debbie's marriage. I didn't want to have to look at Ben and lie to him anymore, and I didn't want Debbie getting angry with me for even talking to Ben about their relationship.

"It's okay." I walked past Ben to the door and opened it, then gestured for him to head out of my office first.

"If you don't mind," Ben said when we were in the hallway, "I'd prefer you didn't mention our conversation to Debbie."

"It never happened," I said, smiling uncomfortably.

"I guess I'm just a bit paranoid," Ben explained as we walked back toward the conference room. "But like I said, forget I ever mentioned it."

"No worries."

No sooner had I uttered the words than we reached the open conference doors. And I sensed the change in Ben immediately as he stared into the room. His expression morphed into something very dark.

And very frightening.

I followed his line of sight—and saw the cause for his instantly foul mood.

Jason.

He must have arrived in the short time Ben and I had been in my office. He already had a flute of champagne and was crossing the room toward Debbie.

An enraged primal sound erupted from Ben's throat. And then he surged forward, straight for Jason.

Jason whirled around, his eyes bulging in shock when he saw Ben. Ben said nothing to him, just threw a punch that knocked him backward onto the conference table. His body slammed into a bottle of champagne, knocking it over.

Collective gasps filled the room. But Debbie's eyes grew wide with outrage. "Ben!"

"Whore!" Ben yelled. "I knew it wasn't over. I knew it!"

Then he spun around and stalked out of the boardroom.

Everyone in the room watched Debbie, waiting to see what she was going to do. Her chest rose and fell in anger, but she let Ben leave without going after him.

I saw the looks of confusion on all of the staff members' faces. They were wondering why Ben would deck Jason.

Debbie realized the same thing.

She walked briskly toward Jason, who was nursing his injured jaw. His eyes lit up when she reached him.

"What the heck's his problem?" Jason asked.

"You need to leave," Debbie said sternly.

"What?"

"You were not invited," Debbie continued, slowly. Clearly. "Leave now."

"Fine." Jason threw his hands in the air and scowled. "Whatever."

Everyone watched as Jason left the room, all of us wondering what would happen next. Someone had even turned down the music.

Several seconds passed. "Enough theatrics," Debbie announced. "Paul, turn up the music. Let's continue the party."

The party continued, but it wasn't the same. Debbie's dirty little secret was now very public.

It was sad for me to even think this, but I was thankful to know that the office rumor mill would now move from my sordid life, to the boss's.

28

An attractive black woman was standing in the lobby of my office building when I was finally heading home from the party for Alaina. I didn't think anything of it until she met my gaze and began to approach me.

"Excuse me?" she said.

She was well-dressed. Some sort of businesswoman, I guessed. An undercover agent?

"Yes?" I said warily.

She produced a business card. "My name is Monica Sheffield. I'm Byron's new girlfriend."

My spine went rigid. "Byron's new girlfriend," I repeated.

"Yes. Rayna's father."

I looked at the card. It read Monica Sheffield, Attorney at Law. The card didn't state what kind of law, and the quality was so cheap, I had the feeling Monica had made them herself on a laser printer.

"What do you want?" I asked.

She hesitated, as though carefully considering her next words. "I wanted you to meet me," she said after a moment. "Meet me and know that I'm a decent person. Not some drug addict."

"So Byron was able to land a decent girlfriend. What does that have to do with me?"

Again, a pause. I studied the woman's face, raising my eyebrows as I did.

"If Rayna is going to spend time with Byron, she's going to be spending time with me. So—"

"Whoa," I said, shooting a hand up to quiet the woman. "What did you just say?"

"If Rayna is going to be spending time with Byron—"

"Rayna will be spending *no* time with Byron," I said. "He abandoned her before she was born."

The woman sighed softly, clearly not liking what I'd said. "We were afraid of this."

"Afraid of what?" I asked testily.

"That you would make this difficult. You're only delaying the inevitable."

"And what would the inevitable be?"

"Sharing custody of Rayna with Byron."

For a few seconds, I didn't speak. I was so livid, I knew I might regret the words that would come out of my mouth if I said anything.

"Tell me something," I began. "You have any jewelry that's gone missing?"

"Excuse me?"

"It might be something small. Something you wouldn't notice missing. At first. Like a bracelet you wear only on special occasions." I glanced down at the woman's feet. She was wearing a pair of designer shoes. "Or maybe you'll find a pair of Ferragamo slingbacks missing from your closet."

"What are you talking about?"

Was there a hint of discomfort in the woman's brown eyes? "Cash. I'm talking about cash. Byron will do whatever he can to get his hands on it, thanks to that little gambling problem of his."

The woman's back stiffened. I had a feeling I'd hit a nerve.

"I'm not here to talk about anything other than your daughter. I know you want what's best for her."

"Trust me lady, that is *not* Byron."

Her soft expression hardened ever so slightly. "You need to know that this is a fight we'll take to the courts."

"Oh, really?"

"We'd prefer it doesn't go that route. That you and Byron come to some sort of agreement."

"What does Byron think—that this is a Tyler Perry movie? That all he has to do is find himself a lawyer girlfriend and he'll suddenly get custody of his child like in *Daddy's Little Girls?*" I paused briefly. "You tell Byron that there's no way in hell I'm going to discuss any sort of custody agreement. He forfeited his rights to Rayna long before she was born."

And with that, I exited the building and stormed down the street.

I was fuming. Absolutely livid at Byron's gall.

But I was also frightened.

This was a nightmare coming true. Rayna's deadbeat father finally wanting to be a part of her life.

★ ★ ★

Things only got worse as I headed home. I had thought—or perhaps hoped—that with Lewis's arrest, I wouldn't see any more suspicious cars tailing me. I'd come to the conclusion that a federal agent, or agents, had been following me around, watching what I did and the places I frequented.

So I was extremely surprised to notice a black sedan that seemed to be keeping a fairly close distance to me, matching the moves I made as I traveled the interstate.

"What the hell?" I muttered. Staring in the rearview mirror, I tried to see if I could glimpse who was behind the wheel. The dark tint prevented me from being able to see inside the car. I didn't know if it was a man or a woman.

But with each moment that passed, I did know the person was following me.

Did the authorities not believe me? Did they still feel I was in some way connected to what Lewis had done?

I maneuvered into the left lane, and the car did the same a moment later. Once I reached the other side of the bridge to South Beach, I turned left onto Alton Road.

The sedan did the same.

My hands grew sweaty on my steering wheel. I'd already had a fender bender, and didn't want another one. Not on account of some jerk who was stalking me from behind the wheel. What the hell did this person want? Instead of following me by car, I wished he or she would just leave me a note, or tell me off somewhere for goodness sake. I couldn't take any more of this surreptitious bullshit.

I drove north, did what I was getting quite good at now, and tried to evade the person in the car. If it was a cop, he was very irresponsible, putting me at risk of getting into an accident by following me around like a stalker. I didn't go quite as fast as I had on the day I got into an accident, but I did try to be clever, making lane changes and turns at the last minute.

After a few minutes of driving like a crazy person, I turned south and headed for home. I no longer noticed the black sedan in my rearview mirror. But I couldn't feel relieved, because I was certain the car would turn up again in the future.

It was kind of like trying to get rid of a cockroach—a futile effort.

Five minutes later, I was pulling into my spot in my building's parking garage. I got out of the car and started for the exit.

That's when I noticed something moving in the shadows, startling the hell out of me. And when I saw a tall, buff man emerge, I gasped.

I stood rooted to the spot, clutching my purse under my arm, trying to decide if I should try and jump back in my car and take off or make a run for it.

To my surprise, I found myself standing my ground. "Are you the person who's been following me?" I demanded.

"Yes," the man said. He was dark-skinned and bald.

"Are you a cop? A fed?"

"Hell, no."

"Then what the hell do you want with me?" I figured it was best to appear tough. If I sounded tough, he might not mess with me if he was up to no good.

"I'm trying to protect you," the man said.

"Protect me?" I asked, guffawing.

"Yes."

"Protect me? You've been scaring the hell out of me!"

"That's because you freaked out when you realized I was tailing you."

"Of course I freaked out. I'm not used to having people tail me on the freeway."

The man took a step toward me. I took a step back.

He stopped, held up both hands. "I've got no weapons. See?"

He might not have any weapons, but he did have two powerful arms. I might be able to put up a good fight, but there was no way in hell I was as strong as him.

"I'm following you because of Lewis," the man went on.

I stared at him, not registering his words. "Lewis?"

"Yeah. Your fiancé."

Ex-fiancé, I thought, but didn't bother to say. "Why are you following me because of Lewis?"

"Because he's concerned for your safety. He wants to make sure you've got constant protection."

I actually made a face, that's how unbelievable this all was. "Why would he be concerned for my safety?"

"Because. Some of his business associates might be a little…unhappy because of his arrest. He worries they might try to get to you to get to him."

The man's words put me at ease. "That kind of stuff only happens in the movies, or on shows like *The Sopranos,*" I said, waving off his concern. "I'm perfectly fine."

"Maybe. Maybe not."

"Have you noticed any sign of trouble when you've been following me?" I asked.

"No," the man admitted. "I haven't."

"I think it's really unlikely his *associates* know about me, much less are after me." And truth be told, I was far more concerned about the fact that Lewis still considered himself my fiancé. We were as done as burnt turkey dinner.

The man continued toward me, his right hand outstretched. "My name's Jay," he told me.

"Vanessa," I said, shaking his hand. "Of course, you already know that."

"I just wanted you to know who I am, so if you see me tailing you, you don't freak out again. Lewis gave me shit for causing you to get into that small accident a couple weeks back. Since then, you haven't noticed me, and that's good."

"Wait a minute. I thought you said you were protecting me because Lewis's associates might be upset regarding his arrest. But when you were following me before, he hadn't been arrested yet."

"No. But Lewis mentioned your daughter's father might give you some trouble."

And what would Lewis do to Byron—take care of him the way he'd taken care of Tassie?

"Really, I don't need your help. But thank you anyway."

"Just let me do my job, Vanessa."

His job. Now I had some sort of underworld character being my bodyguard? How much more bizarre could my life get?

My fiancé had been murdered while in the arms of

another woman, shot dead with a bow and arrow that went through both of their bodies. Then the media—and Tassie Johnson—had made my life hell. I'd met Chaz, fallen in love, then lost him because of a lie. But the most shocking thing, by far, was my humiliating arrest in Grand Cayman.

I'd gone through a lifetime worth of drama in less than four months.

I was ready to move to the suburbs and spend the rest of my days living out a boring, predictable existence.

With Chaz.

"Lewis says he misses you," Jay said suddenly. "He knows you're busy, but still, he'd love a call from you."

What? Was Lewis now letting Jay do his bidding? That wasn't the Lewis I knew.

My stomach sank nonetheless, knowing that Lewis still hoped to hear from me. The last time I'd talked to him, I'd made it very clear that we were through. Was he using Jay as a ploy to get through to me? Hell, was this whole "someone could be after you" thing a ploy to get close to me again?

"Jay, I won't freak out the next time I see you," I promised. "And tell Lewis that I've been really busy. I'll try to call him when I can."

A lie, but Jay didn't need to know that.

"Sure will."

"I'm going into my building now," I said. "You're free to go," I added, not sure what people were supposed to say in situations like this. What I did know was that Jay following me as I traveled around wasn't going to make me feel safer.

In fact, I knew that with him on my tail, I would think of possible danger. And possible danger made a woman feel far from safe.

29

Friday morning, I poked my head into Debbie's office to see how she was doing after last night's debacle.

"Hey, Debbie," I said. "Is it okay to come in?"

Her office chair was facing the window, and she didn't turn around. "Sure."

Her voice sounded...off. I stepped into the office and closed the door behind me. "Debbie? Are you okay?"

"Mmm-hmm. Fine."

And I knew she was lying. I could tell by her voice that she was crying.

I hurried farther into the office now, rounding her desk and stepping in front of her chair. Debbie's eyes were red and swollen.

"Debbie," I said, alarmed. "Oh, no. What happened?" But even though I asked the question, I had a fairly good idea.

Debbie buried her face in her hands and cried for several seconds. I'd never seen her like this, except once when she'd been drinking, and I didn't know what to say. Had there been some sort of disaster with one of her clients?

"Debbie?" I placed a gentle hand on her shoulder.

"He left me," she said softly. "He left me and took the kids with him."

"Oh, no. Oh, sweetie."

Debbie brushed at her tears and fully faced me. "Apparently, he hired some detective to follow me. He got pictures of me in Phoenix with Jason."

"Shit," I muttered.

"I invited him to the party last night, hoping for a new start for us, but he came only with the intention to confront Jason."

"That he did," I said, remembering the public spectacle. Everyone was bound to gossip about it today.

"The hell of it is, I'd decided after Phoenix to end it with Jason. I suddenly realized that I was being completely unfair to Ben, and to our kids. Especially after talking to you. But Ben doesn't believe me. He says he can't trust me. He won't hear anything I have to say."

I eased my butt against the edge of Debbie's desk. "When did he leave?"

"Last night. By the time I got home, he was gone."

I sighed sadly. "Where's he staying?"

"In Tallahassee with his parents." Debbie began to cry softly. "I can't even see my kids...."

I stretched sideways to hug Debbie. There was no point in telling her "I told you so." I'd warned her against taking Jason to Phoenix with her, and like she always had, she'd told me she was a big girl who could make her own decisions.

This wasn't the time to rub salt in her wound. I could only try to comfort her as much as possible.

"I'm sorry, sweetie," I said. "I'm so sorry."

Debbie sniffled. "You warned me. But I wouldn't listen."

"Right now, you have to figure out how you're going to deal with this. You have to call Ben, apologize. Tell him how much you love him and your family, and offer to go to counseling."

"I think it may be too late. Especially since he forgave me the first time."

"It's never too late," I said. I didn't know if that was true or not, but I knew it was what Debbie needed to hear. "But you're going to have to be honest, Debbie. Tell Ben about your father, and how he breached your trust in the beginning of your marriage." Debbie had once told me that on the night she gave birth to her first son, Ben hadn't been there for the delivery. He couldn't be reached. When he did make it to the hospital, he admitted that he'd been with a female colleague who tried to seduce him. Ben had been guilt-ridden, claimed there was no sex, and immediately stopped working with the woman. But Debbie, whose father had abandoned her and her mother when she was only nine years old, had been scarred. Ben's near-affair eradicated any trust in men she might have had left. Unable to deal with her own insecurity, she began having affairs as a way to guard her heart. "And I think that if you tell him you're willing to go to marriage counseling, that will make the difference," I added.

I offered Debbie her tissue box. She pulled out a few and proceeded to blow her nose.

"Can I guarantee that he'll take you back with open arms?" I asked. "No. But all I can tell you, Debbie, is that you have to be willing to fight for your husband. If you still love him."

"I do," Debbie said. "This has made me realize how much."

But she'd hated being vulnerable. Which is what her affairs had been about.

If Ben left her, he'd be well within his rights. That was the problem with infidelity. You didn't just hurt your spouse or lover. You hurt your family. In this case, Debbie's children. They wouldn't be happy if she was suddenly cut out of their lives.

I'd be willing to bet that this was a lesson Debbie would only have to learn once.

But in the end, the ball was in Ben's court. If he didn't want to forgive her, that was the price she would have to pay for her sins.

I was boiling water when the phone rang. I spun away from the stove, grabbed the receiver off the wall base and then turned right back to the pot, where I'd been about to put spaghetti noodles. "Hello?"

Silence. No, wait. Was that a sniffle? Yes, it was definitely a sniffle.

"Vanessa," came the low, sorrow-filled voice.

My spine went rigid with concern. "Nikki?"

"Uh-huh."

"Oh, God. What's wrong?"

"It's—it's Morris."

Lord have mercy. Not more drama with my sister's marriage. "I thought you two had worked out all your problems."

"I think he's cheating again," my sister sobbed.

"What?" I shrieked.

"Yeah."

"I can't believe it. After what happened the last time?" I still couldn't believe my brother-in-law had contracted an STD, then my sister had ended up arrested when she'd torched his clothes on the lawn…and assaulted an officer. Somehow, after all that, they'd stayed together, with Morris swearing he'd learned his lesson and would *never* cheat again.

"I need you, Vanessa. Can you come over? Help me pack up Morris's things?"

"Hold up a second, Nikki. Are you sure? Because after the last time, I find it really hard to believe that Morris would—"

"Fine. Abandon me in my hour of need."

"I'm not abandoning you."

"Then are you coming over?"

I gritted my teeth. "I'm in the middle of cooking dinner."

"I'll order a pizza. It should be here by the time you get here. Please, just come right away."

"Maybe I should call my babysitter."

"Don't be silly," my sister said, her voice suddenly normal. "Rayna can play with her cousins while we talk."

"You're sure?"

"Of course I'm sure." She sighed wearily. "That's the only thing I am sure about," she added sadly.

"All right, then. We're on our way."

★ ★ ★

Thirty minutes later, I was pulling in to my sister's driveway. Morris's car was there—which I considered a bad sign.

Oh, Lord, what am I getting myself into? I couldn't help thinking that the decision to bring Rayna along was a bad one, because if Morris was here, God only knew what kind of fighting was going on inside.

Rayna was content in her car seat, watching a *My Little Pony* movie, so I dug my cell phone out of my purse and called my sister's number. She answered on the first ring.

"Hey," I said without preamble. "I'm in your driveway. Morris is inside?"

"I'll come out to meet you," my sister said, then hung up.

A few seconds later, she was flying out the front door. My heart slammed against my rib cage. I expected to see Morris running after her.

And then I noticed that she didn't look all that upset.

Had I driven over here just for her to tell me that everything was a misunderstanding?

She was gesturing to me, beckoning for me to open the door. I hit the button to release the locks.

My sister promptly went to Rayna's side of the car, opened the door, then unfastened Rayna from her car seat. "Hi, baby," she cooed. "Come to Auntie Nikki."

I stepped out of the car, staring oddly at my sister. She certainly wasn't acting like the distraught woman she'd been on the phone. However, she was likely trying to act normally for Rayna, and if that were the case, I could understand.

"What's going on inside?" I asked, walking around the car to meet my sister.

Her smile faltered. "I need you to talk to Morris."

"What do you want me to say to him? Maybe I should take the kids somewhere while you two work things out."

"Please, just go inside."

"Okay."

I started toward the door, with my sister lagging behind me. It was slightly ajar, so I pushed it open.

I'm not sure what I expected to see—the house in disarray, a couple suitcases, perhaps some broken dishes.

I did *not* expect to see Morris standing casually in the living room, chatting amicably with a tall black man.

"Vanessa," Morris said warmly. The man he was talking to turned, and I saw then that he was very attractive. He flashed a charming smile.

Morris started toward me. Completely confused, I didn't say a word. I was trying to figure out what was going on. Was this guy a real estate agent? A divorce lawyer?

"Vanessa, this is Matthew Bassett."

Matthew extended a hand to me. "But you can call me Matt."

Still confused, I gave him my hand. He shook it firmly, still smiling at me.

"Are you a lawyer?" I asked.

Behind me, I heard my sister's light laughter. "No, Matt isn't a lawyer."

I turned to her. Her smile was so bright, I found myself wondering if she had a split personality. One minute, she was freaking out over Morris. The next, she was acting like she didn't have a care in the world.

"I'm a mortgage broker," Matt explained.

So he *was* here about the sale of the house.

"And Matt," my sister began, moving to stand beside him, "is your date for the night."

"Come again?" I asked, blinking rapidly.

"Nikki?" Morris said, his tone relaying his mild surprise. "I thought—"

"I figured it was best to get her here," my sister said.

"Wait a second." I held up a hand. "What is going on?"

"We're going out for dinner," my sister said cheerfully.

I glared at my sister, who pretended not to notice. "You told me—"

"The babysitter's in the back with the boys. Ready to go see your cousins?" Nikki asked Rayna.

Rayna's face lit up. "Yes!"

"Excuse me," Nikki said, and started out of the living room.

Whatever was going on, I was pretty damn sure that my sister had lured me here under false pretenses, and I was now seething. I forced a fake smile onto my face as I turned to look at Morris and Matt. "I'll be right back."

I hustled through the kitchen after my sister. She had to know I was behind her, and yet she continued, making nice talk with Rayna, until she got to the patio doors. Then she let Rayna down, opened the door and Rayna took off for her cousins outside.

With Rayna out of earshot, I asked, "What the heck is going on?"

Nikki turned around and started moving back toward the living room. "We've got reservations for six-thirty at Bahama Breeze."

"Oh, no, you don't." I grabbed her by her upper arm, forcing her to stop. "That's not what I mean, and you know it."

Nikki gave me an exasperated look as she stared at me. "Okay. I told a little white lie."

"Little white lie? You had me thinking it was World War Three up in here. That's no little white lie." I shook my head. "Why?"

"Because." She blew out a breath. "Because I knew that if I told you what tonight was really about, you wouldn't come."

My eyebrows shot up. "And what *is* tonight about?"

She hesitated, which had me alarmed. My sister was never at a loss for words.

"Nikki?"

"It's about…it's about you and Matt."

Five seconds passed, and then my sister's meaning hit me like a slap in the face. "Are you… This is a *blind date?*"

"He's a nice guy, Vanessa. He's got a daughter, who's five."

"And some wife whose heart he broke?" I supplied.

"No. Matt's not like that. His wife died last year. Of cancer. It was devastating for him. He's finally ready to start dating again."

"Great. So you want to set me up with someone who lost his wife. Probably was the love of his life, too." As far as I was concerned, a guy who'd lost his wife like that—she could be in his heart forever.

"He's a nice guy," my sister reiterated. "Please don't say no. Lord knows your track record in choosing your own men."

"Hey."

"Look, it's just dinner. A nice time with all four of us."

"You could have just told me what was going on."

"Then you wouldn't have come."

"This is true. But still. I'm not even wearing any makeup."

"You don't need makeup. You're beautiful just the way you are."

Was that a compliment from my sister's lips? More likely, she was trying to butter me up.

"The dress is okay," she went on. "It's cute." She reached out and fluffed my hair. "All you have to do is comb your hair a bit, add a little lipstick if you like…" My sister smiled. "This'll be fun."

30

"So," Matt said to me once the round of drinks had arrived. We'd all opted for margaritas. "You have one daughter?"

"Yes."

"She's beautiful."

"Thank you."

"I have a daughter, too."

"My sister mentioned that. She's five?"

"Yes. She's the light of my life." His face lit up as he spoke, underscoring his words.

"I feel the same way about my daughter."

"Rayna?"

"Yes."

"That's a nice name."

"Thank you. What's your daughter's name?"

"Chantelle." He paused. "But I like to call her by her middle name, Janine. That was, uh, her mother's name."

"Oh," I said, my smile wavering. "My sister told me. I'm so sorry."

He nodded. "Thanks." Matt fiddled with his napkin, not quite meeting my eyes. "She was a great woman. A great mother."

"I'm sure she was." I sipped my margarita.

"We always wanted a big family. Then the cancer struck…" Matt's voice trailed off. I wasn't sure that he wasn't going to cry.

Oh, God. This could turn into a total nightmare.

"Matt went to Howard," my sister said, clearly realizing that someone needed to get Matt to stop talking about his wife.

"Howard University," I said, my tone upbeat. "I'll bet you loved it. I'd always wanted to go to a historically black college."

"Yeah, it was great. I met my wife there."

And so the rest of the evening went, with a clearly still grieving Matt talking about his wife most of the time. He was a nice guy, and it was obvious that he'd had an almost perfect marriage for six years.

A new woman just couldn't compete with that kind of history.

Not that I wanted to. I wasn't in the least bit ready to think about dating anyone when I was still heartbroken myself. The good thing was, it was just as obvious to my sister that Matt wasn't at all ready to think about dating, either, and I wouldn't have to come up with uncomfortable reasons as to why I couldn't see him again.

"It's not just the fact that Matthew is still in love with his wife," I said to my sister later. "Even if he wasn't, I wouldn't be interested. Because I'm in love with someone else, Nikki. And not that long ago, I remember you saying that you didn't want to see me jump from relationship to relationship. That if it took ten years, you wanted to see me happy."

"The only reason I suggested the dinner with Matt is because I know he's a great guy. And he deserves a great girl."

"I get that. I believe that. And yes, he seems wonderful. He just...isn't Chaz."

"Wow," my sister said, sounding surprised. "You still miss Chaz?"

"Yes. Yes, I do."

Nikki nodded slowly. "Have you tried to talk to him?"

"Are you kidding? I'm terrified he'll tell me to get lost."

"Maybe he will. But if you don't call him, you'll never know. Do you want to sit around for months and months not knowing?"

"No, but I was thinking that if I sit around for months and months, that'll give him time to forgive me."

"Or time to find another woman. He's a hot property."

"Shit," I mumbled softly, knowing that my sister was right. "You sound like Alaina."

"She said the same thing?"

"Pretty much."

"You know what they say about two heads being better than one." My sister gave me a pointed look. "So...are you going to call him?"

I wanted to, but the thought of doing it terrified me. But with my sister staring at me, I knew I could only say one thing. "All right. I'll call."

My sister hopped to her feet. "I'll get the phone."

"Wait a minute!" I cried, panicked. "You want me to call right *now?*"

"No time like the present."

"But—" My protest died in my throat as my sister disappeared down the hallway. My body tingled with fear.

"Here you are." Nikki smiled sweetly as she passed me the phone.

I didn't take it. "I—I don't remember his number," I lied.

"Nice try. Call him."

"But—"

"But what? You want to spend the rest of your life not knowing, wondering what would have happened if you'd had the guts to call him?"

I snatched the phone from her hand. "Okay. I'll do it."

I stared at the cordless receiver, which felt like a lead weight in my hand. Why the hell was I so scared? Chaz had already rejected me. If he rejected me again, what would I have lost? On the other hand, if he decided to give me another chance…

"What are you waiting for?" my sister asked.

"Some privacy."

She crossed her arms over her chest. "No way. I don't trust you."

I shot her an exasperated look. "All right. I'll do it." I blew out a shaky breath. "Now."

My fingers were shaking as I punched in the digits to Chaz's cell phone, a number I'd committed to memory. As it was ringing, Nikki said, "If he doesn't answer, leave a message."

After the fourth ring, Chaz's voice mail picked up, and just hearing his voice made something stir in my gut.

"Leave a message," Nikki repeated.

"Um, Chaz," I began hesitantly. "This is…it's Vanessa. I wanted to talk, but you're not there. So, 'bye." I quickly pressed the talk button to end the call.

Nikki shook her head as she stared at me. "Not exactly award-winning, but it'll do. At least he'll know you're thinking of him."

I nodded. I could only wait to see what happened next.

I took Rayna to feed the ducks the next afternoon, but what had happened last night at my sister's place still weighed heavily on my mind.

I'd finally called Chaz and left him a message. Almost a day had passed and he hadn't returned my call. I wondered if he ever would.

"Here, sweetheart. Take some bread."

Rayna didn't listen, instead running happily toward the ducks lining the man-made lake. They squawked and waddled away, some going into the water to escape my excited toddler.

"Rayna," I said. "Come and take some bread."

When Rayna turned to look at me, she was all smiles, not at all dismayed by the fact that the ducks had run from her. I held out some morsels of bread to her, and Rayna grabbed them in both palms. One second later, she was flinging all the pieces with all her might toward the ducks, her broken arm not a hindrance to her. The ducks sprinted, and some half flew, to get back to Rayna, where the bread had dropped at her feet.

Rayna squealed with delight as the multicolored ducks surrounded her, hastily gobbling up the food.

Rayna whirled around to face me. "More, Mommy."

I gave her more bread. She threw it, even with the hand that was in a cast. The ducks ate greedily.

I lowered myself onto my butt, getting comfortable on the grass near the water's edge. It truly is the most special of feelings to see your child happy. To watch her face light up over one of life's simple pleasures.

We stayed like that, both Rayna and I throwing bread and the ducks eating voraciously. I snapped some pictures on my cell phone so I could capture the happy memories.

I was angling the phone to take a picture of Rayna chasing the ducks when it rang. Abandoning the picture, I put the phone to my ear. "Hello?"

"Vanessa."

I was stunned into silence. That voice…

"Vanessa?"

Inside my chest, my heart seemed to be doing crazy acrobatics. "Hello," I said, my voice barely audible.

"Vanessa, it's Chaz."

"Yes. Yes, I know." *Sweet Jesus, Chaz was on the other end of my line!*

"Did I catch you at a bad time?" he asked.

"I'm out with Rayna right now," I told him, somehow managing to sound calm. "We're feeding the ducks."

"Oh, that's sweet. I'll bet she's having a great time."

"Mmm-hmm. She is." *And if you were here, it would be even better…*

"Look, I don't want to keep you," Chaz said, "because I'd

really prefer to speak to you in person. I'm glad you called, because it turns out I'm heading to Miami this weekend. I'm going to be staying at the Delano. Arriving Saturday evening. If you're free, I'd love to get together on Sunday."

Calm down, calm down, I told myself. *Breathe.*

"Sure."

My voice must have come out as a whisper, because Chaz said, "Pardon me?"

I cleared my throat before speaking. "Sure," I repeated. "I'd love to get together."

"Great. Like I said, I'd prefer to talk to you in person. But I wanted to reach out and see if you were interested." Chaz paused. "There's a lot I want to say to you. There's a lot we'll have to talk about."

"Right," I agreed. I could only imagine that Chaz had seen or read the news about my arrest, and how I'd been in Grand Cayman with Lewis. I was certain he wanted to talk about that. Part of me wanted to explain everything to him over the phone, but a bigger part knew that it would be better to say whatever I had to say in person, when he couldn't simply hang up the phone if he didn't like what he heard.

Besides, I just wanted to see him. Even if it would be the last time. I wanted to lay eyes on him, drink in the sexy sight of him.

"How about I call you when I arrive on Saturday night," Chaz suggested. "Then we can set a time for Sunday."

"Sounds good." I tried to sound as cheerful as possible, even though my hands were shaking from nerves.

"Oh, and Vanessa?" Chaz said.

"Yes?"

"I miss you."

Three simple words, but they lifted me high on a cloud of bliss. "I miss you, too," I told him.

"I'll call you Saturday."

Flipping my phone shut, I let out a scream of joy. Startled, Rayna whirled around and looked at me in alarm.

"It's okay," I told her. "Mommy's just really, really happy right now."

Rayna turned back to the ducks, and I sighed with contentment.

Happy? Talk about the understatement of the century. There wasn't a word to accurately describe how I was feeling, but my emotions were over the moon.

31

"No, Alaina," I said. "I can't."

"Why not?" she asked on the other end of my line.

"Because I want to wait until he calls me. If I show up at the Delano and he sees me…"

"What?" Alaina asked. "What's the worst that will happen?"

"He'll think I'm…I don't know…pushy?"

"How about he'll think you're so crazy in love with him you couldn't wait until Sunday to see him, knowing he was in town?"

"I don't know."

"I'm coming to your place for five, so I hope Carla can watch Rayna. And if it makes you feel better, we can go shopping for wedding dresses first."

"Shopping for wedding dresses? That's jumping the gun, isn't it?"

"For me, silly."

"Oh," I said, flushing. "Right."

"So, are we on?" Alaina asked, to be sure.

"I'm happy to go shopping for wedding dresses with you," I said, deliberately not broaching the subject of Chaz. "I'll be ready when you get here."

Alaina showed up shortly after five, and we headed to Ocean Drive to look for dresses. We didn't go into actual bridal shops. Alaina wasn't interested in an elaborate white gown. For her second wedding she wanted something sexy and elegant, as opposed to the traditional wedding dress.

But the trendy Ocean Drive shop we were currently in did have some wedding dresses, and after having browsed the other selections in the store, we were now at the back of the small boutique, perusing the various options.

"I can't believe it," I said as I looked through the rack of wildly different bridal dresses. Some were long, some short. Some modest, and others quite skimpy. "You're getting married. My sister's getting remarried. Oh, this is nice." I lifted an ivory-colored dress off the rack. It was a strapless number, with beautiful beadwork over the bodice. The dress's skirt was long and full. I held it up against my body so Alaina could see it. "It's simple, yet elegant."

"It's nice," Alaina concurred, but her tone said she wasn't crazy over it. "But a little too formal, I think. I want something shorter. Sexier."

"I know. I just thought… This is so pretty. And ivory."

"It's going to be a small wedding," Alaina said. "I did the big, fancy wedding with Jorge, and I don't want to go that route again. Mike was also married before, and doesn't want a big wedding, either. We both want something small. Intimate. The kind of wedding that will mean something to both of us."

"Just don't say you want to head to Thailand."

"Huh?"

"My sister. Remember?"

"Right. Right. No, we're not going to Thailand. I'm thinking the Eden Roc hotel might be nice."

"Very nice," I said, raising my eyebrows. The Eden Roc was a landmark hotel on Miami Beach. Very swanky.

"And speaking of hotels…" Alaina gave me a look ripe with meaning. "Why don't we have a drink at the Delano?"

My body tensed. "I don't know, Ally. Tomorrow will be here soon enough."

"What if you get hit by a bus before tomorrow comes?" Alaina planted both hands on her hips. "You'll never get the chance to see Chaz again."

"I hardly think that's going to happen on Ocean Drive."

"Well a Mercedes then. Or a Hummer. The point is—"

"I get your point."

"I say you take advantage of the moment," Alaina went on.

I drew in a deep breath, released it slowly. "We don't even know that he'll be there."

Alaina grabbed hold of my arm. "No more excuses. What, you want a drink first? Some liquid courage? Then let's get a drink. My treat."

I let Alaina drag me out of the store. I didn't protest. Maybe I needed her to force me to do something my heart wanted me to do. Did I want to see Chaz tonight? Absolutely. But I was also nervous. I didn't want to interrupt him if he was in the middle of important business.

I miss you.

I miss you, too.

As my feet hit the sidewalk in front of the boutique, excitement mixed with my nervousness. Chaz had said that he wanted to see me. That he missed me. Surely if he ran into me a day ahead of schedule, he wouldn't be upset.

"All these spots are pretty busy," Alaina said of the various restaurants in the immediate vicinity. "Let's head to Mango's. Although The Clevelander is probably better."

We continued walking up the strip. We passed Mango's, the lively salsa music almost tempting me to head in there. A couple minutes later, we were in front of The Clevelander. House music filled the air, but no one was dancing this early. People were milling about at the bar, or enjoying a meal. My eyes scanned the outdoor area for a table that was open while Alaina babbled happily about Mike.

And then I stopped dead in my tracks.

"I forgot to tell you," Alaina was saying. "Remember how I told you that my mother thought I was moving too fast, especially when we got engaged? Well, now she's done a total one-eighty. It's like she's fallen in love with Mike, too. Which I understand, 'cause he's so good to her. Much nicer than Jorge ever—Vanessa, what is it?"

I whirled around, away from the patio, waves of nausea swishing around in my stomach. "Chaz," I whispered.

"What?"

"Chaz," I repeated, louder this time.

Alaina's eyes bulged. "Chaz?"

"Yes."

Alaina began obviously scoping out the patio. I grabbed her by the arm and spun her around.

"Why are you turning away?" she asked. "We've found him—which is what we wanted."

"I knew I should have waited until tomorrow," I muttered. I started walking, dragging Alaina along with me. But waiting until tomorrow ultimately wouldn't have mattered. It was clear now that Chaz had only been interested in seeing an old friend.

"I don't understand," Alaina protested.

"Vanessa?"

The sound of Chaz's sweet voice stopped me dead in my tracks.

"Why are you running away from him?" Alaina whispered.

"Because. He's here with Maria Lopez. She's wearing a hat and sunglasses, but I know it's her. The bodyguards are a dead giveaway."

Alaina spun around just as Chaz said my name again. Knowing I couldn't very well run, I turned, too.

His eyes met mine instantly. For several seconds, we just stared at each other. Then a tentative smile formed on his face.

I forced a smile onto mine, lifting my hand in a wave.

Chaz held up a finger, signaling for me to wait. Then he said something to Maria Lopez, who looked my way, but didn't stand.

"They're obviously a couple," I whispered to Alaina. "Here in Miami together." I swallowed painfully. "Why the hell did he bother calling me—" I stopped abruptly as Chaz neared me. My heart pounded furiously.

There he was, the man I loved. Smiling at me with that kind expression. I thought I might burst into tears.

"Vanessa." At first I thought Chaz was going to spread his arms wide, offering to embrace me. But instead he seemed to fumble with his hands, ultimately placing them on his hips. "How are you?"

"Good," I said, surprised I could even talk. I wanted to say something about our meeting for tomorrow, but I couldn't. I suddenly understood—all too well—what that was about. Putting the hurt behind us and moving forward as friends.

How big of him.

"I see you're here with Maria Lopez," I said instead. *Tell me you're not a couple. Please, reassure me.*

"Yes. She's doing some shows in Miami."

"Right." I continued to wear the "this isn't hurting me to talk to you" smile. "Well, how very nice that you could join her."

Alaina nudged me.

"Um, Chaz, I don't believe you ever met my friend Alaina."

"But I've heard a lot about you," Alaina said.

"It's a pleasure," Chaz said to Alaina.

"Likewise."

Chaz shook her hand briefly before turning back to me. "I saw you on the news," he said. "Looks like you had quite the adventure in the Cayman Islands."

I rolled my eyes. "Understatement of the century."

"With your ex-boyfriend," Chaz went on, then snapped his fingers, as though trying to recall something. "Lewis. That's his name."

"*Ex* being the key word."

"I guess so—with what he was up to." Though Chaz still smiled, I got the sense that he was fishing. Fishing to see what I'd say about my relationship with Lewis.

"We were just friends," I told him, knowing that had to seem hard to believe. Perhaps impossible to believe.

Chaz nodded. "Right."

What about Maria Lopez? I wanted to ask. *In your message, you said you two were just friends. Is that still true?*

I didn't voice my question. Instead, I simply stared at Chaz. He stared back.

And I don't know why, but I got the feeling that he wanted to say something else to me.

"Did you still want to—" I began, but didn't get the question out before I was cut off.

"Chaz. Aren't you going to introduce me to your friend?"

We tore our eyes away from each other and both looked at Maria, who was now standing at Chaz's side. Her two bodyguards were standing behind her.

"Yes. Of course."

Maria looped her arm through Chaz's elbow, but she was looking at me curiously.

"This is Vanessa Cain, a friend of mine."

A friend of his… I glanced away, unable to stomach anymore.

"And Vanessa, this is Maria Lopez."

I turned back to them, grinning tightly. "Yes. I know."

"Nice to meet you, Vanessa."

"Nice to meet you, too."

Maria turned her face up toward Chaz's. "Chaz, we need to get going."

"Don't let me keep you," I said. I needed to be out of here already. "Well. It was nice to see you."

"And nice to finally meet you," Alaina said.

My stomach lurched as I spun around.

"Wait," Chaz suddenly said.

I closed my eyes briefly. Then turned back to Chaz. "Yes?"

"Are we still on for tomorrow? I'd love to chat, catch up."

Chat. Catch up. I'm not sure how I held myself together. "Call me," I told him, my voice catching slightly.

"Chaz, we really must go now," Maria said. She pressed herself closer to his side while giving me a long look.

I get it, bitch, I thought. *You don't have to rub it in.*

"Take care," I said, and casually waved.

"You, too, Vanessa."

And then I quickly turned around, knowing I was going to fall apart.

I didn't get three feet away before the tears filled my eyes. I walked as fast as I could, not daring to look over my shoulder.

32

"I'm so sorry," Alaina said. She stared at me over her tall glass of lemonade. "I don't know what else to say."

We were sitting at a table in T.G.I. Friday's, at the southern end of the restaurant-and-bar district on South Beach. I'd been walking briskly back toward my condo when I'd decided that I needed a drink, and pulled Alaina into the restaurant with me.

"There's nothing to say." I gulped at my vodka cranberry. "And quite frankly, I don't want to talk about it."

"Maybe Chaz and Maria aren't a couple," Alaina said hopefully. "Maybe there's a logical explanation as to why they're together. Well—other than the logical explanation we're thinking of. I mean, he *does* work for her."

"I love you for trying, Alaina. But if there was any time for me to accept reality, it's now. And you know what, I'll be fine. I've had enough time to deal with the fact that he didn't want me. So, like I said, I'm fine. Perfectly—" I couldn't keep speaking. My throat was so clogged with emotion, it was all I could do to keep it together.

"I saw the way he was looking at you," Alaina continued. "I really feel that if I weren't there, and Maria weren't there…"

I'd gotten the same feeling. And yet, I didn't want to read too much into it.

I'd been so hopeful about my meeting with Chaz, thinking he was going to profess his love for me. I would then tell him that I'd never stopped loving him, and we'd make plans for an immediate future together.

But after seeing him with Maria… It was far more likely that he'd wanted to tell me he was ready to put the past behind us and continue our relationship…as friends.

And if that was what he'd wanted to tell me, I didn't want to hear it. Because I didn't want to be Chaz's friend.

Loving him as much as I did, I knew I couldn't handle talking to him and seeing him—if I could never touch him or kiss him again.

"Can we talk about something else?" I glanced around the restaurant, hoping no one had noticed my emotional state. "Please."

Alaina nodded. "Sure. Like what?"

"Like your wedding."

"My wedding?" She sounded surprised. "You want to talk about my wedding?"

"Why not?"

"I don't know. I just didn't expect—"

"I never did like Maria Lopez's music, by the way," I interjected. "And what was with that whole possessive act with

Chaz? Did you see how she kept touching him? Like she was trying to prove a point to me?"

"I saw."

"I know she's beautiful. Physically. But what does Chaz really see in her? She and I have nothing in common. And if he was in love with me, how could he even be interested in her?"

"I don't know. It could be the sex."

I shot Alaina an unappreciative glance. Then I downed the rest of my drink.

"Or…the conversation. Or, he just really loves her music."

I whimpered, the thought of Chaz in bed with Maria, whispering the kinds of things he'd said to me in her ear, making me ill.

"I'm sorry," Alaina said softly.

I suddenly stood. It was either that or cry. "I need to go out."

"What?"

"You know. Clubbing. We haven't done that in a long time. Tonight, I need to dance like there's no tomorrow. Maybe even meet a Mr. Right Now. Considering my Mr. Right is in love with someone else."

Alaina stood beside me. "Vanessa…"

"Where do you want to go?" I asked her. I was already digging money out of my purse. We hadn't yet gotten the bill, but I threw enough on the table to cover our drinks. "I'm kind of tired of the South Beach strip." And Lord knew I didn't want to run into Maria and Chaz dancing it up at Mango's. "Maybe we can drive to Fort Lauderdale."

"What about my kids?" Alaina asked.

"Can your sister watch them?"

"I can ask."

"Good. Because I need you tonight. Tonight is the night I finally put Chaz out of my mind. And my heart."

Soon Alaina and I were half a block away from my building. Neither of us had said much during the walk to my place. I guess Alaina realized that I needed some time to simply think.

Though maybe talking would have been preferable to silence, because the thoughts going through my head were driving me crazy.

As much as I wanted to hold out hope, I couldn't be naive anymore. Chaz had moved on. Oh, he might want to be my friend, but that was all.

What else could explain the fact that he was in Miami with Maria?

I stifled a cry, my heart aching.

"Oh, sweetie," Alaina said. She reached for my hand and gave it a comforting squeeze.

I glanced at her and smiled bravely, then looked back toward my building. Abruptly, I stopped. Stopped and stared at what looked like a familiar face.

Was that... Tassie?

It couldn't be. It *wouldn't* be.

But, my God, it was. She was standing casually on the sidewalk in front of my building. With Ray Carlton.

As if sensing me, she turned in my direction. Saw me. And the bitch actually waved.

"Vanessa?" Alaina said, her voice ripe with concern.

"Ally, that's Tassie!" I said in an urgent whisper. "Standing right there, in front of *my* building!"

"You're sure?"

"Yes, I'm sure." She had a bandage on her head, obviously from the attack. "And that's Ray, the boyfriend she was still involved with while she was married to Eli."

"Oh, shit," Alaina said. "What the heck's she doing here?"

"Trying to make me sweat," I surmised. "She's got balls, I can tell you that. But today of all days, I am *not* in the mood."

Tassie started toward me, her strut confident.

"Vanessa," she said sweetly. So sweetly, it irked me. "I need to speak with you."

I ignored her, walking to the condo's front door. I opened it, and both Alaina and I went inside.

So did Tassie. "Walking away from me is not going to help."

I whirled around and faced her. "What are you doing here?"

"Enjoying South Beach." Her smile was entirely too syrupy. "Like the thousands of other tourists here."

"In the residential part of South Beach?" I asked, my tone sarcastic. The Cosmopolitan Towers took up an entire city block—albeit a small one—but I doubted that seeing Tassie in front of the building's main entrance was a coincidence. She'd either been trying to figure out a way to get inside, or she'd called, learned I wasn't home, and was hanging around, waiting for me.

She shrugged. "I'm also checking out my new neighborhood." She peered through the glass beyond the building's immediate entrance, into the vast lobby. "I like it." She turned back to me. "I could get used to living here very quickly. The beach is to die for!"

"We've been through this, Tassie. You signed your rights to this property away."

"That was because you had me hospitalized." She touched the bandage on her head, as if for emphasis.

"I didn't touch you. But trust me, I wish I had."

"Temper, temper," she tsked.

Her boyfriend was outside on the sidewalk, which was probably a good thing. If I made a move to slug Tassie, he wouldn't be able to intervene.

Alaina, however, did. "Vanessa, let's just go upstairs."

Alaina was right. Digging in my purse for my keys, I turned to the door that led into the lobby.

"Yes, listen to your friend. You'll want to enjoy this place for the short time here you have left."

My hand stilled on the door handle. I took a deep breath in, but it did nothing to calm me.

"What did you do?" I asked Tassie, turning to face her once more. "Come down here and hang out for hours and hours, waiting for me to show up? Girl, you need to get a life."

"Oh, I have a life. The one you want. That's why you glommed on to my husband, like the gold-digging whore you are."

Just like that, I snapped…and slugged Tassie. My right fist landed solidly on her left jaw. Screaming, she flew backward and landed on her ass.

"Now you've done it!" She glared up at me. "You're going to jail."

"Done what?" I looked around, seeing no one who would be a witness for Tassie. "Ally, did you see anything?"

"I saw Tassie lunge at you. You deflected her blow and she landed on the floor."

"Exactly. If anyone's going to go to jail here, it's going to be you. After all, you came all the way here from Atlanta, obviously itching for a fight."

Tassie's nostrils flared as she glowered at me. Ray threw the door open and stepped into the building's entrance area. I braced myself, not sure what he was going to do.

"Baby," he said, reaching for Tassie.

As Ray helped her up, I returned Tassie's glare. "You're completely pathetic. I'd tell you to grow up, but I doubt that's possible. You'll probably always be petty. But you need to get over the fact I was with Eli. You need to accept that this is my place and back off. Because if you want to escalate this fight—you've been warned. I'm not putting up with any more bullshit from you."

"I told you this was stupid," Ray said to Tassie. He took her by the arm and led her to the exit. "Let's go."

Clearly, Ray wasn't at all interested in Tassie's fight with me, but had come along for the trip.

Huffing, Tassie yanked her arm free of Ray's grip. She marched out the front doors, pushing a middle-aged woman aside as she did so. The woman gaped at Tassie, but Tassie didn't stop. She stalked down the street, with Ray hustling after her.

I could only hope that Tassie would finally be out of my life forever.

33

I still wanted to party, even more so because of the run-in with Tassie. I definitely needed a distraction from the crap going on in my life.

So a couple hours later, after changing and getting dolled up, Alaina and I were in her car with the music pumping. We pulled off of I-95 and onto Broward Boulevard in Fort Lauderdale, heading east toward the beach. Being a single mother, going to a club wasn't a weekly thing for me, but it had been even longer since I'd been out on the town with Alaina.

As far as I was concerned, I wasn't just going clubbing to forget about Chaz, but to celebrate the fact that Alaina had recovered a hundred percent. All physical signs of Jorge's attack were no longer visible.

And Alaina had found love again with Mike, so she was getting a well-deserved happy ending.

As we hit what was known as "The Strip"—the street that bordered the beach here the way Ocean Drive did in

Miami—there was a lot of congestion. Cars filled with twenty-somethings from out of town ready to party.

"We just passed a parking lot," I pointed out. "Why don't we circle the block and go back to that spot?"

Circling the block took longer than I'd expected, with traffic crawling along A-1-A. In a car in front of us, two women in bikini tops were standing through the open sunroof, waving at everyone they passed. Some guys lining the street hooted and howled.

"Looks like the *putas* are out in full force," Alaina commented.

I laughed. "Yeah," I agreed. "Slutty tourists from the Midwest looking for a good time in all the wrong places."

I'd seen more than one young female tourist who'd had way too much to drink being "helped" out of a bar by two young men I was willing to bet she didn't know. I'd often wondered what the morning after had been like for a woman like that. Did she wake up to find herself in bed with one or more strange men? Or did she wake up feeling sore, realizing that someone had had sex with her, but taken off? Or did she just wake up with a bad hangover and need to throw up for an hour? Regardless of how her morning after played out, I was pretty sure the woman realized that her fun times in Miami had come with a bigger price tag than just the plane fare and hotel.

"I'm not going to drink like a fish," I said as Alaina pulled into the lot. "This is simply about hanging out and having a good time tonight."

"And what was that part about finding a man?"

My heart ached at the question. The thought of finding

someone else was inconceivable. And yet, it was clear that since Chaz had moved on, there was no sense in me continuing to pine over him.

"If I meet someone nice…"

Alaina rolled her eyes, then opened her car door.

I put a hand on her arm before she exited the car. "Why did you roll your eyes like that?"

"Because I know you and 'meeting someone nice.' Before you know it, you'll be headfirst into another relationship."

"This is about having a good time," I said. "Nothing more."

"Hmm," Alaina said knowingly, then got out of the car.

I strolled behind her as she went to the booth to pay for the parking, my mind lost in thought. Alaina had mentioned before that she thought I didn't take much of a break between relationships, but it wasn't like I went looking for new guys after a breakup. I hadn't been looking for Eli. And I certainly hadn't been looking for Chaz.

But what was a person supposed to do if love fell in her lap? Push it away like it was a disease?

Having paid for parking, Alaina turned around and smiled at me sweetly. "Ready?"

I smiled back, deciding to let the issue of my love life drop. Because I was over love—Alaina would see. "Let's go."

We ended up at a restaurant that had a band playing, which was perfect for me and Alaina. The crowd was more upscale here—not the rowdy, sex-seeking crowd at most of the clubs.

From our table on the patio, we had a view of the partygoers lining the streets. And what a view it was.

"Oh, my goodness," I said in a low voice. "Turn slowly and look at the woman standing by the light pole, talking to the guy in glasses. What *is* she wearing?"

While sipping her margarita, Alaina casually turned and looked behind her. When she faced me again, her eyes were bulging and she was holding in a laugh. "I'm sorry, but an ass that big should *not* be in a thong."

"Hello," I said, wholeheartedly concurring. "She needs to invest in a nice sarong." I wasn't the type to say that a person shouldn't wear what she felt sexy in, but some outfits I saw women sporting at the beach were so unflattering, I didn't understand how they couldn't see that when they looked in the mirror.

"And look at that one," Alaina said, giving a nod of her head in the direction behind me. "And don't worry about looking—those two are sucking each other's faces off."

I angled my head to see a young couple in a serious lip-lock, the man's hands blatantly squeezing the woman's ass in a way that wasn't appropriate in public.

"Isn't that sweet?" Alaina asked in a mocking tone. "I'll bet they just met."

"Love South Florida style." The couple was still going at it, only now the guy's hand was under the girl's skirt. "I swear, before Rayna hits her teen years, I'm moving to the Midwest. Better yet, Alaska."

"Girl, Alaska is the single man capital of the world."

"Then I'll move to Antarctica. It'll be me, Rayna, some penguins and polar bears. And you, Mike, and the boys, of course."

We both laughed at that one, and as my laughter subsided,

that's when I got the sense that someone was watching me. My eyes bounced over the crowd on the patio—and made contact with another pair of eyes.

"Oh, boy," I said quietly, looking at Alaina.

"Tell me where to look," she said, her tone saying she was enjoying our game of "let's pick out the tacky people."

I snuck a peek at the man several tables behind me. He was still staring at me. "Whatever you do, don't turn around."

Alaina started to turn.

"Don't!" I said urgently. "Because then he'll think I'm talking about him."

"Him? What—someone's checking you out?"

"Yeah, I think so."

"You've already hooked one," Alaina said in a singsong voice.

"No, I haven't!" Although I had to admit, the man was quite attractive. Unlike the baggy jeans and swim trunks most men were sporting on the strip, this guy was wearing a loose-fitting black top and most likely a pair of khaki pants.

I glanced the man's way again, and this time he smiled. Lowering my eyes, I rested my chin on the palm of my hand.

"Okay, now you're flirting," Alaina said. "Can I look at this guy yet or what?"

"No. And I'm not flirting. Although, I must admit he's cute, and maybe he's just what I need tonight to forget about Chaz."

Alaina very deliberately knocked her fork onto the patio

floor. As she leaned over to pick up the fork, she looked behind her.

"Mmm." She wiggled her eyebrows as she rose. "He *is* cute. I wouldn't kick him out of bed in the morning."

"Don't even talk about kicking anyone out of bed. It's not going to get that far."

"*That* far?" Alaina looked at me pointedly. "So, you do think it'll go somewhere?"

"I didn't say that."

"Oh, but I know you so well."

"I'm here to have some fun and forget about—" I stopped speaking when the waitress arrived at our table with two more margaritas. I gave the woman an odd look. "We didn't order more drinks."

"These are courtesy of the two men at that table over there."

The waitress pointed, but she didn't have to. I knew exactly where she meant.

Being respectful, I raised a hand in gratitude. Alaina did the same just as the man's friend turned and looked our way.

The second man looked exactly like the first one.

Twins.

"Oh, boy." Alaina fanned herself. "Twins who are fine as hell. Now that's a fantasy and a half." She finished off her first drink in one gulp. "If I weren't engaged to the sweetest man on earth…"

"Exactly. You're engaged."

"But you're not. I can live vicariously through you."

"One minute you're telling me I need to take it slow. Now you *want* me to flirt?"

"Twins," Alaina repeated.

I shook my head. "Girl, you're too much. But, like I said, I'm here to have fun. A night of dancing with hot men is probably just what the doctor ordered."

I looked at the attractive man again, and wasn't surprised to see that he was still looking at me. Grinning like he hoped to charm the pants off me.

I lifted the drink he'd sent in greeting, then took a sip of the margarita.

Ten minutes later, they were at our table. The twins, Jacob and Jeremy, really could have been models or actors. It wasn't just their very good looks, it was their easy smiles and undeniable charm.

Jeremy sat next to me, while his brother sat next to Alaina. She'd made it clear from the moment they sat down that she was engaged.

"Flipping houses is fun," Jeremy was saying. "But it's not as easy as they show on television. It's dirty. Long hours. And sometimes what you budget just isn't enough."

"But is that all you do?" Alaina asked.

"Now," Jacob told her. "In the beginning, we were both still working at our jobs. Now we've made enough money that we can flip houses full-time. It allows us the ability to pretty much set our own schedules, travel when we want. I wouldn't trade it for anything else."

"Are you the kind of twins who did the same job?" I asked. "Like you both were cops, or both in the military?"

Jeremy shook his head. "My brother worked in construction, installing tile. I was a manager at a bank."

"As different as night and day," Alaina commented.

"But our tastes run the same in a lot of areas," Jeremy explained. Beneath the table, he brushed his hand against my thigh.

My eyes widened in mild surprise. An accident? Judging by the way he smiled down at me, it hadn't been an accident at all.

"Are you all hungry?" Jacob asked. "We already ate, but we don't mind hanging out with you if you're going to order dinner."

"We'll pay," Jeremy said.

I liked Jeremy and Jacob. If nothing else, they seemed like gentlemen. I didn't mind hanging out with them tonight.

But I looked across the table to gauge Alaina's reaction. She read the question in my eyes and gave a subtle nod.

"I'm famished," she said. "And there's nothing wrong with an engaged woman enjoying dinner with friends."

While Alaina and I dined on chicken fajitas, Jacob and Jeremy regaled us with some of their most interesting stories having to do with flipping houses. How they found foreclosed houses and got them at rock-bottom prices, and how amazed even they were with the final results.

"You make me want to flip houses," I said, dabbing at the corners of my mouth with a napkin. "Sounds like a great business if you can make it happen."

"If you can make it happen is right," Jeremy said. "There's a lot of luck involved. Finding the right location, the right property. Knowing exactly what to do to give the place a fantastic transformation without spending more than you can afford."

Finished with her meal, Alaina dropped her napkin onto her plate and announced, "I'm stuffed."

"Would you like dessert?" Jacob asked, looking at her first, then me.

"No way," I said. "I couldn't eat another bite."

"Then what do you say we settle the bill and do a little dancing?" Jeremy suggested.

"Sounds like a plan," I told him.

Beneath the table, he covered my hand, but only briefly. Then he signaled for our waitress.

With the bill paid, we wandered inside and found a space on the dance floor. We paired off—me with Jeremy, and Alaina with Jacob—but remained very much a group. We danced at a respectful distance through an upbeat Shakira tune, letting loose and having fun.

As song merged into song, Jeremy got closer to me, sometimes slipping an arm around my waist so that we were dancing groin to groin. Our group also separated, with Jacob and Alaina behind me and Jeremy.

I glanced over my shoulder at them and saw Alaina pushing Jacob's hands away. She continued to dance with him, but clearly she felt he was getting a little too close for comfort.

Jeremy placed a finger on my chin and angled my face back to him. As I looked up at him, he was smiling down at me.

He really did have a beautiful smile.

"I'm sure you hear this a lot," he said, "but you are mad beautiful."

"Thank you," I said, loving the compliment. "And I know you're used to women tripping over themselves to get to you."

Jeremy threw his head back and laughed, and I found myself remembering the first time I'd gone out with Chaz in the Bahamas. The way Chaz's warm laugh had been like a ray of sunlight on my battered soul. How fun he'd been to hang out with, and the way we'd clicked right from the beginning.

"You having fun?" Jeremy asked, looping his arms around my waist.

I didn't answer right away, as I had to force Chaz out of my head. *Chaz has moved on,* I told myself. *Think about the here and now.*

I blew out a slow breath then answered, "Yes. Yes, I'm having fun."

"Good. I am, too."

There was a tap on my shoulder. I turned to see Alaina standing there. "Can I talk to you a minute?"

"Excuse me," I said to Jeremy.

Alaina led the way off of the dance floor. When we were near the bar, she stopped.

"I don't want to spoil the party or anything, but Jacob is getting a little too touchy-feely for my tastes."

"You want to leave?" I asked her.

She shrugged. "Kind of."

"Is Jacob being a jerk?" I asked.

"Naw. But, I think he's hoping I'll forget I'm engaged."

"All right," I said, nodding. "We can leave."

"Or I can just hang out at the bar for a bit. 'Cause it looks like Jacob has moved on to someone else."

I glanced over my shoulder in the direction where Alaina was looking. Jacob was on the dance floor with another woman, his hands all over her.

"Or come back and hang out with us," I suggested.

Alaina pursed her lips, flashing me a knowing look. "You like him."

"He's nice," I said, my tone noncommittal.

"You go back to Jeremy. I'm gonna order a soda."

"And then what?" I asked.

"I'll be over there soon."

"All right," I said warily.

"Go on." Alaina gave me a little shove.

I weaved my way through the crowd until I reached Jeremy, who was waiting right where I'd left him.

"What's up?" he asked.

"I think my friend is ready to go," I said, deliberately forgetting what Alaina had just said. There was no point in me hanging out here and letting Alaina be a third wheel.

"Are you *leaving* leaving? Or heading somewhere else?"

"Probably *leaving* leaving."

"That's too bad."

"It was fun hanging out," I said.

Jeremy was very clearly giving me a look that said he didn't want our time together to end. "Can I walk you to your car?"

"Sure."

I started off the dance floor again, and saw that Alaina was walking toward me. She had a plastic cup with what looked like water.

"I've told Jeremy that we're leaving," I said. "He wants to walk us out."

"Oh, okay."

Jeremy surveyed the dance floor. "Let me find my brother so you can say bye to him."

"Oh, that's not necessary," Alaina said, smiling sweetly. "Just give him my regards."

"All right," Jeremy agreed. He gestured in the direction of the door. "After you."

We all made our way to the exit. Once outside, Alaina took the lead, walking briskly, while Jeremy and I lagged behind.

"How long are you in town for?" I asked him. Earlier, he'd said that he was from North Carolina.

"A couple more days." He paused. "But if there's a reason for me to stay…"

As his voice trailed off, I looked up at him. I knew what he was saying. That if I wanted him to stick around longer, he would.

I didn't know what to say, so I said nothing.

"Why don't I give you my phone number, and if you want to see me before I leave, you can call me?"

"That's a good idea," I said. It was a win-win situation. If I never wanted to talk to Jeremy again, I didn't have to call him. And if I did, I had a way to reach him.

We strolled up to the stoplight, which turned red as we reached it. Alaina was already across the street and about to enter the parking lot.

"I'll put your number in my cell phone." I dug around in my purse until I found it. "Okay. Fire away."

Jeremy recited his number, and I repeated it back to him to make sure I hadn't made a mistake.

"That's it," he said, his smile warm and sexy.

"All right," I said. "Thanks. For everything."

The light turned green, and I took a step toward the road. But Jeremy put a hand on my arm, making me halt. "Wait."

As I looked up at him, I saw that the warmth in his eyes had turned to lust. "You know, our time together really doesn't have to end." He shrugged. "If Alaina wants to leave, I can give you a ride back home."

I swallowed. And then my stomach lurched as Jeremy began to lower his face toward mine.

Just before his mouth touched mine, I turned my face, and his lips kissed my cheek.

What am I doing? I asked myself. *Why even lead the guy on? You don't want this. You want Chaz.*

As Jeremy pulled away, I didn't meet his eyes.

"What's the matter, baby?" he asked.

"Nothing," I lied. But I knew exactly what was wrong. Chaz might not want me, but what was I going to do—jump headfirst into another relationship as a way to forget him? I suddenly understood what my sister was talking about, what Alaina was talking about. If I was hurting over one relationship, I jumped at the next decent man who wanted me. It was all a way to numb the pain.

And that had gotten me nothing but trouble.

Eli had been trouble. Lewis—hell, that was trouble with a capital T.

But unlike those two men, Chaz had been the real deal.

Jeremy encircled my waist with his arms. "I like you. A lot. And I'd love to continue hanging out with you." He paused. Raised an eyebrow. "You can hang out with me and my brother."

And that's when I got a bad vibe. So much so that I narrowed my eyes as I asked, "You *and* your brother? What does that mean?"

"A beautiful girl like you…we'll show you a great time, I promise. Two identical guys to please you in every way. It's two times the fun. Trust me, the women love it."

With lightning speed, I pulled myself out of Jeremy's arms and gave him a hard shove. "You and your brother? Unbelievable!"

He chuckled softly. "What—you gonna give me the virginal act? Why, because your friend is watching?"

I didn't bother to dignify Jeremy's words with an answer, instead turning toward the street.

"A sister as fine as you—I'm sure you've had your share of experiences. You can probably teach us a thing or two."

I started across the street, even though the light was red. I had to dodge a few cars to avoid getting hit.

"We'll show you a good time!" Jeremy called from behind me.

I broke in to a run and didn't stop until I'd reached the car.

Alaina was already inside, and I quickly threw the door open and jumped into the passenger seat. "Go," I said hurriedly. "Let's get out of here."

"What happened?"

"Drive and I'll tell you."

As Alaina started the car, I craned my neck around to see if Jeremy was coming. He wasn't.

Alaina maneuvered the car around in the parking lot, then made a hasty left turn onto Las Olas Boulevard, heading west. We passed over a small bridge over a waterway. South Florida was known as the Venice of America because of its numerous waterways. There was a marina on the left side of the bridge, with sailboats, speedboats and yachts moored at the dock. From experience, I knew that some of the most beautiful homes in Fort Lauderdale were on the small streets that branched off of Las Olas Boulevard. Houses that backed onto waterways and had their own boats at the end of their backyards.

"I've given you a couple minutes," Alaina said, facing me briefly. "Now tell me what happened."

"Jeremy turned into a jerk, that's what happened." I blew out a huff of air, still unable to believe the drastic turn of events. "Do you believe the asshole had the nerve to suggest I go back to his hotel room—with him *and* his brother?"

"No!" Alaina gasped.

"You and my sister are right. I need to stay away from men."

"I never said you need to stay away from men."

"Yes, you did. You think I date too quickly after heartache. And you're right."

"Better you find out he's a jerk now than later."

I nodded absently, staring instead at the tree-lined street and million-dollar homes.

"You seem really upset," Alaina commented after several seconds of silence.

"I'm not upset about Jeremy." I sighed as I faced her. "I'm thinking about Chaz."

"You're still hurting. That's understandable."

"I wanted to go out tonight, to try and forget about him. But just as Jeremy leaned in to kiss me, I had a revelation. That I couldn't date someone else to get over Chaz. If it's going to hurt for six months or six years, I have to allow myself to feel the pain of losing him. After all, it was my own damn fault."

"You made a mistake, yeah. But if Chaz can't forgive you…"

"But he did forgive me, remember? He called while I was in Grand Cayman—with Lewis." Hearing the words come from my mouth almost seemed unbelievable. That that whole episode had happened, I wanted to completely forget. "I can't even imagine what Chaz thinks of me."

"He certainly moved on to Maria Lopez pretty quickly."

Alaina's words made my stomach twist. I'd seen Chaz and Maria with my own two eyes, and yet I was suddenly doubting *what* I'd seen. Maria had seemed into Chaz, that was certain. But Chaz… The way he'd held my gaze. As though he'd been trying to tell me something he hadn't been able to say with an audience around.

"What if it isn't serious?" I asked. "Maybe I'm deluding myself, but I really got the feeling that Chaz wanted to say something else to me—and would have, if not for Maria." I said her name distastefully, but the truth was, I had no reason to hate the woman—except for the fact that she seemed to want my man. "Even if they are dating, they're not married. And Chaz loved me, I know he did." I paused. "If there's ever going to be a chance with me and Chaz, I have to make my move. I can't just let Maria have him. I have to fight for him."

It was suddenly so clear, I didn't know how I hadn't come to this realization before. Why had I let fear not only hold me back, but send me running?

Maybe Chaz didn't want me, but my God, I would only

accept that after I'd put everything I had into showing him how much I loved him, wanted him, needed him.

Chaz was the only man in my heart. He was worth fighting for with all the fight I had in me.

As my eyes met Alaina's, I saw that she was wearing a silly smirk on her face.

"What?" I asked.

"I'm just glad to hear you say that. 'Cause girl, it's about damn time."

34

I was pumped as Alaina drove me back to my condo. Pumped at the thought of winning my man back.

In fact, as Alaina talked about Mike and possible wedding dates, I hardly heard what she was saying. My mind was on Chaz. I was far more positive about the situation with him than I had been in the moments after seeing him with Maria.

He had called me. He'd requested that we get together. And he'd made sure to tell me that he missed me. It hadn't sounded like a casual comment, but one ripe with emotion.

I was more convinced than ever that there was something else he'd wanted to say to me as we'd stood on the sidewalk. But given where we were—i.e., not alone—it hadn't been appropriate. Not to mention Maria's timing when she'd decided to insert herself into our conversation.

I'd also come to the realization that while yes, Chaz had reason to be angry with me for lying about Rayna's father, I should have fought for him then. But I'd sadly accepted that our relationship was over, and for one reason—because all of my relationships had failed in the past. My engagement to Eli had come to a sudden and tragic end. My relationship with Bryon had ended when I became pregnant, though it was in trouble for a long time before that. I was used to relationships being irrevocably over, with no room for forgiveness. I'd learned to accept a failed relationship and move on to the next one.

But nothing worth having came easily.

And Chaz was worth having.

I was worth having.

Tomorrow, I would prove that to him.

When Alaina pulled up in front of my building, I glanced at her car's digital clock. It was four minutes after nine. Still early. Rayna was scheduled to sleep over at Carla's, so I didn't need to pick her up.

"All right, *chica*," Alaina said. "Let's talk tomorrow."

No time like the present… Alaina had said that to me earlier. She was right.

"Actually, Ally—do you mind taking me to the Delano?"

"You want to see Chaz tonight?"

"Who knows—I could get hit by a bus before tomorrow. Or a Mercedes," I added with a smile.

"Sure, I'll take you. But shouldn't you call him first?"

"I'll call as we drive."

I called Chaz's cell, and held my breath as it rang. *Please answer. Please—*

"Vanessa?"

"Hi." A relieved breath oozed out of me. "Yes, Chaz. It's me."

I could hear loud music on the other end of the line, and wondered where Chaz was.

"One second," he said. The music became muffled. Several seconds passed before Chaz came back onto the line, and when he did, the music was fainter. "Sorry about that."

"Where are you?"

"In the lobby bar at the hotel."

"The Delano?"

"Yes."

"Can I see you?" I asked. "Right now?"

"Sure. That'd be great."

"I'll be there in a few minutes."

I ended the call, turned to Alaina and grinned nervously. "This is it, Ally. Time to fight for my man."

Alaina returned my grin. "Maria Lopez, watch out."

Five minutes later, Alaina pulled in front of the Delano hotel on Collins Avenue. I stared up at it, a towering art deco hotel that attracted successful and beautiful people from around the world. It was white, with sharp angles, and a unique rectangular-shaped structure on the top of the building, something that always struck me as futuristic. I loved the art deco hotels on South Beach, with their bright colors and unique designs. They were interesting and chic, and often quite luxurious.

I lowered my eyes from the hotel's upper levels to the front patio. It was wide and deep and boasted breezy curtains that added an elegant touch, just like the hotel's facade.

The curtains were billowing gently in the warm evening breeze. I looked past them, toward the front door, where I hoped I'd see Chaz. There were a few people milling about, drinks in hand, smiles on their faces, but I didn't see him.

"Go find him," Alaina told me. "And don't leave until you've worked everything out."

I nodded, inhaled a nervous breath, then got out of the car. I made my way up the steps, stopping halfway to turn and wave at Alaina as she drove away.

"Vanessa."

My eyelids fluttered shut as the warmest of sensations washed over me. I turned around, my heart beating so hard I could hear my pulse in my ears.

There stood Chaz, sexy as hell in a pair of pressed black pants and a white dress shirt with the top three buttons undone, revealing his neck and throat. The look was upscale and chic—and totally tantalizing.

I took a moment to just stare at him, drink in the utterly delicious sight of him. The man was so incredibly handsome. Just looking at him sent a charge of lust through my body.

Not just lust, I thought as I met his gaze. *Love.*

First and foremost, there was love.

"Chaz," I said softly, so softly I wasn't sure he heard me. I swallowed, then ascended the last few steps toward him.

The tables on the porch held candles, which provided soft and romantic lighting. I glanced around. Some of the sofas were occupied, but I didn't see Maria or her bodyguards anywhere.

"Where's Maria?" I asked when I stopped in front of Chaz. Not only did he look incredible, he smelled amazing. The scent of freshly cleaned skin combined with a light cologne.

"She's doing a show."

"And you didn't want to go with her?" I asked. But before Chaz could answer the question, I said, "You know what—I don't want to talk about Maria. I want to talk about me…and you."

Chaz offered me his hand. "Do you want to have a seat?"

I took his hand, my skin electrifying at his touch. "Sure."

"But first—let me greet you properly." Chaz gently pulled me close to him, then slipped his hands around my waist and hugged me. The hug lingered. I closed my eyes and savored it, my whole body tingling.

Please don't hug me like that only to tell me you don't want me, I thought.

Chaz eased back, though he didn't let me go. The edges of his eyes crinkled as he regarded me. "Hello, Vanessa."

"Hi," I said, my voice a whisper. Then, urgently, "Chaz, I have so much I want to explain to you—"

"Let's sit. Then we'll talk."

He was right. There were other people standing in the hotel doorway, and even with the sound of jazz coming from inside, I could easily be overheard.

Placing a hand on the small of my back, Chaz led me the short distance to a sofa on the left side of the porch that was unoccupied. He gestured for me to sit, which I did. Then he sat beside me.

"Chaz, I'm sorry I lied about Rayna's father," I began without preamble. "Trust me, I didn't mean to deceive you. And I certainly didn't do it to hurt you." I didn't want to talk about Byron, so I got to the most important issue. "But what I'm more sorry about is the fact that I didn't fight for you, even when you said you wanted nothing to do with me. I know we only dated for a short while, but what we had was real. I know it was. That's why, even when you were so mad at me, I should have called you every day, let you know how much I love you. Instead, I let you walk away from me."

"And then you got involved with Lewis," Chaz said, his eyes searching mine.

I cringed. "Please believe me when I say that wasn't what it looked like. Yes, Lewis wanted to marry me. But I couldn't…I wouldn't. Because I'm in love with you. And he never touched me. It's important that you know that, even though we weren't together. My relationship with Lewis was platonic. I know that might seem impossible to believe." I paused, stifled a whimper. "I can only imagine what you thought when you heard about my arrest on the news… And now you're involved with Maria."

"I'm not involved with Maria. Although that might seem impossible to believe," Chaz said, echoing my words. "With the way the media is spinning things."

Hope flooded my heart at the way. "You're not?"

"I am in love with someone," Chaz said. "But it certainly isn't Maria Lopez."

My pulse pounded wildly, excitement making me light-headed. But before I got too excited, I wanted to clear the air, make sure Chaz had no questions. "Ask me anything you want to about Lewis. Or Rayna's father. I'll answer honestly. I'll never lie to you again, Chaz. I promise."

I glanced down then, feeling a modicum of shame and regret that I'd hurt Chaz with my lie.

"Hey," he said, stroking my cheek softly with his knuckles. I met his gaze, and he continued. "I don't want to get hung up on what's happened in the past. You're not the only one who's made mistakes."

I said nothing.

"Right now is all that matters." He lowered his hand to my neck and grazed his fingers over my skin. "And aren't you curious about who I *am* in love with?"

A radiant smile bloomed on his face. A smile filled with warmth and love. The kind that said his question was rhetorical.

"I am," I said softly. My breathing was suddenly ragged. I knew it would be until I heard him say what I so desperately longed to hear. "Who's the lucky lady?"

Chaz's fingers moved to my chin. He tilted my face upward. "I love you, Vanessa Cain. And I'm sorry I ever walked away from you. I never stopped loving you, not for a moment. I tried. I did—but I couldn't. And when I heard about you and Lewis in Grand Cayman…well, I realized then that my pushing you away might have cost me your love forever. That was a dark day for me, Vanessa. A very dark day."

Was this really happening? Was I really here with Chaz, listening to him say such wonderful things?

"Now that you're sitting here, and I'm sitting here, I don't want to look backward, Vanessa. I only want to look to the future."

"Oh, Chaz." My eyes filled with happy tears. "I never stopped loving you. Not for a moment. And that whole thing with Lewis… It's a wild, crazy story, and—"

"Vanessa?"

Chaz stroked my neck again, lighting my skin on fire. "Yes?"

"Will you do me a favor?"

"Anything, Chaz. Anything."

"Stop talking. Especially about Lewis. Because I want to kiss you already."

"Oh." I chuckled nervously.

"No looking back, remember? I mean that, sweetheart."

"Yes, and I agree. I definitely—"

I didn't get the last word out before Chaz covered his lips with mine. They were just as I remembered them—full and sweet. He kissed me slowly, seductively, and the passion between us simmered like water boiling in a pot.

The kiss tantalized me. Made me light-headed with emotion.

And it healed the wound in my soul.

After several seconds, Chaz broke the kiss. I moaned in disappointment and gripped his upper arms, letting him know that I still wanted to be close to him.

"I don't think it's appropriate for us to continue like this…in public." He paused a beat. "I don't know what your time is like."

"I've got all night," I said quickly, then lowered my head to his shoulder, my face flaming.

Chaz kissed the top of my head. Then he whispered in my ear, "All night works for me. We've got some lost time to make up for."

I raised my head. Met Chaz's gaze. "We do, don't we?"

"Oh, yeah."

I got to my feet, more than ready. But as Chaz stood and took my hand, I said, "Wait a minute—what about Maria?"

"What about her?"

"Are you two...sharing a room?" He'd said he wasn't in love with Maria, not that they hadn't been involved. And I didn't want her showing up while we were in bed.

"Maria and I are not an item. So get that thought out of your head. She booked a penthouse suite. I've got a bungalow by the pool."

I nodded, though what I wanted to do was jump for joy.

"You'll like it. I promise."

I knew I wouldn't be the least bit interested in the bungalow's décor, though as we headed there, I stared in awe at the back courtyard's incredible beauty. There were tall palm trees, neatly trimmed bushes. Candles glowed within lanterns that lined the pool's perimeter, casting the area in romantic light. Some of the poolside cabanas were also lit, with people sitting inside eating dinner and drinking wine.

The place was ultracool and sophisticated, but none of its splendor held any interest for me as Chaz led me to his bungalow near the pool. I briefly registered that everything inside the bungalow was white before Chaz pulled me into his arms.

And then the only thing I could think about was the here and now, and how incredible it was to be back in Chaz's arms.

I finally had my man back.

And this time, I wasn't going to let him go.

I was tired when I awoke the next morning. Tired, but elated. My heart was bursting with love and happiness, something I wasn't sure I'd ever feel again.

I opened my eyes. Saw that Chaz was resting the side of his face in the palm of his hand and staring down at me.

"Morning, sweetheart," he said.

"Morning."

Chaz lowered his face and kissed me, coaxing me fully awake with the skill of his lips.

I was grinning like a fool when he eased back, once again resting his cheek on his hand. Sunlight spilled into the bedroom, reflecting off of the white walls, white curtains and white furniture. The all-white décor gave the illusion that I was in heaven, or on a cloud.

And I was. I was on Cloud Nine.

"How much time do you have?" Chaz asked.

"I've got time."

Someone knocked at the door. I looked at Chaz, and he at me. Then I looked at the clock. It was only nine minutes after seven.

More knocking, but louder this time. And longer. Longer than was necessary at this hour, at least for a person with a conscience.

"Are you expecting someone?" I asked Chaz.

"No, but I'm pretty sure I know who it is. Excuse me a minute."

Chaz got off the bed, and I stared at his naked body as he crossed the room to the white chaise. What a night we'd shared! It was so good to be back in his arms, back in his life.

The knocking persisted as Chaz scooped his black pants off of the chaise and slipped into them. Then he left the bedroom, closing the door behind him.

Moments later, I heard the sound of a woman's voice in the living room with him. My heart slammed against my rib cage.

I knew I should have stayed where I was, given Chaz some privacy. But I was pretty certain Maria Lopez was in the other room, and I guess I just wanted her to know.

I also didn't want to give her the chance to make a play for my man, because I didn't believe for a second that such an early morning visit was about anything other than seduction.

I quickly put one of the hotel's robes on—white, of course—and opened the bedroom door. My stomach fluttered.

"I'm sorry, Maria," Chaz was saying. "It's going to have to be later."

I walked into the room slowly, making my appearance known. Chaz's back was to me, but Maria saw me instantly. Her eyes widened in shock, and I saw her reel backward slightly.

She hadn't expected to see me, and based on her reaction, she was none too happy.

Chaz turned.

"I'm sorry if I'm interrupting," I said. "I was just going to…make some coffee."

Chaz waved off my apology. "Maria, you remember Vanessa."

"Of course," Maria said, then pressed her lips together tightly.

I wiggled my fingers at her. "Good morning."

She didn't respond.

I walked toward them en route to the kitchen, and fully

intended to walk past them and give them privacy. But Chaz snaked an arm around my waist once I was within reach and pulled me to his side. I couldn't help beaming.

"Maria, how about I meet you in an hour? I'd like to have breakfast with Vanessa first."

"Okay," Maria said. Her eyes flitted to me, then went back to Chaz. "But I need you, Chaz. I really need to work through this."

"One hour. I'll meet you in the lobby."

Maria looked forlorn, but nodded. Then she went to the door. As she opened it, I saw at least two of her bodyguards were standing outside, waiting for her.

"Is there a problem?" I asked once she was gone.

"She's having…some issues. I think she's unhappy about last night's show, and she wants me to help her deal with it."

"Like a therapist?" I asked.

"Yeah, I guess so."

I gazed up at Chaz, holding inside the thought going through my mind. I didn't know the exact nature of his arrangement with Maria, but I hardly doubted that she was simply interested in his professional guidance.

She wanted him. I wondered if Chaz knew, or was oblivious.

Regardless, I decided to do something that surprised me. "If she needs you, Chaz—why don't you go to her?"

"Because I want to spend a bit more time with you."

"Oh, we'll be spending a lot more time together. But if she's stressed…I can wait. Maybe even take a little snooze while you do whatever it is that that you do with her." I trusted him, and it was important for me to show him that.

"We won't have much time together," Chaz said. "I have to head to Alabama."

"You do?"

"Yep. I'm doing a three-day seminar there. I carved out this brief time in Miami for Maria—but mostly because I hoped I would get to see you."

I'm not sure how I didn't do a spontaneous happy dance. Instead, I slipped my arms around Chaz's waist. "You really have to leave?"

"Mmm-hmm. Later this morning."

I frowned, a little sadness marring my happy mood. "In that case, please hurry with Maria. If you can. I want to give you a proper send-off." I winked to emphasize my meaning, but I'm sure he already knew.

"I will be back as soon as I can."

Chaz left me a short time later, and I lay on the large bed, sighing with contentment. I pressed my nose into the pillow Chaz had used, inhaling his scent. A smile erupted on my face, and then I started to giggle.

I was giddy with happiness. Everything in my life was finally right.

Twenty minutes later, my cell phone rang. I jumped off the bed and ran to my purse, certain it was Alaina—dying to know what had happened at this early hour. I flipped the phone open and put it to my ear.

"Hello," I sang.

"Where the fuck are you?"

The tone was hostile, loud, and made my happy mood fizzle instantly. That definitely wasn't Alaina's voice.

"Answer the damn door before I break it down!"

I'd been about to hang up, not in the least bit interested in dealing with an irrational Byron. But his words caused my blood to turn cold.

"What did you say?" I asked slowly.

"Answer the damn door, Vanessa!" I heard loud banging. "I'm here to see my daughter. You can't keep me from her."

Byron was at my door? The realization was like a slap in the face. I was sick and terrified.

And grateful.

Thank God I hadn't gone home last night. Thank God Rayna was safe in Carla's apartment.

"You think you can avoid me forever?" Byron asked.

"You have no right to be at my place, Byron. No right."

"Bullshit. I have every right. I'm Rayna's father."

"And you think you'll score points by going to my home and banging on the door? You'll be lucky if the police don't arrive any minute."

"Fuck you," Byron spat out. "I'm through being nice to you. Open the door. *Now.*"

As if I would ever open to the door to someone who sounded like a madman. Much less so he could spend time with my daughter.

"I'm not there," I said, thanking the Lord it was true. "Rayna and I—we're out of town."

"Wh-what?"

"That's right. And we won't be back for a while. And you'd better believe I'm not telling you where we are."

"You bitch."

I knew Byron didn't like me, and the feeling was mutual. But why was he suddenly being so hateful? I couldn't believe he was that desperate to see Rayna. Something else was going on.

"Why do you really want to see Rayna?" I asked. "Lose your car in a gambling debt and need her as collateral?" The words spilled out, irrational as the accusation may have been.

But perhaps it wasn't. I really didn't know what Byron was capable of. I still got chills when I thought of that news story where a father had done just that—given his young daughter over to a loan shark when his gambling debts had gotten out of control.

"I told you, I'm clean," Byron said. "And I've got a lawyer, Vanessa."

I rolled my eyes. "I know. I met her."

"No, not her. A real one. One who specializes in family law," Byron added in a smug tone. "Child custody for men who are screwed over by their baby mamas. He's a real shark, Vanessa."

A chill ran down my spine.

"I just wanted to give you fair warning," Byron said menacingly, suddenly sounding like the epitome of calm and rational. "Cause I'm that kind of guy."

"Right. You could win awards, you're so decent."

"You can always do the right thing before we have to go to court," Byron went on. "Wherever you are, why don't you come home and let me spend time with Rayna?"

I hit the end button, my heart thundering in my chest. For a good minute I sat on the bed, my hands trembling.

Byron was serious. He wasn't going away. He was going to hound me until he saw Rayna. Fight me in court for the right to see her.

And when he had that right, what would he do? What sort of lowlifes would Rayna be subjected to when with him? Other men who gambled their lives away? Bookies with no scruples? Loan sharks who would do whatever necessary to send a message? Even if Byron didn't mean to do Rayna harm, what if someone in his circle of degenerate friends and associates hurt her?

And I couldn't get around the memory of that distraught mother who'd lost her child after her father had handed her over to a loan shark.

Was my fear irrational? I didn't think so. How could I take any chances with my precious little girl?

My hands still shaking, I called Carla.

"Hey, you," Carla said in a singsong voice. "How was your night?"

Just minutes ago, I'd been on Cloud Nine. Now, my happiness had turned to dread.

"Byron just called me," I said. "He was at my door, Carla. Screaming and banging, demanding to see Rayna."

"What?"

"I'm terrified. He was out of control, angry as hell. Maybe he was drunk, but how can he expect me to let him see Rayna when he acts like that?"

"I don't believe it. I can't believe he got into the building. Or that he knows your exact unit."

"That information is easy enough to find out at city hall. Plus, after Eli died, the reporters were all over this place. He probably came by here and asked a few questions, got the answers he wanted." None of which mattered right now.

"I told Byron that Rayna and I are out of town. Whatever you do, Carla, don't leave your apartment. I don't want to risk him seeing her."

"Don't worry about it. We'll stay inside."

Byron's words about the lawyer echoed in my head. "He's not gonna go away, Carla. He wants Rayna, and he's really going for it. He said he hired some bigshot lawyer, and I'm scared." I whimpered. "I'll never trust Byron with Rayna. He can pretend to the world that he's cleaned up his act, but I don't believe it. Not for a minute."

"Calm down," Carla said. "Calm down and tell me exactly what Byron said."

I did. I gave her the condensed version of my reuniting with Chaz, then told her about Byron's call, word for word, as I remembered it. When I was finished, Carla was cursing.

"I'm in Chaz's room now, but I've got to leave. I was waiting for him, but now I have to head home." I had to get to Rayna, take her to my sister's place or somewhere else. Somewhere that Byron couldn't get to her.

And then something clicked in my brain.

Chaz was going to Alabama for business.

There was no reason I couldn't go to Alabama, too.

With Rayna.

Yes, I thought, nodding. I would pack some clothes, get in my car and drive to Alabama. I could spend more time with Chaz—*and* escape Byron in the process.

I needed time—time to figure out what I was going to do. And I certainly didn't want to be home or at work if someone came to my door to serve me with court papers.

Or if an irrational and angry Byron showed up again.

"Carla, get Rayna ready. I'll be there within the hour. We're getting out of town. I'm taking Rayna—to Alabama."

Her babydaddy's a deadbeat.
Her ex-boyfriend thinks
she's a booty call.
Her fiancé was cheating
on her—and his wife...
And now he's dead.

USA TODAY
BESTSELLING AUTHOR

KAYLA PERRIN

Her fiancé's hostile widow, who happens to own the hip South Beach condo Vanessa Cain and her young daughter shared with Eli, wants her out. Vanessa loves her home— but to keep it, she has to come up with money. Lots of it.

Which means bringing in big business for her boss's motivational speaking agency. So with a business plan and a bikini, Vanessa heads down to the Bahamas to convince Chaz Andersen—the biggest name in life coaching—to sign with her.

This single mama is about to get herself into a whole lot more drama!

single mama drama

"A writer that everyone
should watch."
—Eric Jerome Dickey

*Available wherever
trade paperback books are sold!*

MIRA®

www.MIRABooks.com

MKP2551TR